PRETTY
wild

Lacey Black

Pretty Wild

Pine Village Series, book 5

USA Today Bestselling Author

Lacey Black

Pretty Wild

Pine Village Series, book 5

Lacey Black

CHAPTER
one

MARCUS

"Wait."

I pause before slowly turning around to face the gorgeous woman I found stranded on the side of the road. All I want to do is go home, shower, relax, and fill my stomach with whatever leftovers I find in the fridge, but here I am, dealing with a damsel in distress, who's clearly not from these parts.

She releases a deep feminine sigh that screams high-maintenance, the sound doing something strange to my insides. Standing up straight, she lifts her chin and says, "I need your help."

Placing my hands on my hips, I take in the woman. She's wearing one of those little summer dresses in a pale pink color and a pair of sky-high heels no woman should ever wear in Pine Village. How in the hell she's able to walk in them is beyond me. This terrain isn't exactly mountainous, but it's not exactly flat, even ground either. Not to mention one little rock would send her tumbling to the ground in those things. Stilettos, I think they're called. Don't ask me how I know that. It's not because I know anyone who wears them or have heard it mentioned on television.

I exhale, all thoughts of a hot shower and leftovers being put on hold for the time being.

Such is life though, especially when you're the only tow truck driver and residential snowplow driver in the area. Add that to the hellacious hours I keep as one of Pine Village's only auto mechanics, and let's just say, sleep is a commodity I rarely indulge in.

I glance around, the sunlight practically nonexistent now. "This is a terrible place to stop," I find myself saying out loud.

"Well, next time, I'll ask my flat tire to hold it together a few more minutes so it's more convenient for you," she sasses, narrowing her dark eyes at me in contempt.

Ignoring her jab, I walk around to the passenger side of my old truck and move what's on the seat. I place my lunch box and dirty T-shirt from earlier in the day in the bed of the truck and turn to face the woman. "Get in, Princess."

Her eyes widen. "What? I'm not getting into that truck with you," she spits out, her eyes a little panicky as she grips her cell phone tighter.

"Well, if you don't, you'll be stuck on the side of the road until someone else comes along. Could be five minutes, could be five hours." That's a total lie, considering this road is very well traveled. In fact, I'm surprised we haven't seen another vehicle already, especially on the Friday night kicking off Memorial Day weekend.

She narrows her eyes, as if gauging my sincerity. "Are you sure that truck will even make it anywhere? It looks older than dirt."

I glance at my '86 Square Body Chevy truck. This baby is solid, despite being almost forty years old. I'd rather take my chances on this old truck than any of the new ones on today's market. Those things are run on computers and expensive as hell to fix. This old beauty is well-maintained and still has a lot of life left in her. "We'll be fine. Pearl is more dependable than most models on the roads these days." I look over at her expensive-ass SUV to prove my point.

She huffs and walks over to her disabled vehicle. I watch as she opens the hatch and starts to pull three large suitcases from within. She struggles under their weight, and when the third one plops onto the dirt, she turns and demands, "Are you just going to stand there like a mannerless jerk, or are you going to help me?"

A slow smile spreads across my lips. "I didn't hear the magic words."

She mutters something under her breath that sounds like *hick asshole* before leveling me with a gaze. The intensity of it almost knocks me on my ass. "Will you *please* help me with these bags?" I can tell it's taking every ounce of control she possesses not to curse me out right now.

I push off my truck and head in her direction. "See? That wasn't so hard now, was it?"

Her eyes narrow as she flips her long hair over her shoulder. I grab two of the bags, one in each hand, and slowly make my way to the bed of my truck. They're heavy, and I'm a little surprised she was able to load them in the back of her SUV herself. Of course, she probably had someone help her. This woman doesn't exactly scream independent. She probably has a whole slew of employees to handle her every need.

When I glance back, she's just standing there, watching. "You gonna grab that one?" I ask, tossing the first two into the bed of my truck.

She gasps when they land with a thud. "You better not have broken anything in those, or you'll pay for the damages."

Ignoring her comment, I watch as she struggles to drag her third suitcase toward me. Normally, I'm not the type of guy to stand around and watch a woman—or anyone for that matter—battle to carry or move something, but this woman grates on my nerves. So, I'll let her fight it for a few moments before stepping in and helping.

When one of the wheels catches on a pebble and she almost drops the suitcase, I finally head back her way. I grab the handle, our hands touching as I do. A bolt of lightning shoots through my veins. That's the only way to describe it. It's like a static electricity shock when you touch something metal in the middle of winter, or you accidentally touch a faulty wiring system in the car you're working on. It's not enough to kill you, but you definitely know it's there.

Her eyes widen as she looks up at me, clearly having felt the jolt too. I take the suitcase and place it with the other two before walking around to the passenger door. She carefully makes her way toward me, moving surprisingly well in her shoes, all things considered. She reaches my side and looks up into the cab of my truck. It's dirty, but not filthy by any means. There tends to be a thin layer of dust that covers my truck almost as soon as I clean it. Between the dirt road I live on and the gravel lot for my business, nothing ever stays clean for very long.

She tries to hoist herself up into my truck, which isn't very easy, considering this old thing is lifted. When she doesn't quite make it, I grab her waist and help. Her arms flail and a yelp erupts from her throat as I not-so-gracefully set her down on the passenger seat. Her dress is hiked up, which she quickly corrects and adjusts, and turns her attention my way. "Thank you," she grits out.

"You're welcome, Princess."

Closing her door with a thud, I make my way back to her vehicle. The moment I open the driver's door I'm assaulted by her floral scent. It clings to everything, hanging in the air, and embeds in my nostrils. I grab the keys off the console and the pink sparkly little purse sitting on the passenger seat. Once I close the door, I click the lock button and return to my truck.

Just as I go to open the driver's door, a car comes flying around the curve, almost clipping my door. "Oh my God," she bellows, her eyes wide with fright. "They almost hit you!"

With gritted teeth, I climb inside the truck and throw it into drive. "That's why I didn't want you hanging out here in the dark," I mutter, pulling onto the road, passing her disabled SUV, and turning off my hazards. "Where are you staying?"

She pulls out her phone and taps on the screen. The light fills the cab, but I keep my eyes focused on the road. "I need service so I can pull up the directions again," she says, tapping away with a little more insistence.

"Do you know the address? I was born and raised here. I know this place like the back of my hand."

She taps again before answering, "Thirteen sixty Lakeview Road."

I stifle the curse, but not the sigh.

"Do you know it?" she asks, hopeful.

"Yeah, I know it," I mutter, heading in the direction of Lakeview Road and the address she gave.

Is this really happening? It's just my luck the high-maintenance woman I met on the side of the road is renting my cabin for the next month. I mentally pull up the email I received from the management company, informing me of the last-minute rental agreement. I didn't look at the name, because it didn't matter. All I needed to know is someone was going to be my neighbor for the next month.

"So...what's your name?" she asks, breaking through the silence filling the truck cab.

"Marcus."

When the silence surrounds us once more, she says, "Mine's Ryan."

"Ryan?" I ask, my eyebrows drawing upward as I take a quick glance her way.

"Yes, Ryan," she replies in a clipped tone.

"Sorry," I insist, lifting both hands in surrender for a flash. "Didn't mean to insult you. It's just a...unique name for a girl."

"Exactly," she states proudly.

I turn off Lowe Road onto Lakeview. We bounce along the dirt path, the potholes a permanent part of the drive. There are not many houses down this road, and since it's technically just outside the city limits, the road commissioner hasn't made it much of a priority to do upgrades to the roadway, especially since I usually plow it myself when I do my driveway and the cabin next door.

She glances around at our surroundings, taking in the darkened road and the abundance of trees. "Are you sure this is where we're supposed to be going?" she asks, squinting into the darkness. "You're not taking me somewhere to murder me, right? I mean, I'm pretty sure this is how they start most cheesy teen horror movies," she adds with an uncomfortable chuckle.

I can't help but grin. "No, Princess, I'm not driving you to my lair to murder you. Your cabin is actually right up the way."

"It is?" she asks, looking back out the window.

"Yep. There're only two other places on this road. It's pretty secluded and not one of the main tourist areas for the lake. This is all private land around here." We pass one of the only other driveways on the road. "That's the driveway for the owner of your cabin, and if you travel about another half mile up this road, you'll find the other. Just past their house is the main road that'll take you to the Bluff Preserves National Park's camping areas."

"Huh," she says before I turn off the roadway and drive up the private lane. She pulls out her phone and tries typing again. "I still don't have service."

"The cabin has Wi-Fi, but the service is spotty at best. There's an old rotary phone attached to the phone line in the kitchen." I stop in front of the cabin and turn to look at Ryan.

"A what?" she asks, her eyes wide.

I almost laugh as I throw my truck into park. "A rotary phone and a wired phone line. It was all the rage in the eighties and nineties."

She makes a choking noise. "I wasn't even born yet."

Now it's my turn for my eyes to widen. "You weren't?"

"Well, I was in the nineties, but not until the very end. I'm twenty-six."

I close my eyes and groan. She's younger than I expected, a whole eleven years behind my thirty-seven. Not that it matters or anything. It's not like we're dating.

"Anyway, let's get your luggage unloaded, and then I'll run to the shop and retrieve my tow truck to get your SUV."

She meets me around at the back of my truck. "It's a rental," she says, watching as I remove all three pieces from my truck bed.

"All right. I'll take it back to my shop and get it fixed first thing in the morning."

"Not tonight?" she asks, seeming a little uncomfortable.

"I'm not changing a tire on the side of the road there. You saw that car almost hit my truck. It's not safe," I tell her, pulling two of her suitcases toward the cabin's front door.

"I know that," she insists, grabbing the third case and following me up the sidewalk. "I just prefer to have a mode of transportation while I'm out here."

"I'll get it back to you as soon as I can," I tell her, stepping over to the side when I reach the porch so she can enter the security code.

She pulls out her phone again and uses it as reference before entering in the code. When it beeps red, she tries it a second time. Again, it flashes red, a signal the code didn't work. After it happens a third time, I step forward and press the sequence of six numbers into the keypad. The moment it turns green, I turn the knob and push open the door.

When she makes no move to enter, I glance her way, finding her standing ramrod straight, her mysterious, dark eyes gazing back at me. "How did you know that?"

I slip inside the cabin, setting the two pieces of luggage off to the side before giving her an answer. "I'm the owner of this cabin."

Her mouth gapes open and she makes no move to enter the cabin.

"You coming in? You're letting all the cool air out," I state, referring to the air-conditioning as I flip on the living room switch and bathe us both in light.

"You own this place?"

"Yep," I confirm, glancing around. "This place used to belong to my grandpa."

She looks around before slowly taking a tentative step across the threshold. When she closes the door, she asks, "So...that means you live in the place next door?"

"Sure do." After a beat, I ask, "Anything else you wanna know?"

Ryan seems to snap out of whatever trance she's in. She clears her throat and replies, "No, I don't think so."

I nod, moving to the front door. "I'll deliver your SUV in the morning."

"Okay," she replies, still appearing a little stunned by the revelation.

"Oh, before I forget, you were pressing the three twice when entering the code. It's one, one, three, *four*, nine, two."

Her eyes narrow a little. "The email I received had one, one, three, three, nine, two."

"Well, I'll let the management firm know," I tell her, opening the front door and stepping outside. The warm fresh air is welcome as I inhale greedy breaths and close my eyes. "Fuck," I mutter, grateful not to be suffocated by her rich perfume any longer.

The floorboard on the porch behind me creaks. "Thank you for dropping me off."

"You're welcome," I state, practically jumping off the steps to put a little more distance between us. "I'll, uh, see you in the morning."

"All right," she says, glancing around. Just as I take a few steps toward my truck, she adds, "Excuse me, Marcus?"

I glance back, my hazel eyes connecting with her chocolate-brown ones. "Yeah?"

A stick breaks somewhere in the night, causing her to jump a little. "Umm, are there really black bears around here?"

The corner of my mouth curls up. "Definitely. Don't leave trash outside."

Her eyes widen almost comically as realization sets in.

Spinning around, I holler, "Have a great night, Ryan."

Just as I shut my truck door, I see her spin around and practically run back to the cabin. In those ridiculous heels. I let out a chuckle, which feels good after the long day I've had.

Backing into the yard, I turn around and drive down the lane, letting out a deep sigh. It's well after nine and, apparently, my day is not finished. I need to head back to the shop and grab the flatbed tow truck and then retrieve Ryan's SUV. It won't take long to fix her tire in the morning, assuming it just needs a plug. If she somehow tore or punctured the sidewall, then she's looking at a whole new tire.

I pull back into the parking lot for my shop and park beside the tow truck. Just as I'm climbing out, I catch sight of something pink and sparkly. Reaching for the item that slipped beneath the bench seat, I pull out Ryan's purse and sigh loudly.

Great. Now I have to go back.

Though, it's not like it's out of my way. She *is* going to be staying next door.

I run my hand over my face and groan.

Something tells me this isn't going to be as easy as it should. Ryan is clearly not accustomed to staying in a cabin in the middle of the woods. With no cell phone coverage.

A smile spreads across my lips.

Looks like the princess is in for a rude awakening.

Come to think about it, this might be more enjoyable than expected.

No, *no.*

The last thing I need is to have some woman distracting me. I'm a very busy man, with an incredibly demanding job. We're entering the busy summer season. I won't have time to sleep, let alone have time for a woman.

Especially one as high-maintenance as Ryan.

Ain't happening, Marcus, and the sooner you realize that the better off you'll be.

Women are trouble with a capital T.

And Ryan screams trouble.

Best thing I can do is steer clear of her.

Who cares if she's practically living next door to me for the next thirty days?

Not me.

I probably won't ever see that woman again. She'll stay at the cabin and leave at the end of her rental agreement with a summer tan, returning to her high-rise condo in some big city with high-speed internet.

Yeah, I'm sure this'll be the last time I see Ryan.

She'll be gone in no time.

CHAPTER
Two

Ryan

I close the door to my cabin and flip the lock before slowly turning and taking in my surroundings. The cabin is...rustic. The plaid furniture looks well-loved, but comfortable, and the wood floor is marred with years of activity. There's a television sitting in a big cabinet, and even though I can't see it from here, I'm pretty sure there's a box on the back of it, like the TVs we had growing up.

The kitchen and dining room are combined, if you can really call it a dining room. It's more of an eat-in kitchen, with a small table and four chairs in a little nook. There's an old coffeepot on the counter, which I'm grateful for, since I'm pretty certain there isn't a Dunkin' or Starbucks anywhere near me.

That's part of the reason I chose this place. It's an incredibly small town and the cabin's completely isolated. There isn't a camera or a nosy paparazzi screaming my name in sight. I can't help but smile at that thought.

Let's just hope sleeping comes a little easier out here than it did under the bright city lights.

I walk through the rest of the cabin, checking it out. It doesn't take long, since there's only two bedrooms and one bathroom. They all match the rest of the house, with old fixtures, tile walls, and faded linoleum in the bathroom, a pair of twin-size beds and a dresser in the smaller bedroom, and a big antique bed with matching nightstands and a dresser in the master. There's even a big quilt covering the surprisingly soft mattress featuring a wooded scene with big black bears.

Everything is exactly as it was portrayed in the online ad I found, including the warning about black bears. Though, at the time, I thought it was an exaggeration. Apparently not.

My mind instantly flashes back to the man who rescued me on the side of the road.

Marcus.

I remember how hard my heart hammered in my chest when he spoke, startling the crap out of me, as I was standing there on the side of the road. My phone wasn't working, so if his intentions were anything other than honorable, I wouldn't have been able to do a damn thing about it. Even though I could walk a thousand miles in heels, there's no way I would have been able to outrun a man of his...size.

Oh, he most definitely would have been able to take me down and completely subdue me with only his pinky. He's tall and muscular, his dirty T-shirt molded to his biceps like he fell out of some working man's podcast or something.

Do they even have those?

I'm not sure but if I can figure out the whole Wi-Fi situation, I might do a little checking.

Returning to the kitchen, I find the refrigerator completely bare, except a box of baking soda. Grabbing my phone, I start making a list of all the items I'm going to need to purchase tomorrow. Fruit, the makings for salads, sparkling water, and coffee with sugar-free coffee creamer. The website I used boasted about a small grocery store, as well as a few other restaurants in town. There's also some big box stores a few towns over, but it mentioned delivery service wasn't available.

It's been a long damn time since I went shopping for myself, but I'm looking forward to it. It's not because I'm too good for it. I'm not one of those hoity-toity rich folks who have "people" to do their bidding.

Okay, fine.

I have people who do my bidding, but not because I want them to. The reason I have a team is for security reasons. I haven't been able to go out on my own since I was younger, but even back then I was spotted and my photo taken plenty. Now, I can't do anything without having paparazzi up my ass, cameras in my face as they concoct their latest bullshit headline featuring yours truly.

Though, I do admit, if I wanted a quiet, simple life, I was going about it all wrong. It's not like starring in my own reality TV show and developing my own makeup brand was going to create anonymity. Not to mention I'm the product of two beautiful people, famous in their own right, and unstoppable when they got married. I was born under the spotlight, and over the years it's only gotten bigger, brighter, and more intrusive.

Wanting to push thoughts of LA out of my mind, I grab the first of my three large suitcases and wheel it toward the bedroom. This one is packed with summer clothes. Shorts, tank tops, cute little designer tees, and swimwear. Lots of swimwear. When I found this cabin at the last minute, one of the features I looked for was a beach. I didn't realize Wisconsin had beaches, but whatever. I can't wait to see it in the morning light, since the listing had beach access as one of the amenities.

The second suitcase has my summer dresses and shoes. Lots of shoes. Sandals, flip-flops, and a few pairs of my fave heels and pumps, all in a variety of styles and colors to complement whatever outfit I settle on for the day.

I hang clothes in the closet, well, until I run out of hangers. Reaching for my phone, I add more hangers to my shopping list. The rest of my stuff I gently place on the floral-lined contact paper inside the six dresser drawers.

When I have the shoes organized on the floor of the closet, I go in search of my third piece of luggage. I find it right inside the front door and very carefully wheel it to the bedroom. It's heavy and takes a little extra umph to get it onto the mattress. I slowly unzip the bag and gasp when I see the destruction.

"Oh my God!" I carefully start pulling out the contents. Everything is a complete mess. It looks like a bomb went off in here. My hair products are all over the place, and don't get me started on my body care stuff. Some of the lids popped off, and everything is coated in what could either be my heat shield hair protectant or my night cream. Or both.

I gingerly pull out my travel bags containing my makeup and carry them into the bathroom. The entire time I clean white cream off the bags, I curse at the man who clearly took very little care of someone's personal property and just tossed it around without worrying about damage. All I can do is gape at the mess, my anger slowly building.

My mirror is cracked. Even wrapping it in bubble wrap didn't protect it from the wrath of Marcus. What kind of person just throws people's luggage around without having an ounce of respect or decency in regard to the contents? An animal, that's who. A filthy, careless jerk. How would he feel if I haphazardly threw his stuff around, breaking half of it in the process?

Of course, I can only imagine his luggage for a trip. The man probably doesn't even own a suitcase. He'd throw a couple pairs of stained jeans, a few T-shirts, and some boxers into a gym bag and call it good. Hell, he'd probably use a plastic sack!

My mind goes to my travels, and I realize my anger might be a little misplaced. I flew commercial because I didn't want anyone to track my travel plan, and my father's private plane was a well-known source for travel-stalking. It is used by all kinds of people in the movie industry, a who's who amongst actors and executives who don't want to fly commercial. My dad is one of the most giving people I know and lends out his plane regularly, but this was one time I couldn't use it. I needed to be lost, not tracked, and traveling on a commercial jet was the way to do it.

Of course, flying out of an airport like LAX was a recipe for disaster if I was looking to blend in. My name alone was attached to some of the biggest in the industry, which is why I used Burbank. A smaller airport, a bit of a disguise, and a name not always associated with my family is what it took to get from point A to point B without everyone in the world following behind with their cameras, and surprisingly, it worked. No one seemed to pay me any attention, which was something new on its own. Usually, I didn't mind having photos snapped while I was jet-setting for the weekend, but today, I needed to blend in. I wanted to be invisible, and the name Ryan Marcotte is anything but invisible.

I look down at my stuff, realizing the destruction could have very well been caused by the airline. I've seen those horror videos of staff tossing and stacking luggage in the belly of an airplane, so chances are, it wasn't entirely caused by a rugged mountain of a man in Wisconsin. Still, I can't completely squelch my ire at the stranger, even if he *did* rescue me on the side of the roadway.

Just as I get the rest of my stuff cleaned up and put away in the bathroom, there's a knock at the door. It's loud, insistent, and scares the ever-loving daylights out of me. My heart is pounding like a steel drum in my chest as I creep out of the bathroom and move toward the front door. Of course, my heels give me away, the steady click echoing on the wooden floor.

A second knock hits the door, followed by, "Ryan, it's Marcus. Are you still awake?"

I stand up tall and look through the peephole, confirming it's the man who delivered me to my rental just an hour ago. The moonlight illuminates his broad frame, somehow painting him in a gorgeous light.

Wait, what?

No, Ryan. He's not gorgeous. He's...infuriating at best, and completely not your type.

I reach for the lock and turn it before slowly opening the door. "It's a little late to be dropping by, isn't it?" I ask, keeping my chin high as I level him with a look of annoyance.

He seems completely unfazed by my irritation and holds out his hand. Out of my peripheral vision, I catch sight of something pink and sparkly. "You left this in my truck."

"Oh," I reply, reaching for my small bag. Our fingers touch as I grab my purse, the same electrical current from earlier shocking my senses. "Thank you."

He stares at me as we both hold the purse, his penetrating gaze looking straight into my soul. I can't help but wonder if he felt the same zip of electricity I felt and what it means. Of course, the moment he opens his mouth, all thoughts of chemistry and sparks fly straight out the window.

"You should be more careful with that. We're a small, friendly town, but not everyone who'd stumble upon a purse would turn it over to the authorities or the owner. Especially during the summer. Never leave your stuff lying around unsupervised, Princess," he states, muscular arms crossed over his chest as he chastises me like a small child.

My eyes narrow as I snatch the small bag from his grip. "I'm from the city. I'm well aware of the dangers of leaving my purse exposed."

He nods. "Yet, you still left it in my truck."

A wild sound comes from my throat. It's a cross between a gasp and a growl, and if he's supposed to be intimidated by it, he's clearly not. Not if the smirk on his too-kissable lips is any indication. My eyes narrow into little slits.

"Listen, buster, I grew up in LA. I don't need some country bumpkin giving me advice on security and protecting my identity," I reprimand, my bright pink-and-silver French-manicured nail poking him in the middle of his hard chest, right over his crossed arms.

His hazel eyes drop down to where my nail digs into the cotton of his T-shirt. A cocky smirk spreads across his mouth, his eyes sparkling with mischief. "Well, Princess, I don't give a rat's ass where you're from. Ya might want to take better care of your shit."

Then, he takes a step back, dislodging my finger from his shirt. "I'll have that tire patched up first thing in the morning and will get it dropped off to you by ten. That sound good?"

My throat is completely dry, and I have the sudden desire to fidget with my fingers. Crossing my own arms, I level him with an indifferent gaze. "Fine. Great."

He stares at me for a few seconds before nodding once. "See ya in the morning, Ryan."

"Thank you," I say because I'm a polite person and I do appreciate him fixing and delivering my rental SUV, but I don't appreciate his condescending tone.

I close the door, refusing to peek through the little hole in the door to watch him go. He might have a great ass in a pair of worn denim, but his self-righteous attitude makes me want to punch the smug little smirk off his face. And despite what has been printed about me in the tabloids a time or two, I am *not* a violent person.

After making sure the door is locked, I move to the kitchen and set my purse on the counter. There's a detailed list of important information on the counter, including the Wi-Fi password, so I quickly take a moment to enter the access info into my phone. As soon as I do, chimes echo through the room as texts, emails, and missed calls hit my device.

I sigh, knowing many of the texts and missed calls I'll be ignoring, and pull up the texting app. I ignore all of them except the one from my dad.

Dad: Please let me know you made it safely; I don't care what time it is. Love you.

Smiling, I type out a reply.

Me: Made it. Cell service isn't great, but as long as I'm at the cabin, I have Wi-Fi.

The bubbles appear immediately.

Dad: Good deal. Do you need anything? I can have Rosemary overnight whatever it is.

Me: I'm good for now, Dad. Thank you though.

Dad: My phone has been buzzing all day. Vaughn is looking for you.

Me: I don't care. I said what I needed to say and that's that.

Dad: I understand, honey. Just wanted you to know he's looking for you.

Me: Please don't tell him where I am. I made it all the way here without anyone recognizing me.

Dad: Your secret is safe with me, promise. The only person who knows is your mother. She sends her love. She went to have drinks with the reps from the Sullivan Foundation.

Me: Tell her I love her and will call her soon. I better finish unpacking and get to bed.

Dad: Call if you need anything, Ryan. Anything. I'm worried about you.

My heart skids to a stop in my chest and my eyes fill with tears.

Me: I'm fine, Dad. Promise. Love you.

Dad: Love you too. Good night.

Me: Night.

I glance through the rest of the texts, finding several from friends and business associates, all of whom I'll return tomorrow. Then, I find the name I expected to see, yet had hoped wouldn't be there. My finger hovers over his name, and ultimately, I decide not to open the message. Whatever he has to say doesn't matter. From the moment I watched the episode where he told the world how he really felt about me, all blame was placed on me.

You're always busy.
You're making a bigger deal out of this.
It was for ratings, stop overreacting.
This business is ruthless, and we have to stick together.

Why the hell is he still texting me? All he has to do is walk away and we both move on. Instead, he keeps blowing up my phone, calling my family and friends, trying to find out where I am.

I'll tell you why.

Because my last name is Marcotte.

Because my father has more influence in his pinky than half of Hollywood.

Because he's starring in my dad's next movie.

Because it's all about appearances, and he isn't looking so hot right now.

I set my phone down on the counter, knowing I should just block him but not having the brainpower to deal with it right now.

Instead, I go to the cabinet, grab a glass, and fill it up with water. Water that has a slight yellowish tint to it and smells a little musty. I quickly dump out the contents of the glass and set it aside, knowing I'll have to make my trip to town sooner rather than later. As soon as I get my SUV back, I'll retrieve what I need, because there's no way I'm drinking whatever contaminated water is coming out of the tap.

Gross.

I take a look around, for the first time wondering if I made a mistake. I'm not a country girl, one who's fine sleeping in a little cabin in the woods. I've never stayed anywhere that isn't a five-star hotel or resort, so why did I think this was a good idea?

Tears burn my eyes, but I refuse to let them fall.

I can do this.

I am strong, capable, and independent.

I don't need lavish hotels or fancy cuisine.

This space and time away from Los Angeles and the dumpster fire that became my life, when it exploded on national television, is exactly what I need.

For one month, I'll cut off everyone and everything and find out who the real Ryan Marcotte is. Well, except my parents. And my business. Even though I took a small leave of absence, I'm still very much in control of Ryan Holmes Cosmetics.

I don't need anyone but myself.

I've got this.

I just pray I don't see a spider...

MARCUS

I make sure the tire holds air before lowering the lift. As soon as the SUV is on the ground, I jump inside and slowly back it out of the shop bay. Her scent assaults me instantly. How can a woman who only drove a vehicle a short time have her scent embedded into the seats like this?

Parking the vehicle next to the open shop door, I run back inside and holler at Dale, my employee. "Wanna follow me? I need to deliver this SUV."

He nods, setting his tools aside and wiping off his hands on a shop towel. I run over to the sink, washing my hands a second time. I always take great care not to track anything into the vehicles I work on, using paper covers on the floor mat and seat, but this one has white leather seats and light brown carpet, so I use extra degreaser soap again. My luck, I'll leave a smudge of rear end grease on me I didn't notice and get it all over the fancy interior.

Finally, I climb inside the vehicle and wait for Dale, who rolls down the big overhead door and secures the building. When he climbs into an old Chevy I use as a shop truck, we head toward my cabin. It's just after nine, and I can't help but hope I can just leave her keys under the floor mat. The last thing I want is another run-in with the princess from LA. She consumed way too much of my thoughts last night.

And then a few this morning too.

Not to mention, the moment I pulled her rental into my garage, I've been consumed by her floral perfume. It's like I'm surrounded by rose bushes, trapped in some garden without an escape. Like Ryan, it may look beautiful, but the scent tickles my throat and makes me want to sneeze.

Before I even make it a block away, I have the windows down. It's a gorgeous Saturday morning, and the roadways are lined with cars. The diner is packed, as it will be from now to the end of the summer vacation season. I pass a line of trucks and SUVs pulling boats, four-wheelers, and campers, all headed out to the Bluff Preserves National Park.

Growing up in Pine Village, I'm accustomed to the onslaught of tourists who travel to our small northwestern Wisconsin town for time away. Fishing, camping, four-wheeling, and boating in the summer and snowmobiling and ice fishing in the winter. The cabins are rented and the campgrounds full. And my business keeps hopping through it all. I've worked on anything and everything over the years, having spent most of my life in the garage that once belonged to my grandpa.

I head for home, though the trip takes longer than normal, thanks to the added traffic. When I finally pass the lane that leads to my house, I feel a sense of belonging. I grew up in these woods, having lived with my grandparents in the very cabin I use as a rental when I was a young boy. When I was twenty-five, my grandpa deeded off a piece of land for me to build my own cabin, the one I live in to this day. Grandpa passed a few years back, and I just couldn't part with it, despite the more than reasonable offers I received. Instead, I turned it into a rental and let a management company deal with it.

Pulling onto the lane that brings me back to the cabin, I take a moment to enjoy the cooler breeze blowing through the trees. It's heavenly, the welcome reprieve from the impending arrival of the hot summer sun. When I reach the clearing, I park beside the porch, the sound of my shop truck idling behind me. Just as I make sure the windows are rolled up and I climb out of the SUV, the front door opens.

And out walks Ryan.

She's wearing a pretty blue sundress, one that hugs the curves of her waist and the mounds of her tits. It hits just below her knees in a classy way, her toned, tanned calves on full display. This time, instead of wearing those ridiculous heels, she's wearing cork shoes. That's the only way to describe them.

"What the hell are those?" I ask, unable to take my eyes off her feet.

"What?"

"Those shoes."

She glances down. "They're Dior."

"Who?"

She rolls her eyes. "They're designer. These are off the new summer line," she informs me, lifting her heel and showing them off. "They're made from calfskin."

"Okay," I say, drawing out that one word. "I saw those at Walmart last week."

She huffs and crosses her arms. I wish I could say my eyes didn't drop to her chest, but that'd be a lie. "These cost fourteen hundred dollars and were made in Italy. I doubt you saw them at Walmart."

I scratch my head. "Yeah, you're probably right." Holding out the key, I add, "Here ya go, Princess. You're all set."

She snatches the key from my hand. "Thank you. What do I owe you?" she asks, digging cash out of her little bag thingy.

"No charge," I state, turning to head back toward where Dale waits.

"Stop! I have to pay you," she insists, following me to the passenger side of the truck. There's no missing the big grin on Dale's face.

"It's fine, Ryan. Tire fixes like this only cost twenty bucks," I say, pulling open the door.

She reaches out and grabs the door, stopping me from climbing inside the truck. "Here." She thrusts a twenty at me.

"It's not necessary. On the house."

"I can pay," she insists, placing her hands on her hips as she levels me with a glare.

"Didn't say you couldn't, Princess. This is what we call small-town hospitality. I understand that's a new concept for a city slicker like you, but around here, we do things for others without having ulterior motives. Just say thank you."

Her pink, pouty lips gape open before slapping shut. "Why are you so grumpy?"

I climb inside the cab of the truck and close the door. "It's part of my charm."

Her dark-chocolate eyes roll dramatically. "Charming isn't what I'd call you."

A smirk plays across my mouth. "See? It's working already."

"Whatever," she grumbles, her attention turning to Dale in the driver's seat. "Excuse me, I'm being rude. I'm Ryan."

"Dale," he says, reaching across the cab and offering her a polite handshake.

"Nice to meet you, Dale." She lifts her chin and adjusts her dress. "I'm about to head to town and buy things for the cabin."

"How long ya stayin'?" he asks, completely smitten with the woman beside the truck.

"A month," she replies with a bright smile. "Any recommendations for an out-of-towner?"

"The diner has the best home-cooked food. If you're lucky, you'll stop by on meatloaf day."

She wrinkles up her nose. "Meatloaf?"

"Don't knock it till you try it, Princess," I add, inserting myself into their conversation. "Let me guess, you're a vegetarian? Or maybe vegan? I heard that's all the rage out in California." My sarcasm is thick.

"I am neither of those," she retorts. "But I do limit my red meat intake. It takes the body longer to breakdown and process red meat, including meatloaf."

I snort and shake my head. "Well, you better get used to red meat, honey, because we're cow people up here in Wisconsin. Like your shoes." I leave out the part she can find plenty of fish, poultry, and pork on the local menus too, but I seem to enjoy making her squirm in those fancy calfskin shoes she's wearing.

"If you're looking to do a little shopping, we got all kinds of little shops in downtown too, but if you need Walmart or any other big store, you'll have to head to Hudson or even St. Paul, Minnesota."

"Good to know, thank you," she replies, flashing a real charming smile to the old-timer in the driver's seat.

"We gotta get back. Those oil changes aren't going to change themselves," I mutter, ready for him to put the truck in gear and drive out of here.

"Maybe I'll see you around sometime, Dale," she singsongs with a smile.

"It's a small town. I'm certain I will, ma'am." He tips his dirty ball cap and gives her a grin. "Oh, and if you stop by the bookstore, tell Delilah Dale sent you. She's my sister."

Ryan beams and nods. "I will do that, Dale. Thank you for the hospitality and kindness. Maybe it'll rub off on *other* people," she says, glancing my way.

Dale snorts. "Fat chance of that happening. I've been working on this one since he was a young boy." He adds a chuckle, causing me to shake my head.

"We really do need to get back to the shop," I state, ready to put some distance between myself and her floral scent.

"Before you go, can I ask you a question?" she asks, turning her brown eyes on me. When I nod, she continues, "The water...what's wrong with it?"

Confused, I start running through all the things that could be wrong with the plumbing. "What do you mean?"

"Well, the water is kinda...dingy and has a weird smell."

"It's well water, Princess. That's rust."

She makes a shocked face. "Rust?"

I shrug my shoulders and hold her gaze. "The pipes are old but up to code. There's a softener that helps draw it out, but it's not going to be sparkling clear like bottles of fancy water."

She still just gapes at me, waiting for me to tell her I'm bullshitting her. All I do is give her a big, cheesy grin.

"Well, Dale, it was lovely to meet you, and I'll be sure to tell your sister you sent me in," Ryan says sweetly before taking a step back from the truck.

"Enjoy the holiday weekend and your stay in Pine Village, Ryan," Dale says, throwing the truck into reverse and slowly returning to the dirty lane.

I feel her eyes on us as we go, but I refuse to look her way. If I do, there's no telling what I'll say or do. Like tell Dale to go back and drop me off.

That would be the dumbest thing I could do.

We head back to town, the wind blowing through the truck cab and drowning out the old Dolly Parton tune on the radio. I spot a few familiar faces mixed in the masses of people walking down Main Street as businesses start to welcome patrons for the day.

"So...your new neighbor seems nice," Dale says, the smile evident in his voice.

"She's okay," I reply, keeping my answer polite, yet hoping he can tell by my tone I don't want to continue this conversation.

"Pretty too," he says after a beat.

I make a noncommittal sound and continue to look out the window.

"Very pretty, if you ask me. In a classy way, you know? We don't see too many like her around here, outside of Sunday church."

I sigh, knowing I'm not getting out of this discussion. "Yes, she's very pretty."

He's silent for several seconds, and I start to think this little heart-to-heart is over. Unfortunately, luck isn't on my side on this warm Saturday morning. "Looks to be single too, you know. I didn't see a ring."

"Doesn't mean she's not taken," I reason.

"But she's here alone, right? I mean, I didn't see a guy with her, and she is here for a month. Sounds to me like she's single," he says, pulling into the lot for the garage. Instantly, I realize there are customers waiting. "Welcome to the start of summer," he adds, parking the truck by the building.

As soon as I climb out, all thoughts of Ryan, how pretty she looked and whether or not she is single, fly out the proverbial window. There's a line waiting outside my locked door, some locals and some out-of-towners, and I realize quickly my entire Saturday is probably shot. We're usually only here until noon, but by the looks of the line, I'll be here for a while after that. It's a good thing Dale doesn't mind the overtime, because it looks like he might be here for a while too.

Dale started in high school, working for my grandpa. He was friends with my old man, and the continued that friendship until the day my dad died. My dad enlisted out of high school and served in the Army. In his early twenties, he met a woman named Renee while stationed in Texas. They dated until he was shipped off, and six months later, he got word she was pregnant. Thinking he was doing the right thing, he married Renee—my mom—and moved her to Virginia.

Not long after I was born, my dad was sent overseas, where he was killed by friendly fire during a training exercise. The story I was told was not long after my dad's funeral, my mom showed up at my grandparents' doorstep and dropped me off. She claimed motherhood wasn't for her, and she signed over all rights to my dad's parents. Last I heard, she returned to Texas, but I haven't tracked her down. Why would I?

I was raised by my grandparents, Nina and Michael, and I'm proud of that. I grew up in my grandpa's shop, learning how to do oil changes and tune-ups at a young age, working right beside Dale and Grandpa. Besides my grandpa, he was the other man in my life, stepping in and filling the role of Dad whenever I needed it. He's married twice over the years, but neither stuck. He's got a daughter from the second wife, Callie, who's twenty-three and living in Chicago with friends.

"I'll run in and finish that oil change. I don't think we have anything else on the schedule for today, right?" Dale asks as we approach the building.

"Nope. I kept it light for this reason," I tell him, nodding at the customers giving me an annoyed look as I pull the key out and unlock the office door. "Sorry, folks. Had to go deliver a car. Let's step inside into the A/C and see what we can do for all of ya."

It takes thirty minutes to get through the line of customers. I schedule three oil changes for Tuesday, as well as some other mechanical work. If I could put it off until Tuesday, I did. Unfortunately, there are a few tire repairs and a few other issues that can't wait.

My workday doesn't last as long as predicted, but I definitely stay well into the afternoon. I sent Dale home at two and finished out the day by myself. Doesn't bother me though. I prefer it that way, actually. All I had to do was turn up the music and work. I've always loved tinkering with vehicles, though, I do admit, they've slowly become more complicated over the years as computer technology now plays such a big part. It's not just more difficult to fix, it's a hell of a lot more expensive.

After closing up the shop for the night, I head out to the tow truck. I don't usually take it home with me, except I will tonight.

Holiday weekends are always busy, and it'll save me a trip here if I've already got it with me at home.

"Hey!"

I pause and turn toward the voice, smiling when I see Logan Johnson pulling into the lot. "Hey," I reply, nodding to his fiancée, Hallie. I spot their infant daughter in the back seat of her SUV, sleeping soundly in the air-conditioning.

"We're headed to the cabin for the weekend," Logan informs me. He owns the lumberyard and hardware store in town, and his future wife is a preschool teacher.

"Great weekend for it," I say, leaning against the doorframe.

"We're planning to fire up the grill tomorrow evening. Blair and Gabe, TD and Ellie, Gavin and Ava, and all the kids are coming over. You're welcome to stop by. Should be tons of food," Logan says.

As if on cue, my stomach growls, reminding me I barely ate anything for lunch today. I can't help but chuckle. "Yeah, I'll try to swing by. We'll just have to see how busy it is," I state.

Logan nods, understanding what I mean. "We'll be there, and everyone else is coming any time after four. Maybe we can wet a line at some point."

I happily agree to that. Fishing is one of my favorite pastimes, though I don't get to do it nearly as often as I'd like. And don't get me started on taking the old Jon boat out for a cruise. That's even fewer and farther between.

"I'll do my best," I tell him as the baby starts to holler in the back seat.

Hallie reaches back and strokes her infant daughter's foot. "Hopefully we'll see you tomorrow, but if not, we understand. If you text us, we can run you over some food to your cabin."

Wouldn't be the first time someone has dropped off food from a barbecue at my place. I have good friends, even if I don't get to hang out with them as often as I'd like.

"Later, Marcus," Logan says, preparing to pull out of the lot.

"See ya."

"Oh, and Marcus?" Hallie says, stopping me from walking to the truck. "Feel free to bring someone with you. There's lots of single ladies in town for the weekend." She grins and winks before they drive away.

Shaking my head, I make my way to the tow truck and climb inside. My mind immediately conjures up the image of Ryan, standing on the porch in that damn blue sundress and weird shoes. Her blond hair was down, looking soft and luscious, and all I want to do is run my fingers through it.

I blame Dale for this.

He wouldn't shut up about how pretty she looked, and now it's all I think about.

What I need to do is put her out of my head for good. She's not my type, that's for sure, and it's not like we run in the same social circles. She's here for vacation, and I have to work.

I probably won't even see her the rest of the time she's here.

CHAPTER four

Ryan

I set my bags in the booth and slip onto the bench beside them. My eyes scan the diner, looking for a camera, a look of recognition, something to tell me I'd been found, but I don't see any of it. Not one person pays attention to me.

Well, that's not true. When I entered the diner in the early afternoon, several sets of eyes all turned to check out the newcomer, but no one appeared to have recognized me. It felt good, honestly. This is exactly why I chose this place. It's not named on any top destination list for its exotic blue waters and white sandy beaches, and frankly, it's in the middle of nowhere. I had it narrowed down to two places: here and a cabin in the Smoky Mountains in Tennessee. But the idea of driving up and down the mountains didn't really appeal to me, so here we are.

From what I've seen in a short time and from what Dale said this morning, the cuisine is homemade, home-cooked, and delicious.

I splurged on a cinnamon roll from the bakery this morning, enjoying it with a sugar-free iced salted caramel latte with skim milk. The friendly woman at the counter told me calories don't count on the weekend, as she plated me the biggest roll in the display case. I felt a little guilty as I ate the entire treat, vowing it would be my one opportunity to indulge while in town.

Then I arrived here.

Normally, I'd skip lunch altogether, even a late one like today, but as I was walking past the diner, I caught a whiff of something delicious. Like a moth to a flame, it drew me in. I try to keep my eyes cast downward, while still taking in the ambiance of the diner. Several booths are filled, as well as some tables in the middle of the room and barstools at the counter, despite it being midafternoon.

"Good afternoon," a polite woman wearing a warm smile says as she approaches my table and places a small stack of napkins and a menu on the table. "I'm Ellie, can I get you something to drink?"

I scan the list of refreshments, noticing immediately the lack of sparkling water. "Ummm," I say, recalling the water situation at the cabin. "Is your water bottled?"

"Sorry, it's not. It's tap water."

I swallow and return my eyes to the menu. There's a lot of soft drink options, but that's never been my thing. There's lemonade listed, and when I open my mouth to order that, Ellie says, "May I make a suggestion?"

I nod. "Sure."

"Sweet tea. It's like it has crack in it or something," she says with a chuckle.

My eyebrows draw up.

"Oh! It doesn't," she assures me. "It's just that good."

"Okay, I'll try it," I reply, hoping I'm not making a mistake. I can just read the headlines now. *Reality Show Star Drinks Crack Tea in Front of Children.*

No, they'll probably tell the world I was giving it to them with a smile on my face.

"I'll go grab it for you and give you another second to look at the menu," Ellie says, taking off behind the counter.

I browse the menu, taking in the salad options listed, but my eyes betray me. The specials board at the front of the diner proudly boasts bacon-wrapped meatloaf as one of today's offerings. There's also a summer Cobb salad, which is what I should definitely order, but I can't help but stare at the top option, written in bright-blue lettering.

"Do you need another minute?" Ellie asks, placing my sweet tea on the table.

"Well," I start, scanning the salads to make a selection. "I had a big breakfast, so I should probably stick to a salad."

Ellie nods in understanding. "The summer Cobb salad is pretty good. It has fresh avocado and candied pecans and cranberries on the top, but if you're open to another suggestion, get the meatloaf. It's famous and so good. We usually sell out and Saul *never* makes it on the weekend, but he's filling in today. Otherwise, you'll have to wait until Monday to get it and it's usually gone fast."

My vision returns to the board, where the special is posted. Bacon-wrapped meatloaf, mashed sweet potatoes, and fresh green beans, and suddenly, I find myself requesting that particular special over the salad.

Ellie grins widely. "You won't regret it," she informs me. "I'll get your order put in. Let me know if the tea is okay, or if you'd prefer something else."

Once she walks away to the kitchen, I pull out my cell phone. Usually, the first thing I'd do is check my social media pages, but that's not what I'm going to do. In fact, I deactivated them Wednesday, following the season finale of my reality show Tuesday night.

A night I'll never forget.

I swallow over the lump forming in my throat and take a hesitant sip of the sweet tea. I've heard of it, of course I have. Even a city girl like myself would recognize tea on the menu, though it's usually unsweetened where I come from. People who live in LA and work in the industry don't add extra sugar to anything, tea included.

But the moment the sweet, iced drink hits my tongue, it's like an explosion of flavor. It's like summer in a glass, and I take a long drink from the straw. "Holy shit," I mutter, staring down at the contents of the glass.

"Right?" Ellie sings as she walks by, delivering steaming plates of food to the booth beside mine. After dropping off the plates, she pauses where I sit. "Told you. Like crack in a glass."

"It's delicious," I say, preparing to take a photo of the amazing drink to post on my socials.

Then, it hits me. I'm not doing that anymore.

I'm taking a month away to collect my thoughts and to find myself. That's where my focus needs to be, not on posting photos of the most delicious sweet tea ever brewed for my millions and millions of followers. That singular post would cause a flurry of online activity, including the trending of the popular drink and a rush of patrons to flock to the very diner I featured in my post.

A cold chill sweeps through me.

The last thing I want is to cause nice people like Ellie to have to deal with the fallout of my followers inundating the town. Sure, there might be some financial profit from their onslaught of visitors, but I've witnessed the dark side of it too. The online trashing of businesses, people, and everything in between. Going viral has its benefits, but you have to be ready to deal with the negatives too.

"Here ya go," Ellie returns, her cheery smile present as she places a plate in front of me.

"Oh my God, there's so much food," I whisper, taking in the heaping slab of meatloaf, more than generous scoop of mashed sweet potatoes, and mountain of buttery green beans.

Ellie chuckles. "We don't like to send anyone away hungry."

"I guess," I mutter, wondering how I'm going to eat even half the food on this plate. "This is more than I normally eat in a day." Probably two days, honestly.

"Oh, honey. Stick around here for a few weeks. We'll fatten you up."

My eyes widen as I gape back at the server.

My shock causes her to laugh and bat her hand my way. "Oh, I don't mean literally. Though, I'm sure we can definitely help if you're looking to put on a few pounds. Between us and the bakery, we'd be set."

I think about the cinnamon roll I had this morning. "Calories don't count on the weekend."

Ellie laughs. "You met Jillian. We went to high school together. Her treats are sinful, but thankfully, calories don't count on the weekend." She winks before adding, "Holler if you need anything." She heads off to check on others, leaving me alone with my mountain of food.

"Well, here goes nothing," I mumble to myself as I reach for my fork.

The meatloaf, coated in crispy bacon and a mixture of ketchup and barbecue sauce practically falls apart when I cut into it. I tell myself I'll just eat a little and take the rest back to my cabin. This way, I'll have lunch or dinner tomorrow too. But the moment I take my first bite, I realize my mistake. Thinking this is anything but extraordinary is a gross understatement.

"Holy crap," I murmur, closing my eyes and savoring the mouthwatering deliciousness that *is* Saul's bacon-wrapped meatloaf.

Then, I try the mashed sweet potatoes, something I wouldn't even have considered if I saw it on a menu in Los Angeles or New York, but my word, I'm not sure I've tasted anything so uniquely delectable. I've dined in the best restaurants in the United States. I've eaten Michelin-star cuisine from around the world. But this? I'm not sure much beats home-cooked diner food in Podunk, Wisconsin.

Clearly, I'm either incredibly starved or it's been too long since I've traveled to enjoy fine cuisine.

"How's the food?" Ellie asks, stopping by my booth and refilling my sweet tea.

Holding my hand up to cover my mouth, I finish chewing before replying honestly, "It's amazing."

She smiles warmly. "I'm so glad you like it. And I take it by the almost-empty glass, you like the tea?"

I nod, ready to dig into another hearty bite of food. "Thank you so much. I'll have to eat salads for the next week, but I'm so glad I splurged."

"Me too. Oh, and if you have room afterward, there's some peach pie up at the counter. It's best with a scoop of ice cream, but it's still delicious on its own." She winks before moving down the row to help her other customers.

I almost groan. I'm going to gain twenty pounds over the next four weeks if I'm not careful. I most definitely need to pace myself throughout the course of my stay. Diving back into my food with gusto, even though I told myself I'd just eat a little, I end up devouring half the plate. My stomach is full to the point of misery, but I don't regret it. It was that good.

"How long are you in town for?" Ellie asks when she returns with a Styrofoam container for my leftovers.

"A month," I confirm.

"Really? You're going to love it here. It's the best place to visit." She blushes. "Well, not that I have a lot of experience traveling. I've only ever lived here. But it's an amazing little town, and summer is always a great time. It gets warm but not too hot, and if you like the outdoors, there's always something to do."

I make a face at that thought. "I'm not what most would consider outdoorsy, but I'm excited to relax and unwind for a bit."

"Where are you from?"

"Los Angeles," I reply, glancing around to see if anyone overheard or has since recognized me.

"Really? That's cool. I've never been, but I could only imagine. All those stars everywhere. It would be so neat to see some famous people. I've never met anyone. It's not like we get a lot here in Pine Village," she says with a laugh.

Internally, I cringe.

If she only knew.

"Listen, this might sound a little forward since we don't really know each other, but some friends of ours are having a cookout tomorrow afternoon. My husband, son, and his girlfriend will be joining me, and if you don't have anything to do, I'd love for you to join us."

Surprised by her invitation, I don't reply right away. I'm used to being invited to the biggest parties with the biggest names, but this? I wasn't prepared for an offer to attend a barbecue.

"Sorry, that was really direct. I'm sure you already have plans anyway, but if not, here," she says, pulling out her pad of paper and writing. "This is the address for my friend's cabin. There won't be a ton of people there, but maybe fifteen-ish? Four or five couples, some kids, and some single friends. Not that I'm trying to set you up or anything," she quickly adds, rocking from side to side as if she were uncomfortable.

"Umm, I'm not really sure what I'm doing, but I appreciate the offer."

"I think you'd like my friends. They're pretty great," she adds with an endearing shrug, and I can't help but *want* to spend time with her and her friends.

I don't know what it is about Ellie, but she seems genuine and real. Pretty much everyone I know back in California is the exact opposite. They're fake as hell and usually only care about themselves or what you can do for them.

I can't help but think about Vaughn.

The ultimate user.

"Here's your check. You can pay at the counter when you're ready, but no rush," Ellie says, collecting my dirty plate but leaving my sweet tea. "Oh," she starts, stopping before she gets away from my table, "I'm so rude. I don't think I even caught your name."

I can't help but smile. "It's Jade." My middle name rolls off my tongue easily, as it always does when I'm looking to stay under the radar.

She returns the gesture. "Jade. I like that. Well, Jade, hope to see you tomorrow, but if not, maybe I'll see you around. Enjoy your stay in Pine Village."

"Thank you."

I pull out my wallet and retrieve a larger than standard tip, considering my bill is about twelve dollars. I always tip generously, but Ellie was a delight. She was efficient, friendly, and her recommendations were on point.

Taking one final sip of my sweet tea and gathering my bags, including my leftovers, I head for the front counter with cash in hand. "Hi there," the older woman greets when I approach. "How was your meal?"

"It was delicious, thank you."

"Happy to hear. I'm Frannie, the owner," she says, pulling change out of the old cash register.

"Nice to meet you, Frannie. I'll definitely be back," I tell her.

As I make my way toward the entrance, a small group of teen girls are walking in. I lower my head and avoid eye contact, but just as I try to slip through the door, I hear one of them gasp. "Oh my God, that's Ryan Marcotte!"

I keep my gaze down, hoping to slip by them without any inquiries, but unfortunately, luck is not on my side. "Excuse me, are you Ryan Marcotte?" one of the other girls asks, stepping in front of me and blocking my escape.

I look up, startled. "Me?" I ask before giggling in a voice that doesn't sound like mine. "I wish! I get that all the time though."

The four girls all eye me skeptically. "You really look like her," one chimes in, her eyes narrowing as she takes in my appearance.

I wave off her comment and share a closed-mouth smile, doing everything I can to not make myself look or sound like...myself. "If I were, would I be vacationing in Wisconsin?" I ask, rolling my eyes playfully. "If I were Ryan Marcotte, I'd be in like Grand Caymans, Fiji, or Paris."

The first girl seems defeated. "Yeah, you're right. No way would the real Ryan Marcotte come here." She eyes me up and down. "You dress just like her though. You must be a superfan."

Instantly recognizing my mistake, I realize I need to make a wardrobe change and fast. "Oh, yeah, these are knockoffs. No way could I afford the clothes she wears on her reality show and podcasts."

The fourth girl gives me a harsh once-over. "Yeah, those definitely aren't designer," she informs the group, flipping her blond hair over her shoulder. "I'm pretty sure her hair isn't naturally blonde and she's bigger than Ryan," she adds, zeroing in on my waist.

I almost roll my eyes at her assessment and blurt, "Ryan's hair isn't naturally blonde either," but that will only ensure I give away my real identity. Instead, I go with, "Well, have a good day." I move around them, determined to get out of the diner and away from critical, knowing eyes.

The moment I toss my bags into the back and climb into my rental, I pull down the mirror. Of course people would recognize me. It was completely naïve of me to assume they wouldn't, just because I was in Small Town, Wisconsin and the first few people I encountered had no clue. I need to do better at disguising myself if I'm going to survive this entire month without anyone finding out who I am.

The first thing I need is to stop wearing designer clothes in public. Considering that's all I brought with me, that'll require some more shopping. Next, hats. And not the big straw ones I would be photographed in while on the yacht. I need ball caps or those smaller sunhats they were selling at the clothing boutique I visited earlier.

I sigh.

Looks like I'll be making another shopping trip soon.

But most of the shops I went to this morning are closed on Sundays and this coming Monday for the Memorial Day holiday, so it'll be Tuesday before I can do a wardrobe refresh to make me blend

45

in more. Until then, I'll have to make do with what I have, ensuring I don't wear anything too flashy and stylish, like what I have on today.

And I'll just have to stay in my cabin.

For a few moments, I was actually considering taking Ellie up on her invitation. I'm not exactly sure why, but, well, I liked her. She was kind and polite and had no idea who I was. At least, I don't think she did. She could be a great actress, but I don't think so. I never saw recognition flit through her eyes, and I'm usually pretty good at picking up on those kinds of things.

For everyone except for Vaughn…

But we're not going there.

He's in the rearview mirror, remember?

And I'm only looking forward from here on out.

To hell with Vaughn Cramer, user extraordinaire.

I don't need him.

I don't need any man.

CHAPTER *five*

MARCUS

My phone chimes with an alert. Pulling up the message from the rental management company, I shake my head.

> **Arrow Rentals Management:** Received a call from your renter. One of the windows is broken. How would you like us to proceed?

I sigh and close my eyes. These are the times I wish I didn't bother with renting my grandparents' old cabin. It's not like I need the extra income or anything. The old place is paid for, but the rental income covers the property taxes and for the most part, I rarely have to deal with issues. I keep the cabin well-maintained in between renters, and block out days, weeks, and sometimes months when I don't have time to deal with the extra responsibility. But I try to keep the cabin open from Memorial Day weekend through Labor Day weekend. It's the busiest tourist season, and if we ever have a cancellation, it's usually filled right away.

Which is what happened with Ryan.

I had just received notification the previous renter cancelled their reservation, and it seemed just minutes later, I was emailed a new agreement for a new renter. Because my cabin is promoted for long-term rentals with a seven-day minimum commitment, I don't get any weekend stays. You know, the party boys who want to get away for a couple nights, drink beer until they're fall-down drunk, and tear up anything in their path. Logan had a problem with renters like that and eventually removed his cabin from the rental agency. Now, he and Hallie keep it for their own use, and let our friends use it too.

My mind flashes back to the text I received. What could have happened to the window? Was Ryan hurt? Did she cut herself somehow?

I fire off a quick reply as I head for the door.

Me: I'll go check it out.

Arrow Rentals Management: Thank you. Let us know if you need anything.

My agreement with Arrow is they try to contact me first. If it's something I can fix and have time, I take care of it. If not, they'll dispatch the appropriate repair person to take care of the problem.

I bypass the tow truck and head for my garage. Jumping onto my Honda Rancher four-wheeler, I rev it up and take off toward my rental. The dirt roads are dry and leave a trail of dust in my wake as I head toward the path that leads me to the cabin.

When I get close to the clearing, I back off the speed and slowly creep into the yard. Parking the machine beside Ryan's rental SUV, I hop off and make my way toward the old, screen door and knock. The main door is open, the warm breeze blowing through the cabin. It takes only a moment before she appears.

"Oh. Hi." She seems surprised to see me.

"Hey, the agency told me there's a broken window?" I ask, glancing around.

"Yes, well, the one in the bedroom," she informs me, walking over and releasing the lock on the door.

I pull it open and step inside, the scent of fresh air and flowers filling the space. Taking a quick stock of her surroundings, making sure everything is all right, I follow behind her to the master bedroom. As soon as we step inside, I swear her scent is overpowering and the air seems to be sucked out of the room. It's like some Ryan-induced vacuum, and my eyes immediately move to the bed.

Bad idea.

Now all I can picture is her wrapped up in my grandma's quilt, her long, naked limbs sliding against the sheets, her long, blond hair fanning out against the pillow.

"Marcus?"

I startle, ripped from my own head like I'm doused in cold water. Removing my ball cap, I lift it up, run my fingers through my hair and replace the hat on my head. "Yeah. Sorry. Which window is broken?" I ask, turning my attention to the glass panes.

"This one," she says, walking over and grabbing the ledge. "It won't move." She pulls up, but the window doesn't budge.

All I can do is stare at it. "They said a window was broken."

She huffs. "It *is* broken. It won't open."

I close my eyes and take a deep breath. "It's not broken," I mutter, walking over to the window and giving it a tug. It's tight and doesn't move easily, but I get the window up, nonetheless. "There."

Her eyes narrow and she crosses her arms over her chest. It's the first time I realize she changed out of the blue dress she was wearing earlier. Now, her toned, tanned legs are on full display, since she's donning a pair of denim cutoffs and a fitted pink tank top. "You barely got that up. You had to turn all Hulk on it. How do you expect me to get it open?" she asks, tapping her bare foot on the hardwood floor as she waits for my reply.

"Hulk?" I ask, the corner of my mouth threatening to curl up.

"Well, your shirt is stretched across your arms," she says, her cheeks turning a delightful shade of pink. It's as if she didn't mean to confess the fact she was looking.

"So?"

She waves her hand and clears her throat. "How am I supposed to get it closed? Are you going to run back over here and close it for me later?"

My eyebrows draw together in confusion. "Then just leave it closed."

"I shouldn't have to," she proclaims. "All windows should work accordingly, and this one doesn't. It's clearly broken."

I glance at the window and then back to her. "Listen, Princess, it's not broken. It's just tight. It probably doesn't get opened very much."

"It should be fixed," she states.

"It's not broken," I insist.

She throws her hands up in the air and stomps out of the room, leaving me standing here, staring and wondering what the hell just happened. I lift my hat and run my hand through my hair once more before replacing it.

"Women," I grumble before returning my attention to the window.

I mess around with it for a few minutes, lifting and lowering it several times until it starts to move easier. They're old windows, but are still effective, so I have no intention of replacing them anytime soon.

Spinning around, I head out of the bedroom, needing to put some distance between myself and her scent that only seems to have grown stronger since she left the room. I find her standing in the kitchen, sipping from a bottle of sparkling water. "It should be easier to move now," I tell her.

She stares back at me, and I can't help but wonder what she's thinking about. She gives nothing away, just watches me intently. "Are you this crabby and difficult with everyone?"

Propping my hip against the counter, I reply, "Nope, I think it's just you."

She huffs. "Great. I'm honored," she mutters sarcastically.

"Holler if you need anything else," I say, turning around and heading for the door.

Just before I cross the threshold, I hear, "Marcus?"

I pause, glancing over my shoulder.

"Can I ask you a question?"

I don't reply with words, but turn back around, giving her my full attention.

She straightens her spine and lifts her chin. "I need to purchase a hat, and I know most of the shops are closed until Tuesday. Does any other place sell them locally, or do I need to go to Hudson?"

"A hat? What kind of hat?"

"One like yours."

I look up. "A ball cap?" The confusion is evident in my question.

"Yes," she replies with a nod.

"Uhhh, you can get them just about anywhere. The gas stations sell them or the little general store in the Bluff," I reply, reaching up and running my hand across the back of my neck. "Why?"

She shrugs. "I just thought a hat would come in handy when I take walks around the lake. You know, protect my face from the sun?"

I lift my head in understanding, but I can't help feel a little surprised Ryan doesn't already have a hat. You know, one of those big, fancy ones they wear to the Kentucky Derby or on some exotic beach. "Uhh, yeah."

"I'll just swing by some place and grab one. Thank you."

I nod, my hands shoved into the pockets of my jeans. "Anything else?"

"No, that's all."

"Okay," I reply, returning my attention to the exit as I push out the screen door.

As I step off the porch, I hear the door creak open behind me. "Thank you for your help. With the window and...the hat."

I climb onto my four-wheeler and face the beauty in front of me. "You're welcome." Before she can reply, I turn the key, firing up the machine, and press on the throttle. Any words she speaks are drowned out. I lift with my foot, engaging first gear, and press the throttle lever with my right hand. I take off, turning the machine around and heading for the path that leads back to my own cabin. Grandpa and I cut the path when I built my own place as a more direct way for us to get back and forth without having to drive the lanes.

Reaching my property once more, I park my four-wheeler in the garage and close the door. It's a great night for a ride, but I don't feel like dealing with all the tourists on the trails. Stepping inside my cabin, I find myself walking to the room I use as a home office, my boots echoing through my quiet home. I go to the closet and reach for a box. It's already open, since I get in it more often than any other box in the closet, and I pull out two different items.

When I replace the box in the closet, I spot another one right beside it. Reaching inside, I grab a fist full of can koozies and the items from the other box, and head for the kitchen. I check the fridge, ready to pull a beer out, but know I probably shouldn't. You never know when a tow call will come in, and the last thing I need to do is drink alcohol. So I close the door empty-handed and move to the cabinet.

As I fill a glass with tap water, I can't help but chuckle. I can't believe she was throwing such a fit about drinking tap water. I've been drinking it as long as I've lived here, probably longer. We never bought bottled water growing up. It was perfectly acceptable to drink straight from the hose on a hot summer day.

Chugging the contents of my glass, I set it aside and look at the items I grabbed from the closet. I shouldn't do this, but that doesn't stop me from picking up the two ball caps and two of the can koozies and making my way back to the door.

Instead of jumping on the four-wheeler, I opt to walk.

Maybe a little air will do me some good.

And keep me from showing back up at my rental cabin.

It takes me a few minutes to reach the clearing where the cabin is positioned. Her SUV is still here, but as I reach the porch, I notice the door is closed. I almost reach for the knob to see if it's locked but stop myself before I can completely invade her privacy. Instead, I go to the back of the house, where the trees give way to the lake.

She had mentioned something about walking around the lake, except that's not what I find. Ryan's standing in the clearing, her blond hair blowing in the gentle breeze as she gazes out at the expansive lake before her. There's something so...beautiful about her, and it doesn't exactly have to do with her good looks. She looks peaceful, content, and so right standing on the shore of my lake.

Not *my* lake, but you know what I'm saying...

I don't know how long I stand here, watching her as she stares out at the water, but eventually, I realize I need to move. Returning to the front porch, I place the hats and koozies in front of the screen door and take off for the path.

The temperature is cooler under the canopy of the trees, and it's a welcome reprieve from being close to Ryan in the bedroom. I don't know why, but standing there, I started to feel a little flush at her nearness, even though she wasn't even right next to me. I've never had a reaction to a woman like that before, felt her proximity and felt overwhelmed with her presence.

When I reach the clearing for my own cabin, I keep walking. I've always been outdoorsy, spending as much time in nature as possible. My grandpa was that way, always taking me fishing or camping whenever possible. That's why I do what I do for a living. Not only is it all I know, but plowing in the cold and towing in any condition doesn't bother me.

I start walking my property, checking to make sure the signage indicating it's private is still firmly in place and visible. I've got signs at each corner of the property lines, as well as on the trails. It's not too often someone from the park comes onto my land, but it happens. Most of the people visiting don't know where the Bluff Preserves National Park ends and private property begins, even though maps are available throughout the park and most everyone has their property marked with signs.

Moving a few downed limbs, I make some piles of brush to pick up later. I keep moving and end up cleaning a big section of land to the east of my cabin, away from the one Ryan is renting.

Just as I start moving another branch, I hear a noise in the distance. It's the whimper of an animal, which puts me on high alert. Slowly, I creep toward a grouping of young trees with a large stump in the middle, finally spotting what made the sound. There's a dog, hiding behind the stump. He peeks out, his eyes filled with fear and wonder as he watches me.

"Hey, buddy," I say softly, hoping not to scare it. Making eye contact, I drop to a knee about ten feet away from where he's cowering. "Come on out, little fella. I won't hurt you."

It takes a solid minute of me talking to him, but slowly, the dog emerges from his hiding spot and carefully makes his way toward me. Lifting my hand to pet him, he shakes and stops moving. "It's okay, buddy. You're safe."

I keep to my knees and hold out a hand, hoping to coax him to me. He isn't wearing a collar and is on the skinny side. His fur is matted in places and by the frightened look in his eyes, it appears he's been scared and on the run for a while.

After several minutes, he finally reaches my side. I made a big gesture of keeping my hands visible as I bring them down on his head. He jumps under my touch, but leans into me, grateful and appreciative of the mercy I'm extending.

"Poor guy. How long have you been on your own?" I ask, letting my eyes roam over his body, checking for visible injuries. I don't see anything except some cockleburs matted in his fur. I'll try to get those out, but right now, that's not a huge priority.

"Wanna come up and get something to drink?" I ask, wondering if I should pick him up, so he doesn't run off. He's not a terribly big dog, probably about forty pounds. He appears to be a mutt, most likely a mixture of beagle and something else. Lab, maybe? He has long legs and dark hair, but his face looks like that of the smaller breed dog.

When I stand up, he moves back a little, so I place my hands in my pockets. The gesture must comfort him enough that he slowly moves toward me once more. "All right, buddy, we're gonna go up to the house and see what we've got to eat and drink. I don't have any dog food, but I might have something that'll work until we can figure out what's going on, okay?"

He watches me intently, as if understanding what I said and gauging my sincerity. He walks beside me the entire way through the timber, occasionally stopping to sniff the ground or a stick before trotting alongside me as we return to my cabin.

I walk onto my porch and open my front door. The dog hesitates, glancing from me to inside the house. After a few seconds, he takes a couple hesitant steps. "Good boy. Let's get you something to drink."

Making sure he's behind me, I go to the kitchen and retrieve a bowl, filling it with tap water. I place it on the floor and stand back, waiting. The dog watches me for several seconds before slowly making his way to the bowl and drinking. "Good boy," I tell him, holding still so I don't scare him.

When he drinks half the bowl, I carefully move to the fridge. I don't have a lot of options, but I do have a few chicken breasts leftover from the other night. Pulling out the container, I retrieve one fillet and place it on a plate. I cut up the meat, scraping off the seasoning where I can. When it's all chopped into bite-sized pieces, I glance down. The dog is sitting right beside my left foot, watching me. He licks his lips, as if understanding what's to come. Not wanting to make him wait any longer, I place the plate on the floor beside the bowl of water and watch as he goes to town. He chews happily, his eyes bouncing between the food and me.

I've always loved dogs, but never felt like I was in a place where I could get one. My work hours are crazy, but I don't know, something about this guy calls to me. Maybe it's the fact he was abandoned, like me, and reliant on someone compassionate and loving to care for him.

Of course, maybe he's not a stray, but someone's pet. There might be a child out looking for him right now, though by the looks of this guy, he's been left on his own for a while. I guess I should probably start by talking to a vet and going from there.

I run my hand across his head. "You're gonna be okay, boy. I promise."

CHAPTER
six

Ryan

I shouldn't go.

The more I'm out and under the public's watchful eye, the more chances I'm taking at being recognized, and the last thing I want is to have my little world inundated by the press once more.

It's Sunday, only two days since I left LA and flew to Wisconsin, but I'm enjoying this private little bubble I'm in. Of course, at any moment, that bubble could pop. It almost happened on day two yesterday with that group of high school girls, but I was able to convince them I wasn't Ryan. I'm not sure it will be as easy next time, especially if I keep dressing like myself.

My eyes move to the two ball caps sitting on the kitchen table. One dark blue and the other red, both with the same wrench and gear logo with the name Wright Auto printed across it. Beneath the business name is a phone number and the words auto repair, tow truck, and snow removal. It has to be Marcus's business. How else would you explain two ball caps appearing at my front door less than an hour after I asked Marcus about where to purchase one?

Is that his last name? Wright?

I find myself reaching for my phone and doing what I'd normally do when I want information. I Google.

Immediately, I'm inundated with info on Marcus Wright, but with just a quick scroll, I can tell none of them are the Marcus I know. Of course, maybe that's not even his last name. Deciding to try narrowing down my options, I add the town and state behind the name. Instantly, an article from a little more than three years ago in the local newspaper appears on the screen, so I click the link and start reading.

There's a picture at the top of a younger Marcus standing beside an older man, their arms thrown around each other's shoulders. The caption confirms my suspicions of it being his grandfather. The article explains how the business originally started in the fifties with Michael and his wife, Nina, building the small auto repair shop. It doesn't talk about Marcus's parents, just mentions the young boy always helping and being eager to learn from his grandpa and long-time employee, Dale Christian.

Dale.

I read the rest of the article, talking about Marcus purchasing the business from his grandfather before he passed away from pancreatic cancer around the time the article was published. Nina had passed away almost twenty years ago. Over the last several decades, the business grew to what it is now, adding the towing service and snow removal along the way.

There's also a black-and-white photo of the original building, Nina and Michael standing in front of it with wide smiles on their faces. I take in the younger Michael and can definitely see Marcus in him. Was Marcus's mom or dad the connection between grandfather and grandson? I don't know why I'm so interested in learning more about him, especially since he's been less than cordial since I arrived in town.

But even with his grumpy demeanor, I do admit, he's appealing to the female eye. I can see why ladies might lose their minds—and maybe their panties—over a man like him. He's nothing—and I do mean nothing—like the men I've always dated, but I contribute that to the difference in our social circles. He's a small-town country boy and I'm a big-city rich girl.

We'd never work.

I pick up the red ball cap and place it on my head. It takes a few tries to tighten the strap to make it fit, and the moment I have it right, I go to the bathroom to check my reflection. My hair is down in beach waves, and I have to admit, I kind of like this look. I've seen it online, but I've never added the trucker or ball cap to my wardrobe. Can you imagine me wearing one while shopping on Rodeo Drive or at the Americana at Brand? Or in Milan and Paris? The internet would explode with gossip, comments, and opinions, and while they say bad publicity is still good publicity, my current situation doesn't necessarily agree.

I toss the ball cap onto the counter and pull my hair back into a ponytail. When it's secured with a band, I replace the hat, slipping the ponytail through the hole in back and smile. The hat definitely helps camouflage my appearance. It creates a shadow over the top half of my head, hooding my dark eyes and generating a touch of mystery.

"This'll have to work," I tell myself, reaching for my trademark pink lip gloss. Before I swipe it over my lips, I pause and replace the tube on the counter. If I'm looking to blend in a little more, I need to change the things that make Ryan Marcotte stand out.

I take in my cutoff jean shorts and red-and-white striped tank top. I brought a couple of basic fitted tanks for sleeping, so they'll have to do until I can get to a department or big box store and buy some more basic, plain tops.

Nodding in approval of my appearance, I head to the kitchen to figure out what I'm going to take. Apparently, I've just decided to attend the cookout I was invited to, the one where I'll know exactly two people there, including myself, and I can't show up empty-handed. It's not like I can cook more than anything basic, and I don't foresee any restaurant having roasted bacon Brussels sprouts or balsamic asparagus salad I can grab on my way by.

But the moment I open my fridge, I spot a few things I can use. I mean, it's not like I've ever been to a cookout like this, but I assume fruit would be acceptable. Pulling the grapes, strawberries, kiwi, and oranges out, I set out to slicing them up. I find a large bowl in one of the cabinets and start adding the sliced fruit. It only fills about half the bowl, but at least it's something.

I sigh, looking at the contents. I should just stop by the market and grab a bottle of wine or something. Closing my eyes, I take a few deep, calming breaths. This feels right. I'll take the fruit with me and if no one eats it, then so be it. I'll bring it home and eat it myself over the next couple of days. That *is* why I bought all the fruit. They have a higher sugar content, but I've always been a fruit lover and would do extra yoga or Pilates to work it off.

Reaching for my purse, I slip a pair of brown leather sandals on my feet, grab the fruit bowl, and head for the door. As soon as I climb inside my rental, I pull up the address on my phone and plug it into the GPS in the vehicle. Instantly, it starts telling me how to get to the cabin where the cookout is being held.

Fortunately, it's not too far away. It's about a mile and a half up the road, but I'll be heading farther into the national park. The sun is still shining brightly in the sky, reflecting off the water. Boats dot the massive lake, kids swim or float on rafts, and the beach is lined with families. I have to admit, this place looks like a great spot to vacation, and maybe if I were in a better mental place, I'd be able to enjoy it more.

Pushing those dark thoughts out of my head, I follow the last two hundred feet until I'm instructed to turn right at my destination. The moment I pull into the driveway, I spot several vehicles, none of them familiar. It's a reminder I don't know anyone here. Ellie might be the nicest person on earth, but that doesn't mean all her friends are. Or what if it's just an act? Maybe she's the sweet, innocent one, who lures helpless woman to a cabin in the woods and does diabolical things to them.

At that thought I actually laugh out loud.

Yeah, Ryan. The crazy townspeople lure the tourists to a cabin right in the middle of the action, hoping the other out-of-towners surrounding them won't see or hear a thing. And don't get me started on the fact that all their personal vehicles are littered around the property, right out in the open.

Except that could be the perfect crime.

Hiding in plain sight.

A knock raps on my window, causing me to jump and screech. Ellie is there, her eyes wide as she holds up a welcoming, yet hesitant hand. "Hey, sorry, I didn't mean to scare you."

I can't help but chuckle. "It's okay!" I holler through the window then turn off the vehicle. Before I climb out, I check her other hand, making sure she's not wielding a weapon or whatever to incapacitate me the moment I step from the safety of the vehicle. When I don't spot anything, I get out and shut the door.

"Welcome! I'm so glad you came. I mentioned to Hallie and Logan you might join us, and they both agreed, the more, the merrier," she says, flashing me a wide, genuine smile.

"I appreciate the invitation." Remembering the fruit, I reach for the back door and retrieve the bowl. "I brought fruit for the cookout."

"Oh, that's so great, thank you, but you didn't have to bring anything," she replies, leading me away from my vehicle and toward the grassy area where chairs and tables are set up.

"Well, I'll be honest. I don't really cook, but I can cut fruit or chop a mean salad," I reply with a chuckle.

"The fruit is great, really." She threads her arm through mine and adds, "Come on, let's go meet everyone."

Ellie guides me toward a man throwing a football with who I assume is his son. "TD, come meet Jade," she says to the man as he catches a pass from the boy.

The man turns around and offers a friendly smile. He's a good-looking guy, with broad shoulders and brown eyes. "Hey, nice to meet you."

"Likewise," I reply, taking his offered hand and giving it a gentle shake.

"Brody, this is Jade. She's in town for the next month," Ellie hollers to the young man standing at the far end of the grassy area.

"Nice to meet you, ma'am," Brody hollers with a wave, which I return.

"Come on, let's go meet the others," Ellie says, steering me toward the front of the cabin. A group of guys exits, all good-looking in their casual shorts or jeans and T-shirts. "Everyone, this is Jade. She's the one I told you may stop by. Jade, this is everyone. Gabe, Logan, and Gavin."

"Hello," I acknowledge, earning a variety of greetings in return.

"Make yourself at home. We're getting ready to throw food on the grill, and the ladies are finishing up some of the sides. That's code for gossiping in the kitchen," Logan states with a smile and a laugh.

"Come on, let's go meet the girls." Ellie drags me inside the super cute cabin. The décor is a bit more modern than what's in my cabin, and you can tell by all the baby stuff everywhere they use it frequently. "Ladies, the woman I was telling you about showed up! Meet Jade," she says, pulling me into the kitchen to where the trio of woman stand, chatting.

"This is Blair, Ava, and Hallie, and those two little sweet faces are Makenzie and Wrenlee," she informs me, pointing to the two sleeping babies inside a playpen.

The first two welcome me with smiles and waves, but it's the third one that catches my attention. "Holy shit, you're Ryan Marcotte!"

My eyes widen as my chin automatically lowers, hoping the hat shields more of my face. Before I can reply, it's Ellie who speaks. "This is Jade," she reiterates, saying the words a little slower this time.

"No, this is Ryan Marcotte of *Ryan's Reality*! It's on E!," Hallie insists, her eyes alive with excitement. "I've watched every episode of your show!"

All eyes turn toward me. "Holy crap, you're right! I'm Blair, by the way. I just started watching your show because Hallie insisted. I wear your makeup line."

My mouth falls open, but no words rush out. I feel like a fish out of water right now, wishing I knew what to say or do. Instead, I focus on the last part of her statement and mutter a quiet, "Thank you."

Ellie turns to me, her eyes full of confusion. "You're Ryan Marcotte? Why did you tell me your name was Jade?"

I clear my throat, feeling terrible for having deceived her. "My name is Ryan Jade Marcotte, and when I'm trying to fly under the radar, I will use my middle name."

"I can't believe you're here!" Hallie proclaims, practically jumping up and down where she stands. "Everyone is buzzing about where you went."

I can't help but roll my eyes. "I'm sure the stories and speculation are horrible."

"Oh, they are. One entertainment show says they heard you went into rehab after what happened at the end of your show," she says, making my stomach drop to my feet.

"I heard you were spotted in Paris with some prince of some small country no one can pronounce," Blair adds.

I sigh, grateful to be taking a social media hiatus. The last thing I need is to read the rumors and lies being said about me. Not that it would be any different than any other time, but still. Not now, when I'm still reeling from Vaughn's very public betrayal. "I'm sure it'll all die down soon."

Fat chance of that happening. I don't know why, but the paparazzi love me. I'm the Hollywood Princess, as I'm often referred to. The daughter of one of the industry's biggest movie producers and a former beauty queen turned philanthropist. I was practically born royalty.

"So, you're here, hiding out?"

"What made you choose Pine Village?"

"Did you really not know what the big surprise was they were promoting for your season finale?"

"Okay, stop," Ellie says, holding up both hands. "Let's all take a deep breath. I'm sure Jade, or Ryan, has her reasons for doing and saying what she has. Let's not completely overwhelm her in the first couple of minutes. I promised her a great time, just hanging out with my friends, and that's what we're gonna give her. If she wants to tell us more, so be it, but we will not push her," Ellie says, giving Hallie a pointed look. Turning to me, she adds, "If you don't want to stay, I would completely understand. My friends are good people, and if you do want to stay, we will respect your privacy. No one here will say a word about your presence."

My heartbeat starts to settle for the first time since Hallie outed me in front of everyone. "Thank you," I reply, still feeling a bit overwhelmed.

"Come on, let's take this food outside," Blair announces. Turning to me, she adds, "I hope you'll stay, and yes, Ellie's right. We won't say a word about you. No photos or anything," she insists.

I nod, appreciating the hospitality and understanding.

Grabbing the fruit bowl, I follow behind the others outside and to the picnic area. There are tables and chairs set up as they begin preparing to serve the food. I set my bowl next to the pasta salad and step back, watching the dynamics. I have friends—dozens and dozens of them—but this feels different. These women are close.

You can feel their love and bond, and even though I talk to my friends, I realize I may not know them as well as I should.

Sure, I know Calista doesn't like lobster and that Sasha cheats on her boyfriend with her tennis instructor, but how well do I really know them? Deep down, you know? Their fears and worries and biggest regrets.

Just watching the women together for a short time feels different than anything I've experienced, and I don't know why. I don't know these women from Eve, but it's just a vibe I pick up on, like a sixth sense flowing from the group.

"So, what do you think? Are you going to take off?" Ellie asks as she approaches.

I should. These four women know who I am. All it would take is one person telling another for it to slowly work its way to social media. From there, there's no stopping it. It would hit every phone, every computer screen, every TV in America in a matter of seconds. The town would be swarmed, like bees to honey. That's not me being arrogant. It's a fact. I've dealt with life under the microscope since birth, and I know how it goes. I'd have no privacy, which is exactly what I wanted when I chose this place as the spot to hide away for a little while.

"I'd completely understand if you do, and I still promise we won't speak of it."

I nod in appreciation and know what I want to do. "I'd like to stay, if it's all the same."

"Absolutely!" Ellie proclaims, clearly very excited about it. "You'll have fun, I promise." She threads her arm through mine once more. "Come on, let's go grab a drink." Before we can take two steps, she stops. "Oh, what name do you want us to use? If you'd prefer to go by Jade, that's fine."

A part of me wants them to call me by my real name, but I can't take the chance of someone overhearing them use it and out me. "Umm, you can call me Ryan when it's just us, but maybe Jade when we're in public?" I suggest, feeling relieved by her understanding and compassion.

"We can do that, Well, Ryan, it looks like the food is ready. How about we grab us a plate and get to know each other." She turns to the others. "Ryan is going to stay and eat with us. She agreed we can call her Ryan when it's just us, but to keep her privacy, we'll call her Jade in public. Don't make this awkward," she insists, her narrowed eyes leveling on Hallie.

She gapes at Ellie. "I would never." To me she says, "Come on, Ryan. Let's eat!"

CHAPTER
seven

MARCUS

I'm way late when arriving to the cookout, thanks to a tow call following an accident, but if I know Logan, there's still plenty of food available for the latecomers. He's a whiz on the grill and always makes a variety of delicious food. Buddy and I, that's what I named the dog I'm now caring for, hit up the small bakery on Main Street for their selection of cookies. I got lucky there was anything left at this point in the day, especially since she was closing, so I grabbed all four varieties she had available.

I slow the tow truck down and park along the roadway. There's enough grass between the trees and the road to comfortably park, which is what a lot of people do during the busy summer months. Logan's cabin is across from the lake with lots of trees, paths, and access to everything the Bluff has to offer.

Climbing from my truck, I slip the leash onto Buddy's collar and help him from the truck. He instantly starts to sniff around but doesn't venture too far away from me. Grabbing the bag of cookies, I follow the sound of laughter to Logan's property. The guys are standing off to the side, throwing bags, but as I walk past the line of vehicles filling the driveway, I stop beside the one on the outside. I know this SUV, but what I can't understand is why it's here.

My eyes immediately scan the small crowd, looking for the driver of said SUV. It only takes me a second to spot her, sitting over by the fire with the group of women. They're animatedly chatting, about what, I'm not sure. As far as I know, Ryan didn't know anyone in town, so why is she sitting with the women like they've been friends forever?

"Hey, Marcus, quit gawking and come play. You and Gabe got winner," TD hollers.

I turn my attention to the guys, who are all standing there, watching me and smiling. I move in their direction, Buddy happily trotting beside me, and refuse to acknowledge their smirks. "I see you noticed our guest," Logan says, a cat that ate the canary grin on his smug face. "Holy shit, is that a dog?"

"No, it's an elephant," I tease as they all turn their attention to the animal at my side. "Meet Buddy."

"Cool, can I pet him?" Brody asks, dropping to his knees in front of me.

"Sure. He's a little skittish though, so don't be offended if he keeps back a little bit."

I watch as Buddy sniffs the air around Brody, who holds his hand up. "I won't hurt you, Buddy. Come 'ere," Brody says gently, coaxing the dog toward him. As soon as Buddy reaches him, Brody starts petting his head and scratching behind his ears.

"Good boy," I tell the dog, trying to make sure I give him plenty of accolades to keep his spirits up.

"So...the special guest. Want me to introduce you?" Gavin asks, waggling his eyebrows suggestively.

"She's my renter," I mutter, holding up the bag. "I brought cookies. Figured I'd miss the main course, so I brought dessert."

"I think Ellie just put out a cake and some of that strawberry fluff dessert she likes to make," Gabe chimes in.

"And there's plenty of food left. The fridge stuff is in the cooler, but the roaster on the table has chicken wings, brats, and burgers left," Logan tells me.

"Great. I'll run and make a plate and be back. Brody, you okay to watch Buddy for me?"

"Of course," he replies, taking the leash.

"Drinks are in the cooler by the porch," Logan hollers as I start to walk away.

I walk straight to the food table and place the plastic containers of cookies beside the cake. A moment later, Hallie is there, holding her and Logan's sleeping daughter in her arms. "Hey, I'm so glad you could come. Let me get out the cold stuff," she says, carefully reaching down and opening the cooler.

"I'll get it, Hal. Don't you disrupt that sleeping princess," I whisper, bending down and placing a kiss on the top of Makenzie's little head.

"Are those cookies?" she asks, leaning over toward the four containers.

"They are. Picked 'em up just as Jillian was closing. Chocolate chunk, snickerdoodle, peanut butter chocolate, and lemon blueberry."

Hallie gasps. "G'me," she insists, reaching for the first container.

I help open all four so she can grab one of each before shoving the top one into her mouth. "Do you need my help?" she mumbles with her mouth full.

I can't help but chuckle. "I'm good, Hal. Go sit and visit with your friends."

"Thanks," she replies, still chewing, and heads over to where the ladies sit around the fire. My eyes connect with Ryan's brown ones, and it feels...charged. She's watching me warily, but I can't deny the intensity I feel, like I'm trapped in her gaze.

I force myself to return my attention to the food. I'm a meat guy, so I load my plate up with a few wings, a brat, and a burger. I squirt a healthy blob of mustard on the two buns and grab a handful of barbecue potato chips. Heading over to the cooler, I retrieve a bottle of water. Since I could be called out for a tow, I don't want to drink.

Waving at all the women sitting around the fire, I return to the area where the guys are throwing bags. "So, what made you decide to get a dog?" Gabe asks, taking a drink from his beer bottle.

I can't help but notice how Buddy is sitting directly in front of me now, watching my plate of food. "Well, he found me, I think. I went for a walk last night in the timber and heard a whimper. Buddy was cowering behind a tree."

"He's awfully skinny," Gabe notices. He may not be a vet, but you can't take the doctor out of the man.

"He definitely is. We went to one of those big chain pet supply stores in Hudson, and they tried to scan him. He's not chipped. Since I can't get in to a vet until Tuesday, I figured I'd go ahead and look after him."

TD kneels down and pets him on the back. "He looks to be in decent shape, despite a little malnourished."

"That's what the guys said at the pet store. They were doing a vaccine clinic, and the vet there checked him over. Went ahead and gave him a rabies, distemper, and parvo shot, saying it won't hurt him if he's already had them at some point in his life. She thinks he's about a year, year and a half old and is well-behaved. She helped me pick out some food and other supplies for the time being."

"You gonna keep him? I haven't seen a lost dog poster around town," Logan says.

"I don't know. My schedule is crazy busy. Not really fair for a dog, you know?" I look down and find Buddy's sad eyes on me. It's as if he knows I'm considering not keeping him.

"He's so well-behaved though. How'd he do riding in the truck?" TD asks.

"Surprisingly well. It's as if he's been trained and ridden in one many times before."

"He was probably someone's pet, and for whatever reason, they let him go. But as skinny as he is, he's been on his own a while. The only lost pet posters I've seen in the store are for cats," Logan states.

"Where'd he sleep?" Gavin asks while I take a bite of my brat.

I can feel my face blush, and I don't want to answer, but since all eyes are on me, waiting, I know I need to give them something. "I put an old comforter in the utility room for him to sleep on." I pray they drop it, but luck is definitely not on my side.

"He stay?" Gabe asks, now rubbing Buddy's belly. I can't help but notice his touch has a bit of an exam look to it, as if he's checking him over for injuries or issues.

"Uhh, he did whimper quite a bit when I closed the door," I confess, recalling how I lay there in bed for about ten minutes listening to the dog cry.

Logan stares at me and smiles. "You went and got him, didn't you?"

I sigh before nodding. "Yeah, I went and got the blanket and put it in the corner of my bedroom. He did much better when he could see me." I leave out the part about waking up with him snuggled against my side in bed later in the night.

"Oh my goodness, is that a puppy?" Gavin's daughter, Annabelle, hollers. She comes running straight for us.

Buddy moves, jumping behind my legs as if to hide from the excited young girl.

"Hold up, Annabelle, he's pretty shy. You gotta go easy with him, okay?" Gavin says, helping slow his eleven-year-old daughter down before she reaches the dog.

"Can I pet him?" she asks with hopeful, love-filled eyes.

"Sure, you just gotta make slow movements. He's a good boy," I tell the girl, glancing over at Gavin to make sure he's okay with it. I'm still a bit hesitant. Even though he seems to be a pretty mellow, easygoing dog, I don't know him well enough yet, and the last thing I'd want is for him to hurt Annabelle.

But the moment she drops down into the grass, Buddy gives her his nose to pet. The next thing I know, he's licking her face and giving her all kinds of love, which makes her giggle. "He's so cute. What's his name?"

"Buddy."

"Is he yours, Marcus?"

I open my mouth to say no, but to be honest, I kinda like him. A lot. And the thought of keeping him doesn't bother me as much as it should. I wasn't joking when I said my work schedule isn't exactly pet-friendly, but as good as Buddy is, it may not be so bad. He may make a great shop dog too, going with me to work every day. And as long as he keeps up his good behavior in the truck, he can ride along with me for tow and plow jobs.

Of course, I'm putting the cart before the horse. Just because the vet at the pet store didn't find a chip doesn't mean Buddy doesn't belong to someone. Though, the fact he has been on his own for a bit now doesn't sit well with me either. If someone did lose him, they sure as shit aren't too concerned with getting him back. I just need to take it day by day and do what I can until the vet gives me a little more information.

"For now," I finally answer the young girl as she continues to shower Buddy with love and attention. "Can I take him for a walk?"

"Sure, but hold on to his leash."

"And stay where we can see you," Gavin adds.

Annabelle takes the leash and starts to walk around the property with the dog, who stops to sniff different sections of the yard. The women must notice the addition, because someone squeals, and the next thing I know, Annabelle is leading the dog toward where they all sit.

I finish eating my food, while keeping an eye on Buddy and the women. Gabe walks over and takes his baby daughter from Blair, who gets up and fills a plate with desserts. Gabe makes his way back over to where I stand, the tiny girl nestled in his arm. "How's she doing? Sleeping at night yet?" I ask, gently running my finger against Wrenlee's cheek.

"Not even close. Still mixing up day and night, but," he says, shrugging his shoulders, "I don't care. I'll take all the sleepless nights, because she won't be little forever." He moves his daughter up and bends down, placing a kiss on her forehead.

I've never pictured myself in his shoes. I've found comfort in my solitude. Not that I don't seek out female companionship every now and again. I'm not a monk. It's actually pretty easy. There are a few different bars I can hit in Hudson that are always full of eager, willing ladies looking for a little no-strings fun. We go back to her place, spend a few hours together, and then I'm back home and sleeping in my own bed. It works.

I'm not saying I haven't had relationships in the past, but they never seem to go much further than a few months. And that's fine. Happily ever after and together forever isn't a life goal for me. I've witnessed both sides of marriage. My parents, whose relationship was more out of duty than that forever kind of love, weren't exactly the best example for me. I was too young to even remember them together, but my grandparents were very forthcoming with information when they felt I was old enough to handle it. They told me all about my father's death in the military and my mother's decision to drop me off to be raised by my grandparents.

And, yes, before you ask, my grandparents had a great relationship. It wasn't perfect by any means, but they made it work and, at the end of the day, were completely in love and devoted to each other. So that brings me to the other side of relationships. I watched my grandma wither away to nothing from cancer and the devastation it caused my grandpa after she was gone. Why would I want to willingly go through that kind of pain?

"So, Jade is staying at your cabin, huh?"

I'm pulled out of my own head by his question, but I don't know how to answer.

Who the fuck is Jade?

I'm about to ask when Annabelle gets up and starts running with Buddy. He barks and jumps, but not at her. It's as if someone tapped the zoomie button, and she's right there for the ride. Watching how happy he is makes me briefly forget about the fact Gabe referred to Ryan as Jade.

The guys all head to where the ladies sit. I stop by and grab a cookie after tossing my plate in the trash and walk over to the side, out of the way. Annabelle and Buddy are still playing, and everyone is oohing and aahing over the two babies. I glance toward TD and Ellie, who are watching their friends with longing in their eyes. He doesn't talk about it much, but they've been trying for a baby for a bit now, unsuccessfully. They're both great people, and she'd done such a great job with Brody. I couldn't imagine having one in college and one on the way or a new baby, but something tells me Ellie and TD will handle it like pros.

If it happens for them.

"So, a puppy?"

I startle, having not heard Ryan walk up to me. "Apparently," I reply after I clear my throat.

She grins widely, watching the dog jump and play. "He's adorable."

"He's been a pretty good boy so far," I confirm. Taking a few moments while she's sidetracked, I observe.

She's standing beside me, her profile in full view. She's wearing those little cutoff shorts she had on yesterday and a red-and-white striped tank top. But what really catches my attention is the hat on her head. It's one of the two I left for her yesterday with my business logo on it. I've seen them on top of a few heads over the years—hell, I wear one every single day—but I'll admit, I'm not sure I've seen it look so cute. Her long, blond hair is pulled through the back of it and cascades down the middle of her back in big waves. It makes me want to run my hands through the strands as I pull her against my body and claim her mouth with my own.

She's fucking sexy as hell.

"Jade, do you want a cookie? These are from Jillian at the bakery, and they're they best," Ava hollers, catching my attention.

Jade.

My eyes remain locked where they are, on the woman people keep calling by a different name. "Jade?" I find myself asking, the name like something nasty on my tongue. "Why do they keep calling you that?"

Her eyes flash with something that looks like guilt, but it's quickly replaced with defiance. "I sometimes go by Jade, my middle name."

My eyebrows shoot toward my hairline. "Why would you do that?"

She clears her throat and diverts her gaze, even for just a moment. "Sometimes it's necessary."

"Necessary? Lying to people is necessary?"

Anger fills her brown eyes as they narrow. "I'm not lying," she insists, her hands on her hips.

"*Okay*, Jade. Or Ryan. Or whatever the hell your name is." I head over to where Annabelle is playing with Buddy. "Hey, kiddo, I'm gonna take Buddy home now. Thank you so much for playing with him. He'll sleep well tonight," I tell her, taking the leash from her hand.

"He's the bestest boy," she sings, reaching over and giving him one last scratch behind the ear. "See you later, Buddy."

He licks her cheek in response, making her laugh.

"Come on, Buddy. Time to go home."

I wave at my friends, ignoring their confused faces. Clearly they know something's up, since most of them heard me call her Ryan. I wasn't trying to make a scene, but I don't deal with bullshit, and this whole thing feels like one big, steaming pile of it.

Definitely time to put some distance between myself and the lying princess.

Whoever in the hell she is.

CHAPTER
eight

Ryan

I don't know why he left so abruptly, but it annoyed the hell out of me. He dismissed me instantly, throwing a jab about my name and not giving me the chance to explain. I'm not sure if he just didn't care or if he was really mad.

My gut tells me by the look in his eyes it was the latter.

I hang out with Ellie and her friends for a little longer and even help explain my use of both names to the men of the group. I truly enjoying my time with them. They're great people, all several years older than I am, but it didn't feel uncomfortable. And they all respected my privacy enough not to ask questions the entire time. Except Hallie. She snuck in a few inquiries every now and again but steered clear of the major land mines involving Vaughn and the reality show. She asked about my dad and living in Hollywood and what some of my favorite places to travel to are. Even though she is clearly a superfan, she was respectful and polite.

Plus, she let me hold her baby.

No one has ever let me hold a baby before, honest to God's truth. All my friends are more interested in keeping their perfect bodies and being photographed with the right people. None of them are looking at long-term families yet. It's all about who's who and who's fucking who in Hollywood.

"I'm going to head back to my cabin," I tell Ellie after she passes baby Wrenlee back to Blair.

"I'm so glad you came," she insists happily, pulling me into a hug.

I tense immediately, not used to such forward, touchy feely gestures. The people I'm always with do air kisses to show affection or greeting, not crush you against their chest hugs.

But I don't hate it...

I just don't know how to reciprocate.

Sure, my parents hugged me, especially when I was little, but not like this. Dad always places both hands on my shoulders, gives them a gentle squeeze, which is like a hug, and kisses me on the forehead. And my mom, well, the former beauty queen is the queen of air kisses. I don't think they've pulled me into their arms and given me a suffocating hug since I was ten and was suddenly too cool for it.

I realize I'm standing awkwardly, Ellie's arms wrapped firmly around me, so I mimic the gesture. The hug doesn't last very long, fortunately, and she pulls back and smiles. "I hope we haven't scared you too badly, and maybe we can all hang out again soon."

This is the point where I'd tell her I'd call her, knowing full well I won't, but that's not what I say. "I'd like that." And I would. I just attended my first cookout, sitting around a campfire, and I didn't hate it. In fact, quite the opposite. It was way more relaxing and comfortable than I ever expected, and I'm so glad I came.

"Great! I'm sure I'll see you around," she says, squeezing my hand.

"Of course," I reply, feeling only mildly overwhelmed by the offered friendship. Usually, where I come from friendships have strings.

I take a few minutes and say goodbye to the rest of the group, receiving hugs from the other three women and Annabelle. TD offers to help me carry my bowl to my SUV, which I decline, since it's one bowl and I had no issues carrying it to the party myself. The fact he was just being polite is still a foreign concept to me. Where I come from, everyone has ulterior motives.

When I pull out of the driveway, heading back the way I came, I realize I have a smile on my face—a genuine one, not the one I give the cameras—and it feels good. Great, actually. I almost forgot what it felt like to offer a real smile.

As I pull onto the dirt path that takes me to my rental cabin, the smile falls from my face. What the hell is up with Marcus? Why is he always so grumpy and rude? His tone carries a hint of superiority that doesn't match his appearance, and judging by the way he is with his friends, he's not like that with anyone else.

Apparently, he saves that side just for me.

"Stupid jerk," I grumble, the path that leads to his cabin coming into view.

Without giving it a second thought, I whip to the right, turning onto his lane. I've never gone up to his cabin and have no idea what I'm about to drive up on, so when I reach the clearing and find a gorgeous cabin with large windows and a huge wraparound porch, I'm pleasantly surprised. It lacks color or landscaping, but this place has so much potential.

I park my SUV beside the tow truck, which is backed into place in front of the garage. I don't see his old truck, the one he brought me home in the night my tire went flat, but maybe it's in the garage. I don't know, but I'm not here to worry about that.

I climb from the vehicle, ire from his brush-off swirling through my veins. I stomp toward the front of his house, keeping my focus on where it needs to be. The *jerk* inside.

Just as I reach the steps, the front door opens and Marcus emerges. He stands on the threshold, reaching up and grabbing the top of the doorframe. His ball cap is turned around and his T-shirt stretches tautly across his chest and arms in a way that makes my mouth go dry and my panties a touch damp.

It's probably just the heat.

I cross my arms over my chest. I tell myself it's to make myself look intimidating, tougher, but in all honestly, it's to hide the fact my nipples are getting hard.

Silence hangs between us as we engage in a stare down.

"What can I do for you, Princess?"

I blink and give my head a slight shake, dislodging the image of his arms from my brain. "I have something to say to you," I start, straightening my spine.

A single eyebrow raises in question. "Well?"

"You were rude and wouldn't let me explain," I insist, lifting my chin.

Marcus sighs. "I don't care." Releasing his hold on the doorframe and stepping out, the screen door slamming behind him.

I hear the sound of the dog's nails on the hardwood floor, and even though I want to open the door and pet the dog, I can't. I have a point to make.

"Well, you're going to hear it anyway, buster," I state firmly, sticking out my finger and digging my nail into his hard pec.

He glances down, the hint of a smile toying with his lips as he looks at the spot where my finger jabs into him. "Proceed," he encourages, his eyes glinting with mischief.

Clearing my throat, I rip my finger off his body and continue. "My name is Ryan."

Barely finishing my sentence, he asks, "So who is Jade?"

Getting frustrated, I reply, "Me."

He closes his eyes for a moment and exhales. "Okay, you can see where I might be a little confused here, right?"

I let out a growl in frustration. "You are maddening. Let me finish!"

Propping his hands on his hips, he stands there casually, waiting.

Taking a deep breath, I close my eyes for a second to calm my heartbeat and say, "My name *is* Ryan, but my middle name is Jade. I use it when I want to...blend in."

His eyes fill with questions, but he doesn't interrupt.

"Do you know who Douglas Marcotte is?" I finally ask.

Marcus slowly shakes his head no. "Should I?"

"He's a movie producer in Los Angeles."

He shrugs his shoulders, as if the name still means nothing.

"Just," I start, realizing this isn't going as well as I thought it would, "trust me. He's a big deal, and...he's my dad."

"Okay," he says, still not quite understanding.

"My dad is a major name in Hollywood, and my mom is Jade Holmes, the former Miss California, Miss USA, Miss Universe, model, and the face of Feeding Young America, a charity that helps children who face food insecurity. They're pretty much a big deal where I'm from, and because of that, I'm incredibly recognizable."

I leave out the part about my reality show, including the eruption that took place on national television less than a week ago.

None of this seems to ring any bells with him, which is so wild to me, because last I saw, my life was still trending. But then again, this is why I picked Nowhere, Wisconsin. I'm able to blend in easier and hide away in my little cabin.

"Listen, all I'm saying is people know me, and at times, I like to have some anonymity. In order to do that, I go by my middle name. I used it yesterday at the diner when I met Ellie, but the moment Hallie spotted me, the jig was up. She recognized me from my show, but they were so cool about it. They promised to keep my identity to themselves. That's why they were calling me Jade."

Those rich, hazel eyes bore into my soul. After a few second, he asks, "Show? What show?"

I kick at a rock on the porch in front of me. "I have my own reality show."

To that, he rolls his eyes. "Of course you do."

Instantly, my nerves are heckled. "What does that mean?"

"Nothing, Princess," he replies with a cheesy grin.

I huff out a sharp breath and shake my head. "You're unbelievable. Are you always this big of a jerk? I'm a little surprised you have friends," I tell him.

He just lifts his shoulders. "You seem to bring out the best in me."

"Why are you even mad? Who cares if I gave you a different name than I gave someone else?"

"I'm not mad," he insists.

"Clearly," I sass. "You just left because it was time to head home and give your dog a bath, right? It had nothing to do with finding out your friends were calling me by a different name. Well, buster, I hate to tell you this, but your face gave you away. I could tell you were pissed, but since you didn't hang around long enough for me to explain, you're hearing it now. So, quit being a jackass."

A single eyebrow shoots toward the heavens. "A jackass?" The corner of his mouth curls up.

"Yes, a jackass! You're totally being a grumpy butthole, and I'm over it. So...stop it!" I'm breathing harder by the time I'm finished ranting. I don't know why this man gets under my skin so easily. He makes me want to punch him in his condescending, smug face.

I'm about to tell him exactly that, since I'm on a roll, but my ability is stripped away when his mouth presses firmly against mine. One minute, I'm about to tear into this infuriating man, and the next, he's kissing me like I'm the oxygen he needs to survive. His hands frame my face as he coaxes open my mouth with his tongue. He plunders, claims, owns me with his mouth, rendering me speechless and helpless with the slide of his tongue.

A mewl slides from my throat as I grip the front of his T-shirt, holding on for dear life. I've never been kissed like this, and the revelation is both intoxicating and infuriating at the same time. His lips are softer than I expected, with the right amount of pressure, and his tongue is pure magic. It makes me wonder what he can do with that tongue on *other* parts of my body.

But just as suddenly as the kiss began, it ends. Marcus rips his mouth from mine, leaving me dazed and panting. And confused. Very confused. Why did he kiss me, and what's more concerning, why did I like it so much?

Probably because I've never experienced anything like it. No man before has ever kissed me the way he has, leaving me yearning for more and ready to for beg for it. My mind swings to Vaughn, who rarely kissed me with even half the passion I've just experienced, and any man before that is severely lacking.

"I don't know why I did that," he mutters, his voice gravelly and hoarse.

"I..." What do I say to that?

Do it again?

He pulls back, releasing my face and putting space between my body and his. The coloring of his eyes is darker than his normal hazel green, and the front of his jeans look a little snugger than normal.

"You should get back to your cabin."

His words are like stepping under an ice-cold shower. "What?" I ask, taking my own step back.

"*Go*, Ryan." His eyes plead as much as his words, and even though I want to demand answers, I realize I'm probably not going to get them.

At least not now.

So, with my head held high, I walk away, down the stairs and to my SUV. I don't spare him a single glance as I back out of my spot and return the way I came. I keep moving, turning right at the lane and heading to where I need to turn to go to my own cabin. When I park, I climb out, stomping up the steps to the front door. It takes me three tries to key in the code, since my fingers hold a slight tremble.

The moment I step inside, I start to pace, my annoyance strong and powerful. "Who the hell does he think he is? Kissing me like that, and then dismissing me?"

I walk down the hall and into the bedroom, ripping the ball cap off the top of my head and tossing it onto the bed. I pause in front of the dresser mirror and take in my reflection. My swollen lips and flushed cheeks. My eyes are still slightly glassy and dilated with desire. I can't help but touch my lips, recalling how it felt to be kissed by Marcus.

Marcus the...jerkface.

I narrow my eyes and spin around, refusing to indulge in even one more second of looking in the mirror. The best thing I can do is forget it ever happened. I'm sure he has. The moment I stepped off his porch and drove away, he probably forgot all about it. Hell, it was most likely a normal, everyday thing for him. He just goes around kissing women whenever the hell he wants.

Yet, that doesn't feel right either.

Something tells me he was just as shocked by what he did as I was, and that's why he pushed me away. So, there are two ways I can play this. I can be completely indifferent, acting like he doesn't matter, and the kiss didn't affect me whatsoever. Honestly, that's probably what I *should* do.

The other option is, I can have a little fun. You know, show him what he's missing out on? It might be a little fun to bring him to his knees, because I'm certain that kiss meant something to him too.

So maybe he needs a little reminder.

A smile spreads across my face.

Not that I plan to turn into a cocktease or anything, but I can definitely do a little extra flirting whenever he's near. It would serve him right anyway for kissing me the way he did and then casting me aside.

Well, Mr. Marcus Wright, you've met your match.

By the time I'm done, he won't know what hit him.

I quickly change out of my clothes into a pair of pajamas and head to the bathroom to do my nightly ritual of removing my makeup and moisturizing. My makeup line has been slowly moving into more skincare products, and I'm happy to report, I am absolutely loving them so far. After spreading night cream over my skin, I wash my hands and turn off the light.

I make my way to the kitchen and grab a bottle of water. As I sip the cold liquid, I find myself heading back outside. Night has fallen and it's a bit cooler than it was earlier. The sky is dark and full of stars, yet being surrounded by trees causes the night to feel closer and full of shadows. I can hear slight movement in the trees and a dog bark.

Is that Buddy, Marcus's dog?

I look in that direction, but the foliage is too thick to see anything. No lights from his cabin, nothing. We're just far enough away to barely know the other is there.

Probably just how he likes it.

Well, Mr. Wright, you're in for a rude awakening. You might be alone out in your private little section of the park, but your neighbor is about to remind you of just how close she really is.

I slip back inside, close and lock the door, and head toward the bedroom. Tomorrow, I put my plan into action.

Tomorrow, I show Marcus exactly what's missing from his life.

Fun.

CHAPTER
nine

MARCUS

I step outside into the night air, Buddy hot on my heels. Ever since Ryan stormed off, she's all I can think about.

That kiss.

Yeah, I can't stop thinking about it. I've replayed it over and over and still haven't figured out what came over me. Other than I was completely stunned by a mixture of her beauty and the fire that danced in her eyes. It didn't even matter she was basically telling me off. I found her refreshing and not like any woman I've ever met.

That's why I pulled back and told her to leave, because if I didn't, the next step was to throw her over my shoulder and carry her to my bed. *That's* what I wanted to do, not send her away, but I couldn't let my body make any decisions. I needed to use my big brain, not the smaller one in my pants that was ready to get her naked.

Everything about Ryan was wrong. I mean, don't get me wrong, she's *very* right. But not for me. I prefer simple women who don't spend hours upon hours in front of a mirror. One who wants to spend time outside, like me. Feeling the wind in her hair as we take the boat for a ride, the heat of the flames as we cook food by the firepit, or getting splattered with mud as we tear down one of the old trails throughout my property.

Ryan doesn't fit that picture.

She's more of a fancy iced coffee in an artsy café type. Her purse probably costs more than half my wardrobe, and as hard as I try, I just can't picture her laughing when getting covered in mud.

Buddy trots down the stairs and starts sniffing around the yard, searching for the perfect spot to do his business. I've let him out a few times without the leash, and he does well. He usually stays close to the house, checking every few minutes to make sure I'm still there. If he wanders too far, I call, and he comes running quickly.

I recall what Ryan said about her parents. Her dad is some big shot producer? Maybe that's why the name sounded familiar. I just assumed it was someone who lived here years ago, but perhaps the reason was simply because he's well-known. Not that I watch a lot of movies, but that doesn't mean anything. Just because I don't go to the theater or subscribe to movie channels doesn't mean I don't know who Matt Damon or Julia Roberts is.

Pulling my phone from my pocket, I tap on the internet browser and do something I rarely do. I type in someone's name and search.

Ryan Marcotte.

Instantly, the screen is filled with information. News articles, photos, and more all appear. I scroll down a bit, tapping on one of the photographs. The image of Ryan fills the screen, her smiling face, while gorgeous, looking...well, fake. Her smile is tight and doesn't reach her chocolate eyes. She looks completely put together and beautiful, yet so different from the woman I saw earlier with a ball cap on her head.

I scroll down, encountering more and more photos, but it's not the ones of Ryan looking proper and perfect that grab my attention. It's the photographs of her appearing a bit...wild. A party girl, with a drink held high above her head and a guy grinding up on her ass. This persona is...shocking to say the least, because she looks nothing like the Ryan I've met.

There are also a few pictures of her and a guy. He's obviously famous, with his blinding white teeth and his perfectly styled hair. His tuxedo on the red carpet looks like it costs more than I make in a month.

Buddy barks, pulling my attention from my phone. "Buddy, come here," I holler into the night, slipping the device back into my pocket.

The dog comes running, his tail wagging and his tongue dangling.

"What'd ya find? Was there a critter out there?" I ask, crouching into the dirt.

Buddy comes and stands beside me, waiting for his pets, which I happily give. I listen, only hearing the breeze rustle the trees. I stand up, walking over toward my garage. Buddy remains right by my side with each step and waits while I take another listen. When I don't hear anything out of the ordinary, I move to the path that leads to the other cabin. A part of me wants to walk the trail, to make sure everything is all right with Ryan, but unless she summons me, there's no reason for it.

She's my renter for thirty days.

Nothing more.

But then I remember that kiss once more, and all I can think about is how much I'd like to cross that line with her. March over to her place, cup her jaw with my hands, and plunder her mouth. I'm not normally an aggressive man, but with Ryan, the desire is strong. It's a river running deep inside me, with raging waves and an undertow threatening to pull me under.

Buddy sniffs the air and whimpers. He takes a step forward, like he's about to track whatever scent he's on, but fortunately, he doesn't take off. "No, Buddy. Stay."

He drops his ass in the dirt, sitting beside me and watching. When nothing shows itself, I reach down and pet his soft head. "Come on, Buddy. Let's go eat and have a bath."

When the vet at the chain store checked him over, she was surprised to only find burrs in his fur and no fleas. I bought whatever shampoo she recommended and am planning to give him his first real bath in my guest bathroom, since it's the one with the tub. Together, we head inside, and even when I'm tasked with bathing the dog, keeping him off the furniture while he dries, and giving him an extra treat for being such a good boy through it all, I can't help but think about Ryan.

About the kiss.

Even when I go to bed, I lie here with her on my mind. I want to know more about her. I want to click every single one of those links and see more photos, but I don't. Why? Hell if I know. I've got the resolve of steel, apparently, because as much as I want to look, I don't. Half that shit's probably not true anyway, right?

There's only one way to find out what I want to know, and that's from the source herself. Maybe if I get to know her more, the infatuation I suddenly have for her mouth will fade. Perhaps I won't like her at all. Seems to me the only way to get past Ryan is to go through her, figuratively speaking.

So that's what I'll do. Instead of avoiding her, I'll let my curiosity get the better of me. This way, I'll prove to myself we're too different, too opposite to ever be anything more than renter/landlord. The kiss will mean nothing and any desire for more will evaporate like rain. Why? Because who wants to kiss a woman they can't stand? And something tells me the canyon will become apparent between Ryan and me, our differences too big and too deep.

It's a long, sleepless night, filled with images of her and replays of the kiss.

A kiss I long to repeat.

"What do you say we take the boat out for a spin today?" I ask Buddy after he comes in from doing his morning business. His tail wags, and he seems eager, even though he probably has no clue what I'm saying.

It'll be the first big run for my Jon boat this year, though I've had it in the shop and already completed a tune-up. I might even indulge myself on this Memorial Day and grab a fishing pole from the shed and wet a line. It's one of my favorite ways to unwind, and unfortunately, I just don't get to do it as often as I'd like.

I head to the kitchen and pack a cooler. I make a couple of ham and cheese sandwiches, wash a bundle of grapes and put them in a baggie, and add some bottles of water and chips. I make sure to grab a bowl so Buddy has fresh water and start making a pile by the front door. The moment he spots his leash, Buddy gets excited and starts spinning circles. "Yeah, yeah, we'll go for a little walk before we get on the boat." How good the dog is will determine how long we stay out. If he's hyper and all over the place, then we'll cut the trip short. It might take a few trips out in the boat before he settles into the activity. Though, if he's anything like he is in the truck, then we should be fine.

Time will tell.

I step outside, Buddy right behind me, and make my way to the garage. Since my truck is still at the shop and I have the tow here, I'm gonna have to take Grandpa's old one. I love driving this thing, but I don't get it out as much as I should. Mostly because it's hard not to see him behind the wheel anymore.

Pulling open the big roll door on the side of the garage, I step back and take in the 1959 Chevy Apache truck. This beautiful candy apple red, short-bed truck, with step sides and an upgraded 283 V8 engine, was purchased by my grandpa straight off the lot, and was his until the day he died. We'd take this truck out for a cruise on Sundays, grab lunch at the diner, and make sure she stretched her legs for a bit.

Those are the memories I'll carry with me for the rest of my life.

"What do you think, Buddy? Wanna take Betsy out for a ride?"

He barks, as if to tell me he's all in for a ride in Grandpa's old truck.

"All right, let's get it loaded up, okay?"

Buddy stays close by but also checks out the yard as I load the cooler and fishing stuff into the bed. When it's ready, I make my way to my boat behind the garage. Pulling off the cover, I grab a full can of gas and set it inside the boat, as well as verifying I have all my emergency supplies. When it appears I'm set, I turn my attention to my eager pup. "Ready to hit the road?"

His tongue dangles and his ears perk up.

"Come on, boy. Let's go close up the house," I say.

Just as we round the corner from the back of the garage, I catch movement out of the corner of my eye. Buddy notices too and starts barking. I'm unable to say a word before he takes off toward the intruder. "Buddy, stop!" I holler just as someone emerges through the clearing off to the side.

Ryan is there and instantly drops to the ground to welcome Buddy. He eagerly kisses her cheek—causing a bubble of jealousy to pop in my gut—his little tail wagging harder than it ever has. He's practically dancing, happy to see the woman renting the cabin.

She glances up as I slowly approach. "Hi."

"Hey." Something tightens in my chest as I take in her casual, yet completely put together appearance. Or maybe it's the fact she's wearing the other ball cap I gave her, looking like she fell out of one of my wet dreams.

"Sorry to just drop in on you like this. I was exploring and followed the trail." Her hand continues to run over Buddy's back, showering him with lots of attention.

"It's fine. There're several trails around the property. I own twenty acres."

Her eyes widen. "Wow, that's a lot."

I nod, shoving my hands into my pockets so I don't reach for her.

"So, what are you two up to today?" she asks, standing up and waiting.

"Taking the boat out for a spin."

Her chocolate eyes brighten. "A boat? You have a boat?"

"Sure do, Princess."

"Can I go?" she asks eagerly.

Her question stumps me, because for the life of me, I just can't see Ryan on a boat. "Really?"

"Yes, I love boats." She practically vibrating from excitement.

"Uhh," I reply, lifting my own ball cap and running a single hand through my hair. "I guess."

"Yay!" She claps. "I'll run and get ready," she insists, turning and practically sprinting back the way she came.

Buddy jumps, ready to follow, but I stop him. "No, Buddy, let her go. We need to make sure we're set."

Hesitantly, he follows me back to the house, but I don't miss the way he checks over his shoulder for her either. My dog has it bad for the woman.

Take a number, pal.

I go inside, trying to decide if I want to change out of jeans and into a pair of shorts. I rarely wear them, but if I'm going to unwind on the boat, I admit a pair of shorts and athletic shoes are a lot more relaxing, but it takes a lot of heat for me to step out of my comfort zone and May isn't it yet, so I'll stick to my boots and jeans for today.

I do change my shirt, however. I don't know why, but I grab a fresh T-shirt and run my deodorant through my pits once more. I even throw a cleaner hat on my head, changing from the stained-up, dirty one I had on.

I refuse to dissect why.

"Let's get this show on the road," I tell Buddy, who's waiting for me at the front door. We step outside, and I add, "Go use the potty."

Never in my thirty-seven years did I think I would be a man who'd regularly use the term *potty*, but here we are.

Buddy trots off the porch and does his business, meeting me at the cab of Grandpa's truck. The moment I open the door, he jumps inside and gets settled in the passenger seat. Climbing in, I shut the door and fire up the engine, reveling in the sound she makes when she starts to purr.

"God, I love this truck."

I drive from the garage and back to the hitch of the boat trailer. Grandpa made sure he could tow a small trailer with this baby, especially his Jon boat. Once the truck is in position, I climb out and hitch the trailer to the truck. Just as I'm raising the jack, I hear someone approach.

"Wait, we're taking that?"

I glance at Ryan and smile. "What were you expecting, a yacht?"

She bristles and hides her eyes. Yep, that's exactly what she was expecting.

"That's not a boat. It's a postage stamp," she states, crossing her arms over her chest.

I stand up and glance at the fifteen-foot, flat-bottom Jon boat that has served its purpose since I've owned it. It's not huge, but I don't need big. I'm a simple man. As long as it runs well and holds me, my fish, and my cooler, that's all I've ever needed.

Lifting my shoulders, I say, "Well, I guess you don't have to go then."

She steps forward, glancing inside the boat. "Where do I sit?"

Reaching in, I slap my hand down on the aluminum seat. "Right here."

Ryan sighs and shifts her beach bag from one shoulder to the next. When she meets my gaze, she asks, "Is it safe?"

"Princess, I'd never take you out on something that I wasn't one-hundred-percent confident in its ability to not only float but also make it back to shore. This ol' girl is solid," I insist, tapping my hand on her bow.

She inhales deeply and slowly lets it out, her eyes raking over the boat. "Okay, let's do it."

She walks around to the passenger side and opens the door, instantly greeted by Buddy. "Look at you," she sings, scratching his ear before setting her bag on the floorboard and climbing into the cab.

I double-check to make sure everything is connected and slide into the truck. "Might wanna roll down the window. No air-conditioning," I tell her, putting the truck in first and slowly pulling away.

"This truck is...cool. I've never ridden in one this old. Actually, before Friday, I don't think I've ever ridden in a truck at all. SUVs, yes, but never a pickup truck," she says, running her hand over the cracked dash.

"It belonged to my grandpa," As I drive to the dock used by the locals, I tell her the story about my grandpa purchasing it brand new in 1959, and how it was the only truck he kept until the day he passed. "He's the one who taught me how to work on anything with a motor. I used to sit in his shop and hand him tools, soaking up anything and everything he shared with me."

I glance over and catch her watching me. "That's pretty cool."

I nod in reply, keeping my eyes on the road and not her legs. Out of the corner of my eye, I see her gently stroking Buddy's fur. His tongue is hanging out as he sits in the middle of the bench seat, enjoying the ride.

By the time we get to the smaller dock known to the locals, they're both sitting up a little taller in the seat. I carefully back the trailer into the water and engage the parking brake on the truck. Glancing over, I can't help but note the way the breeze gently blows the long hair pulled through the back of her hat. "Ready?"

She smiles. That one gesture reaches into my chest and squeezes my heart. Not to mention what it's doing in the front of my pants. Whoever thought a grin could do so much to a simple guy like me?

"Let's do it."

CHAPTER *Ten*

MARCUS

I can't stop looking at her.

She's so distracting, I've almost wrecked my boat. Twice.

Wearing nothing but a pair of little cutoff shorts and a tank top, Ryan has her feet up on the bow of the boat, her pink toenails for the world to see. Those ever-present long, toned, tan legs are on full display, and it's doing a number on me.

Ryan gazes up at the sun, letting the warmth pass the bill of her hat and heat her face. "So, this is what you do to relax, huh?"

"One of the ways," I confirm, trying to keep my eyes on the horizon and not on her legs.

Spinning around to face me, she places her feet on the bottom of the boat and reaches out to pet Buddy. "What are the other ways?"

I shrug, motoring along as we head for my favorite fishing spot. "Fishing, sitting out on the deck, walking through the woods, four-wheeling. That kinda stuff."

Her nose scrunches up. "I haven't done any of those things," she says almost absently to herself.

"You've never walked in the woods or sat on a deck?"

"Well, not like you have. I've walked in the rain forest and other exotic places while on vacation, but nothing like Pine Village. And the decks I've sat on are attached to penthouses and yachts, not cabins."

I nod, understanding what she's saying. Her lifestyle and mine are totally different. She's caviar and I'm hot dogs, champagne and cheap draft beer. That's never bothered me before—not that it bothers me now—but the difference just feels so drastic.

Feeling her eyes on me, I meet her gaze and do everything I can to ignore the bolt of lightning that strikes my guts. It's crazy how fast my heart starts to beat and how shallow my breathing becomes with just one glance.

"So, where are we going anyway?"

"My secret spot," I tell her, making a left into a narrow inlet.

"Like...the spot where you take all your victims?" she asks, worrying her bottom lip as she glances around.

I snort. "Nope. Just a special place I go that isn't inundated by visitors and boats. I catch lots of fish back here."

She sits up straight on the aluminum bench. "Fishing? We're going fishing?"

"Sure are," I tell her, steering the boat up the waterway.

"Like...catching them?"

I can't help but smile. Her Hollywood is showing. "Yep."

"Umm, I've never done that before."

I pull into the small cove and shut off the motor. Once I drop anchor, I reply, "I'll teach you. It's pretty simple."

She looks around, fidgeting with the hem of her shorts. "I don't know, can't I just...watch or something?"

"Nope," I insist, standing up slowly and moving to grab the fishing poles. "What if you're on one of your big fancy yachts and it crashes. You could be lost on some uncharted island and need to fish to survive."

Her eyes widen and her mouth falls open. "What? That wouldn't happen."

I shrug, unwinding the hook and preparing to slip on the bait. "It might. It's not like you can just call an Uber from a remote island."

As if sensing my challenge, she sits up straighter and holds out her hand. "Fine. I'll fish."

I adjust the pole, moving it toward her so she can grab on to it. Then, I reach into the cooler and pull out the small container of worms. The moment I flip open the lid, she gasps. "What is that?"

"Bait," I tell her, pulling out a long earthworm and holding it toward her.

"Oh my God, I'm not putting that on the hook! Gross," she bellows, making a disgusted face and gagging.

"Got to, Princess. It's the only way to ensure your survival," I insist, shaking the worm at her and fighting a smile.

She continues to stare at it, and even the look of horror is cute as hell. Ryan closes her eyes and swallows hard. "I don't think I can," she mutters, her face pure torture.

"Sure you can," I reassure. "I'll talk you through it."

Ryan continues to stare, and I can practically see the internal struggle going on in her brain. She doesn't want to, but she doesn't like being weak either. The respect I have for her climbs a bit more. "I can't believe I'm doing this," she whispers to herself, holding out her hand. It's shaking pretty hard, and I fully expect her to snatch it away before I can hand off the worm, but to my surprise, she doesn't.

"Oh my God, it's so gross," she cries the moment the tips of her fingers wrap around the worm.

"You've got this, Princess," I insist, letting go.

Taking a deep breath, she holds it up, her entire body rigid. "Now what?"

"Now you're gonna slide it onto the hook."

"Oh God," she groans, her entire body shaking in disgust.

"Now, slide it over the hook like this," I say, gently grabbing her hand and helping her.

"This is barbaric," she insists, making a gagging noise that brings a smile to my face.

"There. See?" I hold up the hook and show her the completed task.

She gapes at the hook and then down at her hand. "I'm all...gross!"

I can't stop the chuckle. "Lean over the boat and wash off your hands," I tell her. "Carefully, so you don't tip the boat."

Her eyes widen to the size of saucers. "What? We can tip?"

"Of course we can," I tell her, even though it's less likely in this boat than others. It's deeper than normal and has the flat bottom, making it a little less tipsy.

She's like a statue, trying to reach over and clean the wet dirt off her fingers. "I can't believe I did that. So nasty," she grumbles to herself, scrubbing the worm guts and muck off her hand.

Buddy takes the opportunity to get close, trying to figure out what she's doing. When he moves, the boat shakes, causing her to reach out and grip the side. "Buddy, stop!"

He does as instructed and looks on with curious eyes.

"He's okay," I say, reaching down and petting his head. "Maybe after we fish for a bit, we can see if he knows how to swim."

She looks on, curiously. "Don't all dogs know how to swim?"

I shrug my shoulders and adjust my ball cap. "I've never owned a dog, but the chances are pretty good."

She nibbles on her bottom lip. "But not definite."

"Nope. I suppose there's a chance he can't swim." I glance down at Buddy and add, "Only one way to find out."

She gasps. "No! You can't just throw him in and pray for the best," she argues, making me laugh.

"I won't. I'm just pulling your leg," I say, prepping the line to be cast. "Ready to catch a fish?"

She sighs. "I guess."

We go through the motions a few times, me explaining when to release the line. She pays attention to me, but closer attention to the dangling worm on the end of her hook.

"Wanna give it a try?"

She nods, almost eagerly, but she covers it well by clearing her throat and averting her gaze.

Be careful, Princess, or you might actually enjoy this.

It takes her three tries to get the motion and release timed right, but when she does, her cast sails smoothly into the water. "See? A perfect cast."

She smiles widely, causing my balls to tighten. If I'm not careful, I'll be pitching a tent bigger than the one my grandpa taught me to pitch when I was seven.

We sit in silence, the only sounds surrounding us the gentle movement of the trees and the frogs croaking. This is the life. I can't see myself anywhere else but here. It's Small Town, USA, where everyone knows you, and I have plenty of opportunity to do what I love. I couldn't get this in a big city, like LA. The thought of living in a city of that magnitude makes me break out in a cold sweat. To me, that's a nightmare I want nothing to do with.

After a few minutes, she starts tapping her feet. "So, now what?"

"Now we wait."

"Wait for what?" she asks, holding her fishing pole carefully while still bending down to pet Buddy.

"Wait for the fish to bite." I reach down and pull two bottles of water from the cooler. The first one, I pour into Buddy's bowl and hand the second one to Ryan.

She takes the water. "Thank you. And what do you mean, wait for them to bite? How long does that take?"

I shrug my shoulders, throwing the empty water bottle into a plastic trash bag and grabbing a fresh one for me. As I twist off the cap, I reply, "It depends. Sometimes they start biting right away, and other times, it could be hours."

"Hours?" she asks, her eyes wide in surprise. "You know, I love seafood, but I never realized so much work went into it. I may have to reconsider the next time I order lobster or crab legs."

I take a hearty swig from my bottle. "Well, you're not gonna find either of those two in northwestern Wisconsin, Princess. You'll see walleye, bass, perch, and trout here."

She scrunches her nose. "I don't think I've had those."

"Well, then you're in luck. We'll fry up whatever we catch."

She seems to consider the thought for a few seconds before nodding. "Why are you being so quiet? I mean, besides the fact you rarely engage in conversation, unless you're being asked a direct question or statement."

"Fish respond to the vibration and noise. That's why you're supposed to be quiet when fishing, so you don't scare them away."

"Quiet? The whole time?"

"The whole time," I confirm, the corner of my mouth curling up.

"That's impossible in my world. Where I come from, silence is unwelcome, especially on reality TV. No one would tune in if you had nothing to say," she says, staring off into the distance.

It's the first time she's brought up the television show. The only reason I know about it is because of my Google search, which continued earlier this morning. It's how I heard about Vaughn, her boyfriend, and whatever bombshell he dropped on TV. But as much as I wanted to learn about Ryan and her life, I refused to click on any of the links. I want to hear it from her, not from some entertainment media source, so while I scrolled through and read the headlines and saw some of the pictures they accompanied, I didn't read any of the articles.

Which brings me to Vaughn. What a smarmy douche, if you ask me. I can tell by his pictures he's a high-maintenance, spoiled jackass, who wouldn't know how to find a clit with a compass and a map. The thought of him having his hands anywhere near Ryan makes me want to kill someone, which I can't understand. They're dating—or *were* dating, depending on which headline you read. Scrolling through my phone, it was a reminder I should stay as far away from her as possible.

Yet here we are.

"Tell me about LA."

She glances up, yet her eyes are shielded by the brim of the ball cap. "I thought we were supposed to be quiet."

Kicking my feet up on the side of the boat, I remove the cap on my water bottle and say, "Humor me."

She sighs and returns her gaze to the water. "LA is...fast. Everything is done in a hurry, but there's so much to do or see, always some place to go, a hand to shake or a cheek to kiss." Her tone is thick with...melancholy, but I try not to dive too deeply into why. Maybe she's missing the hustle and bustle of the big city. Pine Village doesn't hold a fraction of the fame, glitter, and lights that a place like Los Angeles does. I can see how someone who's used to the city life would long for it again when facing a small town like Pine Village. Not everyone is made for this kind of life.

Me? I never want to leave.

"Sounds...fun." There's no hiding the fact it's not my cup of tea.

She giggles. "Yeah, clearly. You'd probably hate it there."

"Probably." I won't hide the fact.

"Anyway, my dad is a pretty big deal, and so is my mom. When I was eighteen, I started doing these online videos for other girls about the right ways to apply makeup, how to pick the correct colors for your skin tone, things like that. It took off, and the next thing I knew, I had my own YouTube channel with sponsors."

"Really? There's money in that?" I ask, trying to understand the concept.

She gives me a look. "A *lot* of money in it. So, when I was twenty-two, I decided to invest my money in myself. I started my own makeup brand."

Okay, that *impresses me.*

"Wow, that's cool."

She smiles warmly. "Thank you. I love it. Some people may not consider it a job, but it is. It's a lot of hard work, honestly. Everything from the product development to testing and marketing. I had no idea how much went into it, but now that I have my hands in it, I feel like I'm finally doing something. Not just for me, but for others too."

Ryan stares out at the water but isn't really seeing it. She's lost in her own head, so I give her a little bit of time to work through it. Buddy rests his head on her bare legs, as if sensing she needs a friend. Her hand runs across the top of his head, her fingers combing over his ears as she gazes off into nothing.

Just as I'm about to ask about Vaughn, her line jumps. It catches her by complete surprise, and she yelps, gripping the pole in her right hand tightly. "Oh my God!" she bellows, her brown eyes wide with shock. "What do I do?"

"You reel it in," I start, reaching out my hand before quickly pulling it back. She needs to do this on her own. "Slowly," I clarify, giving her the steps she needs to pull in her fish. "The hook appears to already be set, so lift up and then turn the reel as you bring the end of the pole back down toward the water."

She follows instructions, her face lined with determination. She does as she's told several times until the fish is right outside the boat. I can tell by looking at it, it's a decent-sized rainbow trout. Grabbing the net, I steady the end of her pole and move to the side of the boat. "Hold still. I'm going to help you get it into the boat."

I bend down and scoop it out of the water with the net. With my hand on the line, I stand up and lift the fish. "Nice catch. I'd say he's probably twenty inches long, and about five pounds."

"Holy shit," she replies, laughing and taking in the fish hanging on the line. Her eyes are sparkling like chocolate diamonds. "I can't believe I did that."

"See? You're a total badass," I say, wearing a smile on my own lips.

"Oh my gosh, that was a total rush. Now what?"

"Now, you take the fish off the hook."

Adamantly, she shakes her head. "No. No way. I'm not touching that...thing!"

"Aww, come on, Princess. You already touched a worm and put it on the hook. You can do this."

"No I can't," she insists, shaking her head.

"Sure you can. Here, hold the fish," I say, practically thrusting it at her.

She screams and jumps back. The moment she does, the boat pitches hard to the right, and as much as I try to find my center of balance, I don't have time to adjust to the quick movement. The result sends me flying. My hands reach out for anything to stop me from falling, but it's no use.

Cold. Water.

And just as I hit the lake, I hear the sound of another splash. The moment I come up for air, I see Ryan's arms flailing about as she bellows for help. I swim toward her, my hands wrapping around her slender waist. "Are you all right?"

She gasps and sputters. "What the hell happened?"

"We fell in," I deadpan.

"I know that, but why?" she screams, kicking her feet. "Oh my God, this water is nasty!"

I look for Buddy, who's still in the boat, tail wagging and tongue hanging, ready to play too. He's jumping around, and I can read his intent all over his face. "No, Buddy. Stay." The last thing I need is to retrieve a dog from the lake too.

I give Ryan a gentle shove toward the boat, helping make sure she stays afloat. "Come on, Princess. Up you go."

She grabs the side of the boat and hoists herself up as I push. She's not graceful, but I'm not sure you really can be at this point. When she falls onto the bottom of the boat, I prepare to pull myself up. "Ryan, move to the other side. We need some counterweight."

She rolls over, Buddy practically jumping on top of her, thinking it's time to play. When she's on the opposite side, I grab hold of the boat and pull. I fall just as gracefully into the boat and sigh.

"I can't believe that happened. It was in my mouth, Marcus."

It takes me a moment to catch up, and even though I realize she's talking about the water, I laugh. Hard. Full belly, lying on the bottom of the boat and unable to catch my breath, laugh.

And do you know what?

It feels good.

Even better, Ryan joins in and laughs along with me. Of course, it could be crying I hear, but I'm pretty sure she's laughing.

"Come on, Princess. That's enough fishing for today."

She turns, sopping wet and still looking absolutely breathtaking. "You know, I think I'm done fishing."

"For today?"

She pins me with a look. "Forever, buster. For. Ever."

CHAPTER
eleven

Ryan

My teeth are chattering as we head back to the cabin. Even though the air is still warm and the sun is shining high in the sky, being soaked to the bones doesn't feel good. I'm cold and dripping water all over Marcus's grandpa's truck. I could tell he wasn't thrilled about climbing inside while we were both wet, but we didn't have a choice. It's not like we can walk home. Instead, he quickly loaded the boat onto the trailer, secured everything in the truck bed, and took off for home.

The wild part about all of this is despite falling into the nasty lake water, having swallowed a big gulp of it that'll probably give me some sort of bacterial infection, and having my nipples poke through my bra and tank top because it's *that* cold, all of a sudden I really want to kiss him.

It was hard not to throw myself at him when we were fishing. Not while I was putting the nasty worm on the hook and not while he was trying to get me to hold the fish, but in between. There were some moments where our eyes connected, and it felt like we were the only two people in the world. Even when he was asking about California.

Then, the whole falling out of the boat fiasco happened, and he's barely said two words since. Well, after he laughed, that is. And if I'm being honest with myself, it was the best sound in the world. His laughter sparked my own, and it was as if I'd never really laughed before. It felt...liberating.

But now, here we are, driving home and barely speaking. I can't tell if he's mad at me, the situation, or maybe a little of both. He uses fishing as his outlet, a way to unwind, and falling into the lake and soaking ourselves doesn't exactly scream relaxation. In fact, quite the opposite. Especially when Buddy decided he wanted to go for a swim too and ended up jumping in after Marcus and I got ourselves back in the boat. Well, I didn't get myself back in. He used brute strength and threw me in.

And I didn't hate it.

Not even a little.

His hands on my hips sparked ideas of his hands on *other* parts of my body, and while being wet is hot, looking like a drowned rat isn't. And despite the fact there's all sorts of thick tension surrounding us right now, all I can think about is getting a shower. Cleaning the lake off my body. Putting on dry clothes.

I rest my hand on Buddy's wet head and sigh. Even the dog can tell there's extra tension riding shotgun with us. He shifts between us, having a hard time getting comfortable on the small section of seat he's given. I try to scoot closer to the window, but that just makes the wind feel colder and stronger, so I remain where I sit.

When we finally reach the lane that leads to the cabins, the air inside the cab is almost suffocating. Not only that, but it smells like wet dog and fish, two aromas I can confidently say I never want to smell again in the same small space.

We pass Marcus's driveway and turn onto mine. I guess that's something. At least he's not going to drive straight to his house and expect me to walk the rest of the way back to my cabin, sopping wet. Under the cover of trees, that would have been a cold, miserable little jaunt, and as uncomfortable as this ride is, I'm grateful for it.

Marcus swings the truck and trailer wide, stopping in front of the porch steps. I reach for the handle and practically jump out. "Thanks for the ride," I holler politely, shutting the heavy, old door hard. I bolt up the steps, anxious to get away from his broodiness. He's already moving, heading back the way we came, before I even have the security code in the door.

I step inside and toss my clutch purse onto the couch. Thank goodness I left it locked in the truck while we were fishing. Marcus had his wallet with him, but it was in a little waterproof lockbox he keeps in the boat. Otherwise, it would have suffered the same fate as we did. I try to picture the contents of my clutch soaking wet, or worse, scattered on the bottom of the lake bed, and I'm so grateful nothing but us got wet.

But it was an accident.

He's the one who thrust the dang fish at me, expecting me to grab and hold it. In what crazy universe would he expect anyone—especially me—to just be okay with that? Of course I jumped back! Of course I screamed! Of course I did what I could to get away from the fish! So if it's anyone's fault we fell into the lake, it's his!

The more I think about his silence, the more annoyed *I* get. I didn't do it on purpose, and it *was* my first time fishing, so why is he mad at me? *I'm* the one who should be upset, not him.

Without thinking, I spin around and walk out the door. I don't bother to lock the entrance, but I doubt it'll be an issue. I've been here three days and the only visitor I've had is the grumpy landlord.

I take off for the pathway clearing and stomp through the woods. Am I cold? Yep! Do I wish I would have at least put on a dry pair of panties? Abso-fucking-lutely! But I'm not letting some wet underwear keep me from letting the big jerk have it.

When I reach the clearing, I spot the truck. It's back behind the garage, dropping the boat and trailer into its spot. So that's where I head. As I approach, Buddy either senses me or hears me, and trots in my direction, carrying a stick. I want to bend down and give him a little pet, but I'm on a mission.

"You have no right to just drop me off and then leave without saying a word. It was your fault we fell into the stupid water to begin with," I seethe the moment I reach where he's standing.

Even though he's bending down, turning some handle on the trailer to raise the tongue, he tenses. Slowly, he releases the handle and stands to his full height. For some reason, he appears taller than normal, like a big sopping wet ogre. His shirt is plastered to his hard chest and arms, and the moment he turns, I catch the hint of dark ink beneath his gray T-shirt. Not to mention, his jeans are practically painted on his legs. I can see the outline of everything—and I do mean everything.

With his ball cap on backward, I can see the hard lines and rigid features on his too-handsome face as he narrows his gaze at me. "My fault?"

"Yes, your fault," I insist, taking a step forward. My finger automatically jumps out, poking him square in the hard chest. "You practically threw a fish at me! Not only is it rude and very ungentlemanly, but it's disgusting. So, the fact I jumped back and rocked the boat is clearly your fault."

He snorts and inches closer. My fingernail digs into the wet material of his shirt and the skin underneath it, but it must not bother him much, since he doesn't move. "Ungentlemanly?"

"I said what I said, buster."

The corner of his mouth curls into a smirk and his eyes seem to dance with humor. "Well, that's a first."

I bark out a laugh, but it lacks any humor. "I seriously doubt that. You've been nothing but grumpy and brash this entire time."

He gets even closer, his lips dangerously close to my own. "You bring it out of me, Princess."

"You're nastiness?"

"My ungentlemanliness."

"Same thing," I insist, throwing my hands in the air. "Here I was, trying to be nice and getting to know you better, but nooooooo, you have just been all...difficult."

He laughs hard. Again, he moves a hair closer, his lips practically touching my own. I can feel the warmth of his breath against me and almost reach out and wrap my arms around his waist. "If you want difficult, honey, you better look in the mirror."

"And what about you?"

"What about me?" he asks, just as his right hand wraps around my waist. I can feel the heat of his palm through my wet clothes, searing my flesh with his touch. "What you see is what you get."

I lift my chin, almost daring him. To do what? I'm not sure yet, but I think I have a list. We can start with strip off our wet clothes and running those full, kissable lips across every inch of my body.

"So, what do you want, Princess?"

Isn't that the loaded question? What do I want? Again, there's the list, and it's growing longer by the second. "I want..."

Just say it.

"I want...you to kiss me. Like you mean it."

If my request surprises him, he doesn't show it. He watches me, studying me for a few seconds before doing exactly as I asked. He kisses me.

And curls my toes.

His tongue delves inside my mouth, tasting and commanding more. I give in, letting him lead me to wherever in the hell he wants to, because I'm completely at his mercy. His lips are a touch rough, but I don't seem to care. All I want is more.

I reach for his wet T-shirt, pulling his chest to mine. Marcus's hands frame my face, his thumbs lightly caressing my cheeks. I can almost feel those very thumbs touching me between my legs. Gentle, yet firm, and driving me straight to orgasm.

The kiss is everything I didn't know I needed, wrapped in a big pink bow.

A glittery one.

Then, he spins me around. I'm pinned against the side of the truck, my wet legs wrapped around his waist. I can feel every hard inch of him, from his muscular chest to his erection pressed firmly where I need him most. His hands grip my ass, kneading it, as I rock myself against him.

I gasp as pleasure races through my veins. Any discomfort I feel at having wet clothes is forgotten. All I feel—all I want—is him. Every hard, square inch of him. In his work boots and ball cap. Jeans and faded T-shirt. No name brands, no fancy watch, no Italian shoes.

Just him.

Marcus.

A small-town, blue-collar country boy with stained fingernails and an I-don't-give-a-shit attitude.

When it feels like I can no longer breathe, he rips his mouth from mine. We're both panting as he rests his forehead against mine. "I don't know what to do about you."

"What do you mean?" I ask, confused and a little concerned.

"We're so damn different, and yet, I want you so fucking bad it hurts."

Judging by how hard he is in his jeans; he could be referring to a physical ache.

My mind swirls like the spin cycle on a washing machine, but it's desire that's making it turn. This is temporary, right? I'm only here for a few more weeks, so why not make the most out of my time? Spending some of it wrapped in these strong arms might be just what I need to put everything that happened in LA behind me.

Besides, I'm wild, right?

Might as well live up to my famous persona.

"What if...we act on this attraction. Unless a temporary summer fling isn't your thing."

He smirks. "Princess, that's just my thing."

"Well," I start, tightening my arms around his neck, "how about we enjoy the next three and a half weeks. At the end of my vacation, I head back to California with a tan and some memories."

He holds my gaze, as if waiting for me to tell him I'm joking. "You're serious?"

"As a heart attack." Shrugging, I add, "I think we both deserve a little fun, and there's definitely some attraction here. I can't miss it." I roll my hips over his erection.

He grunts and closes his eyes for a brief moment. "Just sex?"

"Or whatever the hell we want, Marcus. We're consenting adults. We're both single...right?" I ask, realizing I really have no idea. I assume he is, but maybe he's not. And if that's the case, I'll climb down off his body, head back to my cabin, and forget all about him.

Well, maybe not forget, because the size of his dick is something a girl won't ever forget anytime soon.

"Very single." He pauses before adding, "You?"

"Definitely," I confirm. The first thing I did after watching my show's season finale was break up with the asshole who used me. "So, what do you say, buster? You game?"

The corners of his mouth slowly curl upward, revealing that rare, yet gorgeous smile. "I'm game, Princess."

My blood starts to hum through my veins, my panties even more soaked than after the dip in the lake. "When do we start this fun little adventure?"

He leans forward, running his lips down the front of my neck. "I don't have anything going on now, do you?"

Just as I go to answer, Buddy barks. I glance down and find him sitting right beside us, watching like the voyeur dog he is. "Ummm, we have an audience."

Marcus looks down. "I thought you'd be used to that."

My snort is very unladylike. "Usually, yes, but not for...that."

"That? You mean sex?" he asks, grinning widely.

I nod, my shorts starting to feel a little uncomfortable.

Suddenly, he's setting me down on shaky legs. I'm a bit confused, since we were just talking about sex. Why isn't he carrying me off to his cabin to have his wicked way with me?

"I have an idea," he starts, stepping back and putting a little distance between us. "How about we each head back to our cabins, get showered, and cleaned up. When you're done, come back and I'll cook that fish for dinner."

There's so much I want to ask, but I don't know which should come first. He doesn't want to have sex right now? What guy wouldn't jump at the chance for immediate no-strings sex? Like, seriously, at this very moment. Instead, he wants to shower and cook dinner first? Not to mention, he wants to cook the fish we caught that got us in the wet mess we're in.

"I can see the wheels spinning, Ryan," he says, reaching up and placing a strand of limp, wet hair that fell out of the hat behind my ear. "I figured you'd prefer to get cleaned up first. Not that I wouldn't throw you over my shoulder and take you straight to my bed right now, but I assumed you wanted to wipe the raccoon eyes off your face and maybe scrub the lake water off your skin."

My eyes widen and my hand darts up to shield my face. "I have raccoon eyes?"

He chuckles a low, gravelly noise that goes straight to my clit. "It's cute."

"Oh God," I grumble. Why didn't I think to at least check myself in the mirror before I stormed over here to give him a piece of my mind?

Buddy jumps up on Marcus's leg, tired of being left out of the conversation. "I need to get the boat and truck taken care of and clean this fish. Unless you want to stay and help? It is part of the whole fishing adventure."

I scrunch up my nose and make a face. "No, thanks. I draw the line on fish guts."

"Figured," he replies, taking another step back and putting even more distance between us. "Go get cleaned up and come back when you're ready."

"Okay," I agree, realizing he's right. I can't hang in these wet clothes much longer, and the more I think about it, I don't want to get all sexy with this man smelling like lake, worm, and fish. "I'll be right back."

He nods, grabbing a stick off the ground and throwing it for Buddy. The dog immediately takes off running to retrieve it. "So, you'll be back in like thirty, forty minutes?"

I laugh. Hard.

"What? What woman gets ready in thirty or forty minutes?" I ask, incredulously.

Marcus shakes his head and picks up the stick Buddy drops at his feet. "How long do you need?" he asks curiously.

Without having a watch or my phone to check the time, I reply, "Two hours. Will that give you enough time to get your stuff done?"

His eyes go wide. "Two hours? It takes you two hours to get ready?"

I shrug and slowly start to head toward the path. I can feel his eyes on me as I walk, so I add a little extra swing to my hips. Glancing over my shoulder, I reply, "Two hours, buster, but it'll be worth it."

With a wink, I walk away feeling better than I have in I don't know how long. There's just something about this man that makes my blood pump. Maybe it's the desire I saw reflecting in his hazel eyes. It's a heady feeling knowing it's reciprocated. Something always felt...off with Vaughn. Now, at least I know why. If only I had realized it before now, and maybe I wouldn't have wasted three years on the asshole.

But Vaughn isn't anywhere close now.

Tonight, it'll be just Marcus and me and what I hope will be a very sexually gratifying three-week vacation. Sure, he might be a dud

113

in bed, but something tells me Marcus is anything but. He knows how to use what God gave him.

I'd bet my trust fund on it.

CHAPTER
Twelve

MARCUS

I glance at the time once more. I've been doing that a lot since I came inside to clean up. The anticipation of her arrival is killing me.

After taking care of the boat and getting Grandpa's truck put away, I got everything out to clean the fish. Usually, I wouldn't worry about one singular fish, but I want Ryan to experience it all. Sure, we might have experienced a little too much, considering we both took an unplanned dip in the lake. Eating our catch is all part of it.

Anytime Grandpa and I went, we always cleaned and cooked our catch. When Grandma was still alive, she'd be waiting back at the cabin, the supplies ready for our return. I remember asking Grandpa why she didn't help, and I'll never forget his answer. *Cleaning the fish and doing the dishes afterward is all part of it. If we catch the fish, we clean 'em. Never expect a woman to have to clean anything, especially when we're perfectly capable of doing it ourselves.*

Not that I have a woman to clean—or do anything else around here—but I've never forgotten that. Grandpa would always help clean the house, insisting we pick up after ourselves. And likewise, Grandma was always capable, and sometimes very happy to help keep up the outside chores. She mowed and would pick up sticks. Even handwash vehicles in the driveway. It wasn't until the cancer took over her body that she stopped, and within a few months, Grandpa and I were the only ones left to do all of it.

Since I've been fishing and taking care of my catch since I was little, it took me no time to get our dinner cut and soaking in a bowl of salt water. Then, I went inside to shower. My dick was still hard throughout the whole thing, as memories of Ryan and that kiss filtered through my brain. I almost reached down and grabbed a hold of it to relieve some of the pressure but decided against it. My luck, she would have shown up early and found me stroking one off in the shower. Not exactly the impression I want to make with her.

Now that I have the lake and fish washed off me, I'm in the kitchen, trying to figure out what to make with the fish. Spotting a few potatoes, I pull those out and start dicing. They'll be great with some avocado oil and seasoning, roasted until brown and crispy.

Just as I pull a few fresh vegetables out of the drawer, a knock sounds. Buddy instantly starts barking, his legs carrying him as fast as possible to the front door.

"Hi, Buddy," I hear Ryan say as I round the corner, and the front door comes into view.

"You can come in," I say, reaching the entrance and pushing open the screen door. "You stay and be good," I tell the dog, who's eager to jump and play with our new visitor.

She enters my home and glances around. "Wow, this is just as beautiful as the outside."

I glance around the open living room, with the floor-to-ceiling windows and the stone fireplace. The furniture is comfortable, and the TV is mounted over the fireplace. It's a tad bit too large for the space, but it suits me just fine, even though I don't watch it much. "Thanks," I reply, stepping back so she can take it all in.

My eyes are on her.

She's wearing another one of those sundresses with the thin straps. This one's green with little white and pink flowers on it, and it hugs her slender waist and the curve of her breasts like it was designed specifically for her.

Hell, for all I know it was.

Someone of her status and wealth can surely have their designer clothes custom made, right?

My eyes travel down to what's covering her feet. They're strappy little things that tie in some intricate bow around her lower calf. I don't know why I find them so sexy. Maybe it's because they remind me of lingerie. You know, ties and bows and if you give it one little tug, it exposes the goods behind it?

"Do I get a tour, or can I just wander around and snoop?" she asks, glancing back at me with a mischievous smile on her pink lips.

"I can give you a tour," I confirm, hands shoved in my pockets, so I don't reach out and touch her. "Buddy, go lay down." He does as instructed, walking over to the elevated bed I bought for him. He grabs his bone and starts to go to town.

Ryan falls in line with me as I move toward the back of the cabin. "Let me guess, bedroom first, right?"

I crack a crooked smile. "After I feed you," I reply. "You're going to need the nutrients."

I swear I witness a shiver run through her body at my comment. "Okay then."

"There's one bedroom down here," I tell her, showing her the guest bedroom. It has a full-size bed and a dresser, but other than that, I use it for storage. Not that I have a lot of stuff, but sometimes it's easier than taking it down to the basement.

"Nice. Do you have a lot of visitors?" she asks curiously.

I don't even have to think about it. "Not one," I state, earning a laugh.

"Then why do you have a guest room?"

I shrug my shoulders, glancing around the room. "I don't know. I guess when I built this place, it was customary to have one. But all my friends live in town here, and I don't have any family, so I don't really need it."

Her chocolate eyes transform into sadness. "You don't have any family?"

I shake my head, hating this conversation. Not that I've had it a lot over the years. The locals know my story, and the women I tend to sleep with don't really care. I'm there for one reason, and it's not small talk.

"Come on, let's finish the tour," I say, exiting the spare bedroom. "Bathroom here," I say, pointing to the open door, "and laundry room. The original house plan was for two bedrooms downstairs and the laundry room either in a small room off the kitchen or in the basement, and I didn't like either option. I barely use one guest room, let alone two, so I turned it into the laundry room and made the bathroom bigger."

"It suits the space," she says. "And with those enclosed cabinets, you get a lot of storage."

I nod, turning and heading for the stairs. Ryan doesn't say a word as we move up. Each step we take echoes off the hardwood, and once we clear the landing, the master bedroom comes into view. It's completely open with a picturesque view. In the front, there's a railing that looks over the living room, as well as the windows at the front of the cabin. So even when I'm in my bedroom, I can see the driveway and front of the property. And at the back of the room, more of the windows that aim directly at the back of the property where it meets the lake.

"Wow," Ryan whispers, stepping into the open space. With her hand on the railing, she moves into my bedroom, taking it all in. I can't help but realize she's one of the very few women to ever be in this room.

I stand back and watch her. She slowly walks to the bed, a king-size masterpiece I handmade when I built this cabin. It's rustic, made from old barn wood from the original barn beside my grandparents' cabin. It suffered severe damage from a tree falling on it when I was in high school and ended up being torn down and replaced.

"Closet's the first door on the right and bathroom the second."

She walks over to the closet, places her hand on the knob, and grins. I don't stop her, so she turns the handle and steps inside. "Holy shitballs!"

I can't help but chuckle.

Her head pokes out, her eyes wide as she meets my gaze. "This is...huge!"

I shrug, knowing I fill very little of it. When I say I'm a simple man, I mean it.

She returns inside. "I could totally fill this bad boy," she says, and even though I know she's not meaning literally, right now, my heart skips a beat at the idea.

When she makes her way out of the closet, she shakes her head. "Did you use an interior designer? Because most closets don't have anything more than a shelf and a basic hanging bar. But *that* is perfect."

"Hallie helped me," I state with a shrug.

"Well, she has an amazing sense of style. She really used the space to its full potential."

"It's the same size as the bathroom. When I built it, it was just easier to divide the whole space in half."

Her eyes widen. "Wait, you built this? Like...the whole thing?"

"Well, not the shell. I paid a contractor to pour the basement, do the entire outside of the cabin, and all the support beams outside. I did the inside."

Her mouth drops open. "Yourself?"

Again, I shrug my shoulders. "I had help. My friends would come over, especially Logan. He owns the lumberyard and hardware store in town, so he helped a lot."

She looks around the room once more. "I can't believe you built this."

Feeling uncomfortable with the kudos, I say, "It wasn't too hard. My grandpa was great with his hands. Not only as a mechanic, but he could build about anything. He taught me a lot and helped through the whole process."

She looks around the lofted room with the high ceilings and exposed beams. "Wow, I guess, I've never really known anyone who actually does the building. I've seen some amazing architecture, but I suppose never really thought much of the build." She gives me a look I can't decipher and turns her attention to the bathroom. With a wide grin, she heads straight for the doorway and walks inside.

"Oh my God!" she bellows from within. "I don't know which I love more, the closet or the bathroom."

That makes me smile, because personally, I love the bathroom. I put a lot of extra work into the shower, since it's one of the most-used spots upstairs, and there's nothing better than a long, hot shower after a day of work. Especially in my line of work. But I can see the attraction for a woman like Ryan. The soaker tub was something Hallie pushed for, claiming most women would lose their minds—and their panties—for a chance to sit in the tub. Personally, I find it gross to sit in my own filth, but whatever. And chances are slim to none that a woman will ever be here long enough to enjoy the very tub Hallie insisted I get.

But I can see Ryan sitting in there, the jets creating bubbles around her glorious breasts as she leans back and relaxes.

In fact, that just might be one of my fantasies.

"Wow, Marcus," she starts, returning from the bathroom. "I have to admit, I wasn't expecting all this."

"All what?" I inquire, even though I pretty much know what she's going to say. People have been making assumptions and underestimating me my entire life, thanks to the fact I'm just a small-town grease monkey raised by his grandparents. Just because I don't mind getting my hands dirty doesn't mean I can't do anything else. I'm good with my hands, period, and that includes small or large construction projects.

"Such a lovely home. Not that your cabin isn't beautiful from the outside, but there's no...I don't know, woman's touch? Flowers or landscaping or those little garden welcome flags. But the inside, while sparsely decorated, has beautiful bones and features. It's like a woman, sometimes they just need a little makeup and skincare products to enhance their natural beauty."

I watch her, noting the passion filling her eyes at even the mention of makeup. I may not understand the obsession some get with makeup, but I can certainly respect her take on it. It seems like she's not just out to make millions of dollars, peddling crappy product. If what she's wearing is from her own line and her videos teach women how to apply it tastefully and without looking like it was done with a paintbrush and a putty knife, then good for her.

She walks toward me, that glint in her eyes darkening. It makes my cock jump in my jeans. "I bet the women are lining up to use that tub," she says when she reaches me. Her manicured nails dance across my pecs.

I shrug my shoulders, trying not to be a total douche and just stare down at the cleavage of her dress. "I wouldn't know. No one has ever used it."

Her face reflects her shock. "What? Seriously?"

My hand wraps around her slender waist, gently drawing her body closer to mine. "Nope. Never."

"That's...criminal, Marcus."

I snort. "I can think of a lot of things that are considered criminal, but no one taking a bath in my tub isn't one of them."

Exasperated, she huffs out a long breath. "No, I'm serious. Any woman would fall at your feet for just an hour in that bad boy. I mean, the jets, the steam, the massager."

"There's a massager?"

Her mouth falls open. "Are you joking? That pad with the little knobs on it is a massager, Marcus. How did you not know that?"

Again, I lift my shoulders casually. "I don't know. Hallie picked it after I had the space specifications ironed out. That's probably why the damn thing was so expensive," I say, scratching my chin with my available hand.

"Uhh, yeah. I imagine it wasn't cheap," she states incredulously. "I can't believe it's never been used. I bet you'd like it. You know, after a long, hard day, you can fill it with hot water, some lavender oils, and use that massager. Your back and your muscles would thank you."

"A shower does all that," I reason, even though it really doesn't.

"No, it most certainly does not. One of these days, I'll show you. We'll get you all set up with a nice, relaxing bath, and you can try out the jets and massager."

My eyebrows shoot toward my hairline. "You're gonna show me...from inside the tub? That's pretty much the only way I can envision enjoying that thing."

"So, there has to be a naked woman in there with you in order to take a bath?"

A smile stretches across my lips. "Absolutely."

She sighs. "Don't sound like there'd be much relaxing going on."

"Oh, there won't be," I assure her, giving her side a gentle squeeze before releasing my hold on her. "What do you say we head down, and I start dinner."

"I assume that's not a euphemism for anything dirty, right?"

I snort a laugh. "Nope. Unless you want it to be," I reply with a wink.

"For an hour in that bathtub, I might be willing to negotiate," she says, moving toward the stairs.

My cock? It goes completely hard in my jeans. I can practically feel her mouth around me, which makes it incredibly difficult to walk down the stairs without looking like I'm suddenly bowlegged.

When we reach the kitchen, Buddy jumps up and joins us. Ryan enters the open space and looks around. "Wow, this is beautiful too."

"Do you cook?" I find myself asking, approaching the bowls with the cut potatoes and sliced vegetables ready to go in the oven.

Ryan laughs. "Uhh, no. I'm a pro at reading a menu though." She makes a face, knowing how that makes her sound. "That probably makes me snobby or spoiled, and I suppose I am. My parents had a live-in assistant, and by that I mean a woman who cooked, cleaned, and practically took care of everything house-related. Not to mention the gardener who came two times a week to take care of any mowing, landscaping, and the pool.

"You had a pool?" I ask, starting the oven to roast the potatoes.

"In Southern California, everyone has a pool," she states with a smirk.

"Well, in northwest Wisconsin, not many do. Especially with the lake so close. If people want to go swimming, they just go there."

She makes a face. "Charming."

I bark out a laugh and place the potatoes on a greased cookie sheet. "You get used to it."

Once the timer is set, I get the vegetables situated in the steamer basket. I have carrots, asparagus, broccoli, and red pepper all sliced and ready. The water starts to boil, so I turn down the heat and place the basket inside, tossing a slice of raw carrot straight into Buddy's open mouth. I read online that carrots and broccoli are a healthy snack for dogs, so he's been given just a couple of small pieces while I was slicing them earlier.

"What is that contraption?" she asks, peeking inside the steamer before I close the lid, giving Buddy a pet on the head as she does.

"It's a steamer. I bought if off Amazon." Turning around, I lean against the counter and cross my arms over my chest. "I try to grill my food as much as possible, but I love steamed vegetables. So this twenty-dollar appliance is one of my best friends."

Her face turns a cute shade of pink. "I'm embarrassed to admit, I didn't even know how they made steamed vegetables," she confesses with an uncomfortable laugh.

"Well, now you do," I reply, trying not to make a big deal about it, even though her privilege is showing.

The air starts to thicken around us, filling with sexual tension. It seems to accompany us whenever we're together. It rode shotgun in my truck earlier today, and it's just as heady now in my kitchen. It's one of the reasons I invited her to join me tonight.

Knowing I only have a few minutes until I need to cook the fish, I let a lazy grin cover my lips and ask, "So, let's negotiate this whole bathtub thing."

CHAPTER Thirteen

Ryan

I can't stop laughing. It's to the point I have tears in my eyes, threatening to stream down my face. "He did not!" There's nothing left on our plates, the food long consumed as we sit at the table and talk.

"Oh, he did. The moment TD opened the door to the locker room, Logan released the baby pig. It went screaming through the room, running over anything and anyone he could."

I continue to laugh, picturing this cute little *Charlotte's Web* baby pig running through a locker room, slamming into a room full of burly, sweaty high school football players. "What happened then?"

"Well, the pig stress-shit all over the locker room, and when someone finally caught it, there was quite the mess."

"How much trouble did they get in?"

He grins. "Well, they had to run the entire football practice, and as soon as it was over, run some more. Then, after the shit sat in the locker room and baked, they had to go in and clean it all up."

I shake my head, picturing the disgusting scene and wishing I hadn't. "That's so nasty," I say, wiping the moisture out of the corners of my eyes with a napkin.

"I was told it was a pretty gross scene, but neither regret it. In fact, I think they're weirdly proud of that prank."

I study him, the crinkle around his eyes as he smiles and the relaxed way he leans back in his chair. Marcus is older than me, that's obvious. He was approximately my age when he built this cabin. His grandpa helped him build it, and he's been gone a few years now. That means he's probably mid-thirties, roughly eight to ten years older than my twenty-six.

"Did you play?" I ask, wondering more about his youth.

He shakes his head. "Nope. I worked. Sports weren't really my thing."

"Me either," I say, making a face. "Well, I didn't work," I add with an awkward chuckle. I didn't exactly need to work either. I grew up with everything I could have possibly wanted. Considering my trust fund is large enough to support a small country, I don't have to work now, but I can't imagine my life without what I do. I know it's not curing cancer or saving endangered animals, but I love it and feel I'm doing something worthy.

"You work now," he reasons.

"Yeah," I reply, remembering how cruel the media was when I announced my makeup line. My mom wouldn't let me dip into my trust fund to back it, so she helped. Once word got out that *the* Jade Holmes was financing the start-up on my business, they were relentless about digging into my life. They found photos of me at parties and brought to light any and all of my shortcomings. They were ruthless, parading my dating history in front of their viewers and making me out to be some wild child.

"Wanna take a walk?"

His question pulls me out of my head. "Sure."

Marcus stands up and collects our dirty dishes, setting them beside the sink. "I'll take care of these later. Come on," he says, holding out his hand.

I take it willingly, letting him lead me toward the French doors at the back of the house. Buddy is hot on our heels, clearly anxious to go outside. "Do we need his leash?"

He drops my hand and holds open the door for me to exit. "No, he doesn't venture too far away from me. If we were going somewhere new, I'd say yes, but as long as we stay in my backyard, I trust him to stay close."

The moment we're outside, Buddy runs over to pee before returning to our side. He picks up a stick along the way and carries it as we head toward a pathway opposite from the one I use to move from his cabin to mine. "Where are we headed?"

"Does it matter?" he asks, hands shoved in his pockets.

I consider his response. "No, I suppose it doesn't."

The temperature drops the moment we're under the coverage of trees, and I wish I would have brought a sweater. I bring my arms to my chest, running my hands over my upper arms. "Cold?"

"Just a bit chilly."

"Hold up," he says, turning around. "Stay."

I'm not sure if he's talking to me or the dog, but we both stop and wait. Buddy lies down and starts chewing on the stick he was carrying, as if he has not one care in the world after his owner took off at a fast pace toward the house. "What do you think he's doing, Buddy? Leaving us alone in the woods to get eaten by bears?"

The dog glances up at me but ultimately goes back to tearing apart his stick.

"You'll protect me from a bear, right, Buddy?"

After a couple of minutes, I hear the snapping of a stick behind me. I spin around and spot Marcus jogging toward us, something in his hand. "Here," he says the moment he reaches my side.

It's a sweatshirt, and as he holds it up for me, I can tell it's a big one. "Thanks," I reply.

The next thing I know, he's helping me into the oversized sweatshirt. Not only am I surrounded by instant warmth, but I can smell him. It's embedded in the fabric, wrapping around me like a big hug. Unable to help myself, I bring the sleeve up to my nose and inhale.

"It should be clean. It was in my closet," he says, taking a step back. His eyes rake over me and suddenly darken, as if he really likes what he sees. I'm sure it's not the massive sweatshirt I'm swimming in, but perhaps the fact it's his.

"It's perfect, thank you."

After a few more seconds of him watching me, we continue our stroll. Two squirrels run past us, chasing each other up one tree and down another. Buddy runs ahead, jumping around and watching the two animals play. A raccoon scurries from behind a tree and slips into a hole at the base of another tree. I've never experienced this kind of nature, with woodland creatures just running amuck, before.

It's a bit...thrilling. And more enjoyable than I ever expected.

When the pathway gives way to a clearing, I gasp. The beach isn't like any I've been on before. It lacks the clean, white sand and crystal blue water I'm accustomed to. Instead, there's just this beautiful sunset over the lake that reflects a thousand shades of oranges, pinks, and yellows. A few boats dot the expansive body of water, and I can see cabins scattered around the shore with families outside enjoying the night. It's...simple.

Breathtaking.

I've witnessed hundreds of sunsets accompanying amazing views, but this one rates pretty high.

"This is one of my favorite spots," Marcus states, breaking through my private thoughts.

"It's beautiful."

"Yep," he says.

Something in his tone has me turning his way. Only, he's not looking at the gorgeous sunset. He's looking at me. A rush of arousal sweeps through me, landing firmly between my legs.

I don't know who moves first, but the next thing I know, his hands are holding my head as his lips press firmly to my own. This kiss doesn't turn ravenous, at least not right away. It's gentler, sweeter, almost romantic. His mouth still takes control, but I don't feel possessed by him. I feel...cherished.

Kissing Marcus is unlike any kiss I've ever experienced. My first few boyfriends were always rushed and fumbly. They were all tongue, usually too wet to make it enjoyable. I dated the son of a movie star for a handful of months, and he was awful. Worse than the ones I had when I was a teenager. I ended up breaking up with him because I couldn't get over the fact he was constantly trying to tongue fuck me, and not in the good way. His tongue action in the form of kissing was a touch on the eager side.

Then there was Vaughn, who, surprisingly, didn't seem that interested in much kissing. He hated PDA, so I assumed it had something to do with that. But that doesn't explain why he didn't want to kiss when we were in private and especially when we were intimate. Of course, now, I know why.

Fucker.

That leads me to Marcus, who practically has a PhD in the act. His lips are firm, his tongue masterful, and his spit not overwhelming. Kissing him is quite enjoyable, actually, and it just goes to show how lackluster my sexual life had been up to this point, because if a man can kiss this good, surely, he can do other things just as well, right?

Buddy barks nearby, letting us know he's getting tired of being ignored.

"Was that not okay?" he asks, a bit of hesitation filling his hazel eyes.

"No, no, it was *very* okay," I reassure him, holding on to his arms and praying he wants to continue the kiss. I clear my throat and add, "You're quite good at this."

"At what?" he asks, a hint of mischief reflecting in his eyes as a grin plays on his lips.

"Kissing. It must be your thing," I reply with a little giggle.

A single eyebrow shoots up toward the bill of his hat. "My thing? I don't think it's my thing. I rarely do it, actually. I think my thing has more to do with this other thing I can do with my tongue," he says with a very playful and slightly husky tone.

His comment makes me smile. This mischievous side is one I've not really seen of Marcus yet, and I like it. But even though I'd love to talk more about this *thing* he does with his tongue, I can't get past the first part of his statement. "Why do you rarely kiss?"

He holds my gaze for a few moments before dropping down and picking up a stick, severing our connection completely. He gives it a toss, sending Buddy sprinting after it. We both watch the dog grab his prize and run back through the water and dirt, leaving puppy footprints in his wake.

When Buddy drops the stick at his feet, Marcus scoops it up and gives it another toss. As the dog takes off to retrieve it once more, the man beside me gives me his full attention. "Kissing usually means intimacy. I don't usually do much of that."

Now it's my turn to be confused. "Really?"

"Nope," he replies, picking up the stick and tossing it a third time.

"Ex-girlfriends?" I ask, trying to figure him out. He's like a one-thousand-piece puzzle and you don't have the box that shows you the picture.

He shrugs his shoulders and watches Buddy return with his stick. "A few. I work a lot. The hours I keep can be hard for a woman to deal with." He meets my gaze and says, "When you run your own repair business and have the only tow truck in the area, the hours can be long. Women tend to find coming in second hard to deal with."

His words are heavy and eye-opening. My job can be difficult and stressful, the day is long, but there's always a break somewhere.

For Marcus, he's at the mercy of everyone else. After working long days, he could also have to work long nights, something I've never had to do.

"That's kind of sad," I state honestly. "You're really good at it."

The corner of his mouth curls up. "Yeah?"

"Definitely. I like kissing you," I find myself confessing, feeling a tad vulnerable in the moment.

He steps toward me, placing a big, rough hand on my hip. His fingers hold a touch of pressure, but not enough to hurt. "I don't seem to mind kissing you either," he says, his eyes burning darker than I've ever witnessed.

"Then, perhaps we include kissing in whatever happens, even though it's intimate and you don't do that. I mean, our time together has an expiration date, right?"

"Correct," he replies, pulling me toward him so my body is pressed to his. "I can handle it if you can."

"I can," I confirm, dancing my fingers up his rock-hard chest. "One more thing."

"Yeah?"

"You mentioned something about using your tongue for *other* things. When do we get to that?"

His slow grin turns wolfish. "Whenever you want, Princess."

"Well, I seem to have a little time now."

His sudden movement almost causes me to fall on my face, because instantly, he's no longer standing in front of me. He grasps my hand and all but drags me back in the direction we originally came. Marcus whistles for Buddy, who instantly falls in line beside him.

"I can't believe how well he listens to you. You'd think he's been your dog for years, not days."

"Yeah, I realized pretty quickly he's well-trained, which is why I can't believe someone just tossed him out."

I move quickly on the pathway, careful to avoid sticks and anything else I could trip over. "You don't think he's just lost?"

Marcus glances down at the dog. "I don't think so. He doesn't have on a collar, and as skinny as he is, he's been on his own for a bit. Plus, Pine Village is a really small town and none of my friends recognized him or recalled seeing a missing dog flyer around. Honestly, I think he was dumped, probably from a neighboring town or maybe even by someone who visited the Bluff Preserves National Park."

"I can't believe someone dumped him," I say, my heart breaking for the dog who most likely has experienced a rougher life.

"Me either. We're going to the vet tomorrow. Hopefully I'll have some more answers then."

"Are you going to keep him?"

We break through the pathway into the yard surrounding Marcus's gorgeous cabin. He looks down at the dog, who seems to be smiling up at his new owner. Even without Marcus responding, I know the answer to my question. I can see it in his eyes.

"Yeah, I think I will."

We reach the porch and jog up the steps together. Before he opens the door, he spins around and pins me with a look. "Before we go in there, I need you to know you can stop this at any point. And we don't have to do anything when we get inside."

"You don't want to?" I ask, my heart starting to gallop with both anticipation and dread. Is he breaking this off before it begins?

"Oh, I want to, Princess. Bad." To confirm his point, he takes my hand and places it on his crotch. His cock is...wow. Huge. Hard. Ready. "But if you're not ready, that's okay."

"Marcus?" I ask, stepping into his personal space and pressing my body against his. "Take me inside."

The door opens as I'm swept into his embrace. With one arm, he carries me inside, my feet never touching the ground until we're in the living room. His eager mouth presses to mine. Immediately, I open, allowing his tongue to delve inside. He spins me around and lifts, setting me on the back of the couch. Stepping between my legs, he pulls me against him as my legs wrap around his waist.

"I've been thinking about this since the night I found you on the side of the road," he whispers, running his mouth down the column of my neck.

"Really? I thought you hated me."

"I was incredibly attracted to you, and it bothered me."

"Why?"

He pulls back enough to meet my gaze. "Because I didn't like the way you made me feel. I wanted you, but didn't want to want you. Does that make sense?"

I nod, understanding completely. "Same, buster. Same."

He takes my mouth with a bit more urgency this time, deepening the kiss and making my toes curl. "What do you say we get this off?" he asks, sliding my dress up and exposing my thighs.

"Sounds like an amazing idea."

Lifting my arms and balancing on the couch, I hold up my arms as he assists me in removing the sweatshirt. "I've been dying to get beneath one of these little sundresses since that night too."

"Well, tonight's your lucky night," I say, slipping one spaghetti strap down my bare arm.

He follows the motion, his eyes riveted to the strap.

Suddenly, he reaches up and stops me from slipping my arm completely out of the strap. "Hold up."

"What?" I ask, wondering what could possibly be wrong. Getting naked is sort of the first step before embarking into a sexually gratifying night.

A lazy grin plays across his lips. "I have an idea."

He reaches around me and picks me up off the couch, my legs wrapping tightly around his waist. "What are you doing?" I ask, holding on for dear life, even though I know he can carry me. Marcus has proven to be plenty strong.

He walks over and makes sure the front door is locked before taking off for the bedroom. Neither of us pay Buddy any attention, even though he's right behind us as we head up the stairs. Once we reach the bedroom, he all but tosses me onto the bed. I bounce a little and can't help but giggle as I settle into the middle of the mattress.

He stands beside the bed, his eyes devouring me. "I'm going to eat your pussy, Princess, until you come. Then I'm going to fuck it and make you come again."

Holy shit, Marcus Wright is a dirty talker.

My mouth goes completely dry at his direct words. My nipples pebble hard and my panties are soaked.

Is this man real?

Gorgeous, rugged, and a filthy talker. He's the trifecta of ultimate masculinity, something I never expected to be attracted to or crave. And I definitely crave Marcus and what he's promising. That big dick energy you hear others boasting about? Yep, he totally has it. In spades.

There's only one thing I can say right now.

"Sign me up."

CHAPTER
fourteen

MARCUS

I was dangerously close to exploding in my jeans. Like a teenager.

Feeling her body pressed against mine, having her rock her pussy against my cock was enough to make me lose my mind. All I want to do was thrust, to take what she's offering. To feel the walls of her pussy squeeze and milk everything I have to offer her.

But first, I need to taste her.

It's as if my life depends on it. I've never felt this urgency, this frantic craze consumes me, and even though the desire is so strong I swear I'll always feel it, I refuse to let it take control. I'm a man who prides myself on remaining in control at all times, and I'll be damned if I'm going to lose it now, with Ryan.

I take in the gorgeous woman lying on my bed. Her blond hair is wild across the blue bedding, and her dress is hiked up her thighs. I can almost see a sliver of panties. But what holds my attention right now is those damn shoes. The ones with the ties running up her calves.

Placing my hands just above the ties, I gently push her legs apart. "I don't know what kind of footwear this is, but I like them. A lot. When you arrived, I thought of you wearing them and nothing else."

"They're Monika Chiang. I love these sandals," she tells me, her eyes sparkling like chocolate diamonds. "I have them in a nude four-and-a-half-inch heel that ties about halfway up my calf."

A groan that sounds both animalistic and painful slides from my throat. I run my hand over my face, picturing these shoes with sexy as fuck heels, and now my cock is leaking precum. "I want to see them," I find myself saying, though it comes out husky and more like a demand.

She smiles. "I brought them with me."

I place my palms against the inside of her calves and slowly start to move up. Her skin is so damn smooth and soft. "I want you in them one night this week."

She nods and swallows hard.

Returning my attention to her legs and dress, I gather the material and push. Her silky thighs have me all but panting, but it's what I find when I move the dress over her hips that has me coming out of my skin—and almost coming in my pants.

She's bare.

No panties.

No hair.

Bare fucking pussy.

"Fuck," I groan, closing my eyes and still picturing it. I do everything I can to remain firmly grasped on whatever control I have left, which isn't much.

"Problem?" she asks, humor laced in her question.

"You've been bare all night?"

She nods. "I figured panties would just get in the way," she reasons proudly.

I run my hand over my face once more and return my focus on the gorgeous sight before me. "You've been naughty, not wearing panties."

The smirk on her lips tells me she knew exactly what she was doing, what going sans panties would do to me.

"Well, you figured correctly," I tell her, running my fingers along her thighs before gently gripping her hips.

Pointing to the dog bed in the corner, I politely, yet slightly urgently tell Buddy to, "Lie down." He immediately does as instructed, though I can tell he doesn't want to. He'd much rather jump up on the bed and lie with Ryan, and that's not going to happen. At least not now.

I pull Ryan to the corner of the bed and squat. She gasps at the sudden movement and immediately places her legs around my neck. Tossing my ball cap down onto the ground, I ask, "Ready?"

She nods eagerly. Her pussy is glistening and directly in front of my face. What's a man to do but enjoy?

I lean forward and take a long, leisurely swipe with my tongue. Her scent surrounds me, her taste consumes me. Placing my hands on the insides of her thighs, I go to town eating her pussy. My tongue flicks across her swollen clit before sliding inside her body. Her hips roll as she starts to move in rhythm with my mouth.

Ryan grinds against my face, seeking more. I catch a nice pink tint developing on her thighs, no doubt from my facial hair. I don't have a beard, but I've always had scruff, and seeing the redness mar her tanned skin sends another bolt of lust straight to my groin.

Returning my mouth to her clit, I press two fingers into her pussy. She's tight, hot, and soaking wet, and all I want is to thrust my cock inside her. But first, I need her to come on my mouth and fingers.

I turn my hand so my palm is facing up and curl my fingers along the top of her insides. I know what magical spot I'm looking for and know the moment I stroke it. Ryan cries out, her legs wrapping firmly around my head. She's getting close to coming, just needs that little nudge over the edge.

Latching on to her clit, I suck it hard into my mouth, running my tongue across the hard nub, while burying my fingers deep inside her and massaging her G-spot. She detonates like a beautiful bomb, coming hard as she grinds against my face. I can barely hear my name falling from her lips, since her thighs are pressed firmly to the sides of my head, covering my ears. I suck and lick away every drop she gives me, ready and eager for more.

When I move my mouth, her legs fall open and I'm able to sit back on my heels. "Holy shit," she murmurs, her voice heavy with satisfaction. "That was...wow."

I can't help but smile. What man doesn't want to hear those kinds of accolades?

Standing up, my eyes scan her flushed cheeks, her wild hair, and the smooth, set skin of her pussy. Her legs are still spread, hanging open, and all I can think about is what's to come. "You okay there?" I ask, reaching behind my neck and pulling my T-shirt off.

Her eyes pop open, drinking in my chest. I don't work out regularly, but thanks to a very physically demanding job, I keep in shape. Her eyes take in my ink, and I can't tell if she's intrigued or repulsed. I don't have a lot, but my chest holds a couple pieces in memory of my grandparents.

But they're the last people I want to think about right now.

I only want Ryan on my mind.

When I reach for the fly of my jeans, her eyes follow my movement. She licks her lips as I lower the zipper. I can practically feel her gaze in my balls. They're heavy with need and craving release. Pushing my jeans and boxers over my hips, I realize my issue as soon as the clothes reach my knees. Quickly, I do what I can to unlace my boots, and thanks to the bunched-up material halfway down my legs, it's difficult.

Fortunately, my attention is drawn elsewhere.

Ryan reaches between her legs and starts rubbing her clit. All I want to do is lean forward and bury my face in her sweetness all over again. "You got that, Marcus?" she asks, her eyes dancing with humor, as I blindly try to unlace my boots.

"Yep. Got it." I don't have it, but I will. I don't care if I have to rip my own foot off to get these damn pants off, I will do it.

When I finally remove my boots, pants, and boxers, I bend down, placing both hands on the bed, and press my mouth to hers. "That wasn't very nice. You were trying to distract me."

She giggles, reaching around and gripping my ass in her hands. "Sorry?"

I snort and stand back up, heading to the nightstand for a condom. "You don't sound very sorry. For that, I might have to spank you."

Her eyes widen and dilate, and I'm not sure if she's turned on or shocked. Probably both. "Y-you wouldn't," she sputters.

Spanking really hasn't been my thing in the past, but the thought of seeing her pink ass in the air, my handprint on the round globe, has me harder than I've ever been. "I think I would, Princess. On your knees."

She doesn't hesitate.

Ryan flips around onto her hands and knees, but I realize she's still wearing the dress. I push it up, helping remove what's covering her abdomen. The moment it's over her head, she returns her palms to the mattress and glances back at me. Her bare breasts hang, and even though I long to suck her nipples into my mouth, there's something else I need more.

The most beautiful woman in the world is primed and ready for me, looking like every man's wet dream right now.

"You can still stop this," I say without touching her.

"I'm not stopping anything, so suit up, buster."

Ripping open the package, I quickly cover myself with latex. I run my hands up her thighs, squeezing her ass. "Ready?"

"So ready," she groans, drawing out those two words as she waits.

Taking my position behind her, I line myself up at her entrance. I drink in the sight of her, hearing the heavy pants of her breath and mine. Her ass is right there, and I know what I have to do.

I bring my hand down onto her skin, the crack of the contact echoing through the room. Before she can respond, I thrust forward, filling her in one long stroke.

Her gasp turns to a groan. She's so tight, I have to grapple for every ounce of control I possess. Fully seated inside her, I hold still so she can adjust to the invasion. I run my palm over the smarted skin, cupping her ass, as she pushes back against me.

"More," she begs, arching her back.

I give her exactly what she wants.

What we *both* want.

My grip on her hips tightens, and I pull back until it's just the head of my cock still inside her body. Then, I thrust forward once more, rolling my hips and repeating the movement at a quickened pace. It's not frantic, but there's definitely an urgency. She meets me halfway, pushing back against me and taking everything I give.

Ryan arches her back and I almost lose it, but I refuse to come first.

I let my body move, driving us both toward release. My hands grip her hips as I thrust, but I eventually shift my right hand to cup her ass. The globe fits perfectly in my hand, which is tingling as we speak. I lift it up and bring it down firmly on her smooth skin. The slap echoes through my bedroom as she yelps. Instantly, I feel her pussy clench my cock. I sooth the smarted skin with my palm and continue to rock my hips.

"You liked that." It wasn't a question. I felt her reaction around my dick.

"I didn't hate it," she whispers between pants.

She drops to her elbows, her ass pointed directly at me. My handprint is visible against the tanned flesh, and all I want to do is mark her again. I won't—at least not right now.

My balls draw up as the familiar tingle erupts at the base of my spine. I'm going to come, which means I need to get her there. Now.

I roll my hips and reach between her legs. Gliding my fingers across her clit, I feel her entire body tense. "Oh, fuck," she groans, pushing back and taking my cock harder.

"Come on my dick, Princess. I want to feel it," I demand, sweat starting to drip down my forehead. "That's it. I feel how close you are. Squeeze my cock with your pussy."

And she does. With a firm finger brushing over her hard clit and my cock buried deep inside her, she comes hard, crying out as her release rocks her to the core. "Marcus," she says with a gasp, riding the waves.

I follow suit, pushing myself as deep into her body as I can and stilling, coming with an intensity I haven't experienced in a long damn time. My orgasm seems to drag on and on, my body drawing every ounce of pleasure it can get from her body.

When the spasms finally subside, I drape myself over her back and kiss her bare shoulder. "Jesus," I whisper harshly, trying to catch my breath.

"That was...wow," she confirms.

Even though I don't want to, I pull out of her body and reach for the condom. I move to the bathroom to dispose of the used protection and clean up a bit. I definitely need a shower, but maybe we can hit that together after round two.

Smiling, I grab a washcloth and wet it with warm water. When I return to the bedroom, I stop in my tracks and stare at the woman before me. She's slipping back on her dress, clearly preparing to leave.

"I, uh, brought you this," I say lamely, holding out the washcloth.

"Oh, thanks," she replies with a quick smile. "I'm just gonna head back to my cabin. I can shower when I get there."

I'm struck completely speechless. She's leaving? Before I have a chance to? I almost don't know what to do with that information. I don't think that's ever happened before. Usually, I'm the first one to start dressing and get on the road to home.

Before I have a chance to invite her to shower with me, she gives me a happy little satisfied grin as she approaches where I stand. "Thanks for everything, Marcus."

My brain is still slow on the response, because all I say is, "Yeah."

Going up on her tiptoes, she places a soft kiss against my lips. I'm a millisecond away from throwing her over my shoulder and carting her back to my bed when she pulls away. She gives me a wink and walks away from where I stand, rooted in my spot.

"See you around," she says, waving her little fingers and heading for my stairs.

I watch her blond hair bounce until she's out of sight completely. If I could get my feet to move, I'd go after her, but they seem a little leaden right now, as if they've recently been encased in concrete.

The front door opens and closes, leaving me still trying to figure out what the fuck just happened.

I'll tell you what happened. That was some of the best sex ever, and she just got up and walked away after. And it was completely unexpected. Never in all the years I've been sleeping with women has one ever turned the tables on me like that. It's a little heady and makes me smile. The sexy vixen bested me when I least expected it.

Tossing the washcloth into the laundry basket and knowing I eventually need to go downstairs to let Buddy out one last time for the night and to make sure the house is locked up; I crawl onto the bed. Her scent hangs heavy in the air and on my bedding, and I don't hate it. I lie here, replaying our night together, and smile.

Ryan Marcotte is nothing like I expected.

And it's the memories of what we shared that accompanies me when I finally fall asleep later in the evening.

CHAPTER
fifteen

Ryan

I'm all smiles as I stretch once more in the kitchen. My body is deliciously sore in the best way possible. The kind of sore only good sex can provide. Well, that's an assumption, because I've never felt this achy after having sex before, and after sleeping with Marcus, I can safely say I've never had good sex before either.

Being with him was...wow.

I slept better than ever before. Like a baby. Or a woman who was royally sexed up from head to toe, her vagina thoroughly stretched and filled. And that was after being eaten to orgasm, which is another thing I've been lacking in my life. It's something I love, but Vaughn just wasn't a fan, so he rarely did it.

The fucker.

But Marcus enjoyed it. In fact, he may have enjoyed it more than me. Well, not *more* than me, but he was a serious fan. Seeing my juices glisten on his face, coating his lips and chin, was epically erotic, and my thighs are clenching at the thought of seeing it again. Is it bad to shoot him a text and ask? I'm not above begging.

At the end of our sexed-up night, I left with an extra pep in my step and thighs that burned from his stubble. It was perfect.

Now, I'm trying to decide how to spend my Tuesday. Marcus is at work, so it's not like I can buzz through the pathway to his cabin and jump his bones. Or specifically, a very large bone. If I thought he had big dick energy before, last night only confirmed it. He's practically the president of the big dick man club.

Grabbing my phone, I take a sip of my coffee and grab a seat at the small dinette. I haven't paid much attention to my device since I arrived on Friday, so I'm sure I've got plenty of communications to catch up on. The scent of fresh caramel infused coffee with yummy sugar-free Italian cream fills the air. It may not be an eight-dollar cup of Joe from a coffee shop or café, but it'll do, all things considered.

The number shown above the text message icon is staggering, so I tap the email app first. I scroll through, deleting spam and advertising emails, and click on one from my business manager. Ariana was the perfect fit for the job when I was searching for someone to help run the day-to-day business for Ryan Holmes Cosmetics. She has a decade of experience under her hat and came highly recommended by several in the industry.

I read through her message and make a few notes in my calendar for when I return to Los Angeles. We'll start working on our winter line then, introducing a new palate of gorgeous colors, as well as more skincare products. I'm incredibly giddy at the thought, ready to show the world I'm not just a one-hit wonder, that my business has the staying power.

When I've finished my notes, I click over to the phone app and hit her name.

"I was starting to get worried you were eaten by a bear or something," she says in way of greeting.

"Don't put that out there," I say, taking another sip of coffee. "I was told there are bears in the area."

"Well, you need to get bear spray or something," she replies.

"Do they have bear spray?" I wonder. Maybe I should order some.

I'm greeted by a pregnant pause. "I'll check Amazon."

Smiling, I jump into business. "I received your email. Everything looks good to me. I've added notes to my calendar and can meet you when I return."

"Perfect. I've asked the design team to start putting together compact layout samples. Last we talked, you didn't want to do traditional marketing and product displays for the winter release. Is that still the case?"

"Yes. I want to combine classic with edgy for this release," I confirm, ideas swirling through my brain.

"That's what I told them. I'll reach out and make sure we're all on the same page. Maybe by the time you return to LA they'll have some design concepts for you to look at."

"I like that," I say, taking another sip of coffee.

We talk business for a few more minutes, running through sales numbers and projections. By the time that's over, she switches gears on me. "There's one more thing. The network called the office. They said you weren't answering your phone."

"I'm not answering anyone's calls," I reply lamely.

"And with good reason. I gave—what's his name? Bradley?— a piece of my mind when I had him on the phone," she states, starting to get a little heated.

"I don't need you to fight my battles, Ari," I reply. The communication from the network isn't unexpected, but I *did* ask them to give me space while I sorted a few things out.

"Well, if that guy was standing in front of me, I would have kneed him straight in the balls."

I can't help but giggle. "You're not the only one," I mumble, mostly to myself.

"Anyway, this is me giving you the message, like I said I would. I can't tell you what to do, but as your business manager *and* friend,

I think you should do exactly what you told him you were doing. Take the time off and work through the crap in your head. What he and the network did to you on that finale is bullshit, Ryan. Pure bullshit. They deserve to sit and sweat a little bit."

"I signed a contract for two years," I remind her, wishing I hadn't, but when the network pitched me the idea, they swore it would be a ratings gold mine and that two years was nothing in the grand scheme of things. Look at the Kardashians.

I was eager to get my name and new brand out there, and what better way to do so than a behind-the-scenes look at what I was doing. Two years seemed like nothing at the time. Two seasons. Forty total episodes. I could totally allow cameras to invade my life for a few hours a week, right?

"Get out of it. Contracts like this always have early-out clauses, right?"

I close my eyes and think about the clause that's printed in black and white with my name scribbled on the last page. Not only would I have to pay a huge sum of money to terminate the contract, I'd have to cover costs for every episode not fulfilled, and the number wasn't pretty. Not that I couldn't dip into my trust fund to get out of it, if I absolutely had to. I'm sure Mom would understand. She invested in my initial start-up, so I wouldn't feel right to ask for her help either.

"They do, but mine has some pretty heavy financial and legal repercussions."

"Well, that's bullshit," she sputters out, angry on my behalf.

"Agreed." After a beat, I add, "I'll figure it out, Ari."

"I know you will, honey. You're very business-savvy for someone so young, but if you need direction, call your lawyers. That's why you retain them, right?"

I nod.

"So, enough about all that. Tell me about that little place you're staying," she says, excitement on my behalf pouring through the phone.

My mind instantly flashes to Marcus. "It's...fine." I shift in my seat, my clit starting to throb a bit as memories filter through my mind.

"What? What happened?" she digs.

"Nothing." Of course, my reply is way too quick and with too much force.

She gasps. "Something happened. What? Tell me!" she insists.

"Ariana," I reply through a groan.

"Ryan," she mimics, waiting me out.

"Fine. I met someone," I say quietly.

"Really? Good for you! Tell me more. Where did you meet?" she hedges.

"Actually, we met on the side of the road."

"Seriously?"

I recall the night we met, just four short days ago. "Yeah, my tire went flat, and he stopped to help. I thought he was a murderer or something."

"Did he kill you with his charms?" she asks with a laugh.

Not his charms, but his big dick tried to kill me.

"Something like that," I reply, feeling my cheeks heat.

"Oh, I can practically see you blushing through the phone. Don't make me FaceTime you," she chastises.

"Stop it."

"*You* stop it! Is he checking under the bed for bears?"

I roll my eyes. "No, he took me fishing."

I'm met with silence. "Are you serious? You went *fishing*?"

A shiver sweeps through my veins as I recall putting that nasty worm on the hooks. "It was...interesting."

"I bet," she replies. "I could never go fishing. I'll stick to ordering it at a restaurant."

"I'll never look at fish the same," I tell her, even though the fish Marcus made for dinner was delicious.

"So, the sexy mountain man took you fishing, huh?"

"He's not a mountain man, Ari. There aren't any mountains here. He serviced my car."

"Okay, fine, I get it. But tell me this." After a beat, she asks, "Are you at least getting your vagina serviced while you're there too?"

I open my mouth, but nothing comes out.

"Atta girl," she replies, and I can feel her grin through the phone. "You keep servicing it. Have fun."

"I am, Ariana."

"Good. I'll let you go, so you can get back to the vagina servicing," she blurts out with a hearty laugh.

"Goodbye, Ari."

"Bye-bye, sweetie. Oh, wait! Don't forget about the release celebration when you get back. It's the following night. You're still coming back for that, right?"

How could I not? The release celebration has been in the works for the last three months. It's a culmination celebration of the reality show, the summer release of my line, and a preview of what's to come. "Yes, I'll be home on that Friday."

"Good. Anything I can help with?"

"No, the party planning company is on it, and my mom is their point of contact, working on all the behind-the-scenes details. You know she loves these kinds of things." Jade Holmes is the ultimate party planner and event organizer.

"I've got a meeting scheduled for later this week to go over what she needs from me on this side. Plus, we're working together on announcing Desi as the new face of Ryan Holmes Cosmetics, since the network completely fucked you over and didn't include it during the finale."

No shit. I was totally fucked, and not in the good way.

"We're working on it. The celebration is in good hands. Don't let a single worry enter that pretty little head of yours. Take this time and decompress. Everything will be here waiting for your return, and then we'll hit the ground running. Until then, we have it handled, and if there's something we need help with, we'll reach out."

"Thank you, Ari."

"You're welcome, Ryan. Talk soon."

I hang up the phone and shake my head. Everything is being handled.

My vagina is still in firm agreement with Ariana, hoping to get a little more servicing soon. The way blood keeps humming through my veins and my panties are slick with desire, I might be sitting on his front porch, waiting for him to get home.

Or maybe I'll stop by the repair shop.

No, that won't work. Not that I think the paparazzi are hanging out near Marcus's auto shop, but the last thing I need is to be photographed coming out of his office after being "serviced." I wouldn't mind having his fingers in my hair, but I don't necessarily want the world to see the aftermath.

I scan through the rest of my emails, replying to the ones I need to and putting the rest off until later. My fingers hover over the ones from Bradley and the network, but I don't tap to open them. I should—I'm under contract—but I told him I needed time, so that's what I'm doing.

Taking time.

That stupid reality show.

No, I can't exactly blame the show. It did exactly what I was hoping it would. It gave me the exposure to elevate my makeup and skincare line into a global sensation. My name is being carried in some of the biggest department stores in the world, and I couldn't be prouder.

Now, all that feels...inconsequential.

Why? Because what should have been dubbed a success—meaning the end of a great first season and the skyrocketing global sales—was completely overshadowed by the fact my boyfriend betrayed me.

On television.

And I found out along with the rest of the world.

Bradley told me they were planning a big bombshell during the season finale, but it wasn't what I expected. I *thought* it was going to be the announcement of my new product line and the fact one of the biggest stars in Hollywood was going to be the face of my company. That's what I was expecting.

That's not what I got.

Instead, I watched in horror as the man I'd been seeing off and on for three years confessed his darkest secret—and biggest lie—to the world. Sure, the network got exactly what they wanted. Ratings gold. Me? I get to clean up the mess.

After replying to a few emails from my mom and the party planner, Veronica, about the celebration event, I closed down my email and flipped over to my text messages. I scan through the list, tapping out replies to the few friends who reached out following the finale. Most were shocked, repulsed by what they saw, and a couple even had comments about Vaughn's duplicity and the fact he should be shunned right out of Hollywood.

Couldn't agree more...

I scroll past the man himself and tap on my father's name.

Dad: Just checking in. Hope you're enjoying your vacation.

Again, Marcus flashes through my mind, but I can't exactly tell my dad about him. I'm sure he'd be real proud of the fact his daughter—his only baby girl—slept with the grumpy neighbor just three days after meeting.

Me: The relaxation is exactly what I needed.

The bubbles appear immediately, which doesn't surprise me. Even though California is two hours behind, my dad has always been an early riser. I can picture him sitting in his home office, his second cup of coffee steaming on his desk as he works.

Dad: Good. You know, I've been thinking, maybe after this movie, I'll take your mother away for a little while. Find us a cabin in the mountains somewhere, like Tennessee, and just decompress.

I can't help but smile, because picturing my father in a cabin in the mountains, let alone one in Tennessee, was a bit absurd. But then again, what did I know? I seem to be enjoying my time in a little rustic cabin, so maybe Douglas Marcotte and Jade Holmes would too.

Me: I'm sure you'd love it. It's unlike anything I've ever experienced.

Dad: I'm proud of you, Ryan.

Tears fill my eyes. I've always been close to my parents. They did their best to make time for me in their busy schedules, but it could be difficult at times. Dad traveled a lot, on location for whatever movie he was producing, and my mother was incredibly busy with her charity. Yet, I always felt their love, even if we weren't together.

Me: Thank you.

Dad: I mean it, honey. You've grown into an amazing woman and business owner. You're making your mark all on your own and doing it with class and dignity. You're so much like your mother. Beauty and brains.

The tears start to fall. My mother was the epitome of class. I have looked up to her my entire life. I've been compared to her too, especially under the powerful lens of the camera. The criticism has been brutal over the years, the digs about the ways I don't measure up. But in the end, it's all bullshit. None of it mattered then.

And it doesn't now.

Something I'm learning as the days go by.

I'm also learning about myself, about who I really am and who I want to be.

Dad: Anyway, I've been thinking...about Vaughn.

I fire off a text before he can continue.

Me: No.

Dad: I wish you'd let me. It's not right. He doesn't deserve the part.

Me: No, he doesn't, but he won it based on his talent, not because he was dating the producer's daughter. Right?

I worry my lip, waiting for his response.

Dad: Right. He was the only one we saw for the part.

Me: Then you stick with your gut. Just because he turned out to be a lying fucker doesn't mean he deserves to be fired. Keep the line between business and personal in place. You can't fire him because of what he did.

Dad: I can.

Me: But it wouldn't be right. He was a business decision. You said he was perfect for the part, and I'm sure that hasn't changed.

Dad: No, it hasn't.

Me: Then you have to let it go.

Dad: I'll never let it go. He hurt you. I won't tolerate that.

Me: I love you, Daddy.

Dad: I love you too, baby girl.

Me: I should let you get back to work.

Dad: I always have time for you. Always.

Me: Likewise. Have a good day.

Dad: You too.

I ignore the rest of the text messages—for now—and set the device on the table. I sit here, enjoying the morning quiet with a cup of coffee, and a smile. It may not be Hollywood or Los Angeles or a fancy coffeehouse, but that's okay.

This is growing on me.

Wisconsin, this small town, the cabin—it's all starting to feel...good.

Better than good.

Comfortable.

Sure, it's only been four days since my arrival, but I don't know. There's something magical about this place. It makes me feel hopeful for the first time since my entire life seemed to implode on national television.

This is me taking control. Not letting the media and gossip rags and loudmouths of California dictate my story. It's my life, dammit, and I can do whatever the hell I want with it.

Starting with the gorgeous mechanic next door.

I think I'll add him to the top of my to-do list.

CHAPTER
sixteen

MARCUS

"This alternator is fucked," Dale hollers from under the hood of the Buick LeSabre he's working on.

"I figured," I reply, finishing up the tire rotation on the Ford F-150 on the lift.

"Good thing you already had one coming from the auto parts store," Dale says, wiping his hands on a shop towel as he approaches.

The parts store is in Hudson and makes two trips a day to Pine Village, a morning and afternoon run, and thanks to me adding the new alternator to my order before the morning deadline, we'll be able to get the part replaced and the vehicle out the door before noon, freeing up the bay for the next repair.

I grunt, keeping my focus on lining up the front right tire to the lug holes. I feel a little behind today, since I had to use part of the morning to take Buddy to the vet. She confirmed he's not microchipped and in good health, despite having been out on his own for a little while. She checked with area clinics and shelters, but didn't find any missing pet information, but promised to look again in a few days. At this point, he's starting to grow on me, so I'm not sure how I'd feel if his owner appeared finally, looking for the dog.

"You're awfully quiet today," Dale says, breaking through my concentration and loud enough to be heard over the country music playing through the speakers. Not that I need to concentrate on a wheel rotation. I could do them in my sleep.

"Just working," I reply, reaching for the torque wrench to tighten the lug nuts.

I can feel his gaze on me, but I keep my focus on the task at hand.

"How's Ryan?"

"How would I know?" I ask, raising the wrench and lining it up with the first lug nut. I had already researched the correct amount of torque to use when tightening the wheel.

He chuckles, grabbing my attention. "Your actions and your words don't match."

I can't help but give him a confused look. "What are you talking about, old man?"

He just grins. "You like her."

I scoff and tighten the first lug nut. "You're crazy."

"Am I?"

I turn in his direction. He's casually leaning against the rear of the Buick he's working on. "Yep. Certifiable."

That just makes him smile bigger.

When I realize he's not going away, I make a big production of lowering the torque wrench and giving him my full attention. "She's not so bad."

He laughs.

Fucker.

"No, I don't suppose she is," he says, turning back to the front end of the car he's working on. "Oh, Marcus? It's okay to have fun every now and again, and I'm not talking about whatever in the hell you do when you go to Hudson. She's here for a few weeks. Have fun.

Enjoy life a little. There's a lot more to it than just working all the time."

With that, he spins around and disappears beneath the hood of the car.

I return my attention on the wheel, but I can't help but think about Ryan. I recall every second of our night together, including the fact she practically jumped up and walked back to her cabin after we were done. She told me thanks for the good time and disappeared before I even had a chance to redress.

Kinda like how I am with the women I encounter in Hudson.

It was the arrangement I was familiar and comfortable with, yet I can't help but wish she would have stayed. For another round? Sure. But also because I craved her in my bed.

Ryan turned out to be a lot more...adventurous than I expected. From the moment she rolled over on her hands and knees, I was a goner. And not just because I was horny and hadn't had sex in about four months. It was her. She was a slice of wild I wasn't expecting and drew out every domineering and alpha side I possessed. And the best part was, she seemed to crave it too. Letting me take control. Straddling the line between rough and too rough, which I don't think we crossed. Not if the satisfied smile on her lips was any indication.

I shift myself so Dale can't see the wood I'm suddenly sporting, thanks to the vivid memories of my night with Ryan. I just get the wheel completely tightened when I hear my name being called across the shop.

"Marcus! You have a visitor!" Gladys hollers over the noise.

I glance over at the office but don't see anyone through the picture window. With a sigh, I grab the towel and wipe smudges of grease and dirt off my hand. I wonder who it is? Usually if it's a customer, Gladys takes care of them. That's why she works here, even if it's just part time in the mornings.

"A visitor, huh?"

I glance over to the Buick and find Dale sticking his head around the hood, waggling his eyebrows suggestively.

"Stop it, old man," I grumble, making my way to the shop office, his laughter following me with each step I take.

Pushing through the doorway between the shop and the office, I come face-to-face with the woman I spent a portion of last night with. Ryan looks completely out of place here, even if she's wearing tiny little black shorts, a fitted T-shirt, and a ball cap on her head. She still looks regal and beautiful, and while the office isn't completely coated in grime and filth, it's still an auto shop office. Gladys helps keep the floors clean and the counter dusted off, but it's nowhere near the standards or cleanliness I'm sure she's accustomed to.

"Hey," I say when she offers me a small smile.

"Hi."

I glance over at Gladys, feeling her eyes on me. She's grinning, taking in our exchange with an eagerness I've never seen before. "Everything all right?" I ask, wondering if there's an issue at the cabin.

"Oh, yes," she replies with an awkward chuckle. Her chocolate-brown eyes move to Gladys at the counter. "Umm, do you have a minute? I know you're busy, so I won't take long."

"Sure." I point to the open office door behind Gladys. "In here."

Ryan follows me inside the small space and turns around as I shut the door. I can't help but wonder if Gladys is running to find a glass to place against the wall or door.

"I won't take up much of your time," she quickly says. "I know you're busy working. I was in the neighborhood," she adds, making me internally smile, because Pine Village is small enough, it's kinda one big neighborhood. The whole town.

"Anyway, I was nearby," she continues, holding my gaze. "Do you want to grab lunch?"

Her question surprises me, and I'm certain it shows on my face.

"If not, that's okay. Like I said, I was just in the neighborhood, and it's almost lunchtime, so I thought—"

"Okay."

"Really?" Her entire face lights up.

I take off my ball cap and run my fingers through my hair. "Yeah, well, I'll have to say something to Dale and Gladys. I don't usually take lunch."

"Why not?"

I shrug. "There are only so many hours in the day, I guess, and I want to get as much done as I possibly can."

"You don't have to if you don't want to," she insists.

"No, it's fine. I haven't eaten anything today, so a quick lunch wouldn't hurt."

She smiles, and rocks on her heels. "Great! Where should we go?"

There aren't too many options in town, and no matter where we go, we'll be under the microscope. We'll be the talk of the town within an hour, and for once, I don't care. Usually, I'd avoid the spotlight in any way, shape, or form, especially in this town. It's easy to become gossip fodder, which we've all fallen victim to from time to time. Not that I care what anyone thinks of me, but I do prefer to have my name kept out of their mouths.

"How about the diner? It's just down the road and they're usually pretty quick," I suggest.

"That sounds good. I ate there on Saturday, and it was delicious."

"Saul is an amazing cook. We might get lucky, and they'll have their bacon-wrapped meatloaf on special, since yesterday was a holiday."

Her eyes bright at the thought. "I had that Saturday. Ellie recommended it."

"She's a wise woman. Worked there forever," I tell her, reaching for the doorknob. "Gladys, I'm gonna take a quick lunch."

She seems surprised by my announcement. "Really?"

"Yeah," I mutter, walking past the counter and heading for the shop. Glancing over my shoulder, I make eye contact with Ryan again and add, "I'll be right back."

She nods, so I push through the door and head for where Dale is working. First thing I do is wash my hands, making sure I get as much grease and dirt off them. When I tear off a paper towel, I mutter to Dale, "I'll be back. I'm gonna take a quick lunch."

He pops his head out from under the hood and levels me with a look of shock. "What?"

"I'll be right back," I say, making my way back to the office before he can say another word. I'm sure I'll get an earful when I get back, especially after he talks to Gladys. Don't need to hear it before I go.

When I return to the office, I hold open the door and wait for her to exit first. She steps outside ahead of me and starts to head for her rental car. "You mind walking?" I ask, loving the warmth of the sun above me.

"No, I don't mind," she replies, falling in line beside me.

"Hi, Miss Ryan."

I glance over and find Dale standing outside the first garage bay, a big grin on his face as he waves.

"Hi, Dale. Lovely day, isn't it?" she asks, waving back.

"Sure is. You two have fun," he says, whistling as he returns to work. I don't miss the knowing smirk on his face either. Yeah, I'll definitely hear all about it when I get back.

We're quiet as we hit the sidewalk and head toward the diner. It's not far, only a couple blocks up the road. It would take longer to find a parking spot at this time of day than it would to just walk there.

"How's work going?" she asks as we approach the first crosswalk.

"Good."

She nods. After we cross the street and continue on our way, she jumps back into more conversation. "I went shopping today. I realized I needed a different wardrobe if I wanted to fly under the radar while I was here. As much as I love my dresses, they're too Ryan Marcotte, so I drove to Hudson and found some basic shorts and tees at Target."

I glance her way, sidestepping a woman and child exiting one of the small boutiques. "Personally, I kinda like your sundresses."

She giggles, looking at me from beneath her lashes. "That's what you got out of all that?"

I shrug, my hands shoved in my pockets.

"Well, I could always wear them...later," she says softly, keeping her head down to shield her face from those around us.

"I like...later," I confess, this playfulness is something new with me.

We reach the diner as she adds, "Me too."

I open the door, and we step inside the cool building. Instantly, we spot Ellie, who waves us in. "Hey, guys," she greets. She looks around the room and nods toward the far back booth. She knows who Ryan really is, even if she thought she was Jade at first, so I can't help but think she put us in the back corner to offer a bit more privacy.

She slips into the booth with her back to the room, while I take the side with the view. Sure, everyone will wonder and speculate about who I'm with, but that's fine. At least she's shielded from prying eyes.

"What can I get you to drink?" Ellie asks when she approaches.

"Sweet tea," Ryan requests eagerly.

Ellie laughs. "I've created a monster." Then, she glances at me.

"Same."

"Special is country-fried steak with all the fixin's or chicken salad on a croissant with fresh fruit and coleslaw. I'll grab your drinks and be back for your orders."

Ellie heads to the counter and fills two glasses with ice and tea. I take a quick glance around the room, finding most of the tables and booths full. Considering it's near lunch hour, you can tell we're officially jumping into the busy summer tourist season. Fortunately, no one really seems to be paying much attention to us. Sure, a few of the locals wave and send me a curious glance, but no one approaches the table.

Yet.

"Do you know what you're having?" Ryan asks, looking over the menu.

"Probably the chicken salad special. I don't usually eat too heavy for lunch, otherwise I'd have the country-fried steak. It's always delicious."

She nods, replacing the menu in the napkin and condiment holder. "I think I'll do the same. Usually I wouldn't have the croissant, but I'm on vacation, right? Might as well live a little," she says with a chuckle.

"Live a little." I don't know why those three little words hold so much weight, but they do. It reminds me of what Dale said earlier.

"All right, did you two decide?" Ellie asks, setting two glasses of sweet tea on the table.

"Chicken salad special, please," Ryan requests.

"Same."

"You two are easy," she replies, jotting our orders down and offering a smile. "It'll be up shortly." Then she's gone again, stopping by other tables and checking on patrons.

We're both silent, and honestly, the quiet doesn't bother me. I'm that kind of guy naturally. I sit back and watch. Always observing.

"What do you think of these sandals?" Ryan thrusts her leg up by my leg so I can see her footwear.

"Umm...they're nice?"

She grins. "I got them at Target. Aren't they cute? And, they were only sixteen dollars. Can you believe that? Most of the sandals I wear cost at least five hundred," she informs me.

If I was taking a drink, I would have spit it out. "Five hundred dollars? For shoes?"

She shrugs, as if it were no big deal. "Everything is expensive in LA."

"But five hundred dollars expensive? My leather, steel-toed work boots don't even cost that." Jesus, I can't imagine spending that kind of money on fashion.

She sighs, placing her foot back down on the floor. "It's all about who you know, who you blow, and who you wear out there. It's just...different. I've lived that lifestyle my entire life. It's all I know. But when I'm here, it's just so simple, and I don't mean that to be an insult. No one cares what your last name is and what they can get out of you. It's a refreshing change. Honestly, I like it."

I consider her words for a few moments. We lead such different lifestyles. Everyone knows everything about everyone in Pine Village, but because it's a small town, not because we're being photographed and publicly put on display for everyone's entertainment. She's lived a life of just that. Public.

"I guess I never really thought about the other side of the fishbowl. Sure, everyone knows you here, but I think it would be worse having them know all about you without actually knowing you. Does that make sense?" I find myself saying before taking a long drink of sweet tea.

"Totally," she replies, running her fingers through her long, blond ponytail that's hanging over her right shoulder. "The fishbowl is the best way to describe it. My life is so public, everyone can see it looking in."

Ellie arrives, interrupting our conversation. "Here ya go. Two chicken salad sandwiches on croissants, coleslaw, and fresh fruit. Can I top off your teas?" she asks, noticing both glasses are almost half empty.

"That would be great, Ellie, thank you," Ryan replies politely.

"I'll be right back," she says, scurrying off to grab the pitcher of tea.

Ryan takes a bite of her sandwich and groans. "Oh my goodness, this is amazing." As she chews, I spot a little drop of chicken salad smeared across her lip, and all I want to do is reach over and wipe it away. Maybe even with my tongue.

"Here ya go," Ellie says, topping off our glasses. "How is it?"

"It's amazing," Ryan confirms. "I've never had a sweeter chicken salad before."

"The secret ingredient is grapes," she says with a wink. "It complements the smoky chicken."

"So good," Ryan says before taking another bite of her sandwich.

"I'll leave you two to it. Holler if you need anything." She glances between Ryan and me before adding, "Let's get together soon. Apparently, we have a lot to talk about." She smiles widely and heads toward her next table.

"Great, she's going to ask me all about us having lunch together," Ryan says, stabbing a piece of pineapple with her fork.

"Yep. It's part of that small-town charm you're starting to like," I tease with a grin before taking a hearty bite of my sandwich.

We eat in comfortable silence, and the moment our plates are cleared away, I pull out my wallet to pay. There are people standing at the door, waiting for tables, and I need to get back to work. So while this lunch was on the quicker side, it served its purpose, and now it's time to go.

"I can cover lunch," Ryan says, reaching into her tiny little purse and pulling out cash.

"I got it," I insist.

"I invited you," she counters.

"Yes, but call me old fashioned. If a woman is ever out with me, I'm buying," I state, tossing a healthy tip on the table for Ellie.

She opens her mouth, but closes it just as fast, choosing not to argue. "Well, thank you. I'd like to say I'll buy next time, but I'm not sure you'll let that happen." Her smile is small, her eyes dancing with humor.

"Probably not."

I stop by the front counter and pay our bill at the cash register. Ellie doesn't say a word until she hands me my change. Then, she leans in and whispers, "I like you two together."

"We're not together," I reply, shoving my change into my front pocket.

"Really? Huh," she says, closing the register drawer and propping a hip against the counter. Her eyes glance over my shoulder to where Ryan waits. "Then you're totally fine with her talking to that new guy in town, the one who bought the gym?"

I've seen that guy the few times I've been in lately. He's a total tool. Muscular and always smiling at the women, screaming to be noticed. The thought of Ryan talking to him—of him flirting and hitting on her—causes a ball of fire to erupt in my gut. I spin around, ready to do everything necessary to get Ryan away from the guy, only to find her standing along the wall by the door, looking at the historical photos dotted around the room.

When I turn back to Ellie, she's standing there, smiling.

"That was a dirty trick."

"I think I proved my point. Have a great day," she sings, grinning even wider.

"I'm taking your tip back," I state, even though I wouldn't do that.

She just laughs. "Talk to you soon, Marcus."

I walk toward Ryan, feeling eyes from around the room follow. "Ready?"

"Yes," she replies with a smile.

Instantly, my heart does this weird little rapid beat. Like a tap dance, but without the shoes. It's a foreign sensation, one that concerns me slightly. I'm not one to go to the doctor, but maybe I should get it checked out.

Except it only happens when Ryan smiles, and something tells me what's happening won't show up on any test or scan.

Sneaky little Ellie's comment filters through my mind, and now I can't get rid of it.

Dammit, this is why I keep to myself and most people at arm's length.

She put thoughts in my head, and now they're stuck there.

I need to put the jealousy—*and Ryan*—out of my mind.

It has no place here.

At least that's what I'm going to keep telling myself.

CHAPTER
seventeen

Ryan

He's quiet. More so than normal. He hasn't said a word since we left the diner, and I can practically hear the thoughts swirling around in his head.

"You all right?" I finally ask as we cross the final street before we reach his auto shop.

"Yeah, fine," he replies quickly. His entire body is rigid, his hands shoved in his pockets.

"Okay," I reply, picking up my pace a bit to keep up with him.

When we reach the parking lot for the repair shop, I realize he's heading straight for the open garage bay, while I need to go to the left to my rental. Needing to say something, I blurt out, "Thank you for lunch. Sorry to have bothered you while you're working. I should have considered your time more, but I was in the neighborhood and saw your business, and well, I just stopped. My friends and I get together every now and again for lunch, so I just fell into that old habit."

He stops. I see his shoulders rise as he takes a deep breath and slowly turns around. I don't know why I expect to see anger in his eyes, but I don't see an ounce of it. Probably because of his complete one-eighty from the time we ate to the time we left the diner. But his eyes reflect awkwardness and maybe a touch of embarrassment.

"I made it uncomfortable. I'm sorry," he says softly.

"It's fine," I reply quickly, waving it off.

"No, it's not." He takes a deep breath before continuing. "Ellie said something about us being together, and I guess it just hit me wrong. I don't mean to be rude, but," he pauses, lifting his hat and running his hand through his hair, as he tends to do when he's thinking. I don't know why, but I find that act incredibly sexy.

"We're not together," I insist. The moment the words are out of my mouth his shoulders physically drop. In relief. "I mean, we had a great time last night, right? And I'm out of here in a few weeks, so it's not like I'm looking for a relationship. And if I'm being honest, I've recently gotten out of one and not looking to start anything anytime soon."

His eyes burn with something that resembles...jealousy. "You did?"

I nod. "Before I came here." I take a deep breath, almost relieved he didn't research me. "Listen, Marcus, last night was great. It was more than great, really. I had fun. If we do that again, I'm game, but you don't have to worry about me wanting more from you. Like I said before, this is temporary. A summer fling."

He continues to stare at me. "A fling. Yeah."

"Don't worry, big guy. Your big dick energy is phenomenal, but at the end of my month here, I'm heading back to California," I state, reaching out and patting him on his big, hard chest.

The corner of his mouth curls up, giving me a hint of a smile. "Big dick energy?"

"Oh yeah," I reply, wondering where this bold woman has come from. "You just possess this broody, confident big dick energy, and lucky for you, it was confirmed last night."

Now he openly smiles, making my heartbeat skip a little in my chest. "Interesting."

"My point is, we talked about this yesterday. Whatever happens here, stays here, so to speak. I'm not looking for anything but maybe a few orgasms." Again, *who* is this woman? I can't believe I'm actually saying this out loud.

He steps forward, but not close enough we could touch. His jaw seems tight, his eyes laser-focused on me. "My place. Eight o'clock. I have a bit more *energy* to show you."

My core clenches, my panties soaked. Instantly. I have *that* sort of reaction to this man.

Clearing my throat, I lift my chin and nod. "See you then, buster."

With my head held high, I walk to my SUV. Do I add a little extra swing to my step as I go? Sure do. Am I excited about what's to come later this evening? That would be a very loud, overly anticipated Hell yes!

I check the clock for the one-thousandth time, only to find it still thirty minutes before our scheduled meeting time. Why is the time passing so slowly? Is this the sex-laced equivalent to a watched pot doesn't boil? Because the clock is refusing to move, essentially drawing out the length of time until I'm supposed to head to Marcus's cabin.

The front door is open, the warm breeze blowing through the screen door, so when a large truck approaches, I hear it. I walk to the door and find a tow truck approaching. I recognize Marcus's truck and step outside as he turns and backs into the lawn beside my SUV.

He climbs from the driver's seat, Buddy hot on his heels. "Hey, change of plans," he says as he approaches the steps.

"Is everything all right?" I ask, crouching down to give Buddy some pets.

"Yep. We're going for a ride. Get in."

I stand up and blink. "A ride?"

"Yep," he says with a crooked grin. "Got a tow call and won't be done by our eight o'clock appointment, so I figured we could have another adventure."

"An adventure," I grumble, taking a step closer to where he stands. "I'm not sure this is the adventure I was looking for."

He openly smiles now, lines crinkling around the edges of his eyes. "Ever been in a tow truck, Princess?"

"Uh, no, can't say I have."

"Well, you're in for a treat. And if you're lucky, I'll let you honk the horn."

I can't help but bark out a laugh. "Lucky me."

"Get whatever you need from inside. We gotta go."

Spinning, I move up the stairs and reach for the door handle. "Oh, Ryan?"

Before I slip inside the cabin, I look back at Marcus.

"Leave the panties here."

All I do is smile. Why? Because I'm not wearing any.

When I got home and unloaded my shopping bags, I spent a little time removing tags and checking out my purchases. None of it was items I'd choose—or find, frankly—in any of the boutiques I frequented in Los Angeles and Beverly Hills. I purchased bags worth of clothing for the same price as one or two shirts back home. Everything I found would work perfectly for my little vacation here, helping me blend in better than my usual attire.

I flip on the small light above the kitchen sink, so I can see when I get home later, and grab my clutch purse. However, as I walk back to the door, I set the bag down. I shouldn't need it, right? I don't need keys to get into the cabin, and if I'm just going on a tow run and then back to Marcus's place, I shouldn't need money. I mean, he's already made it very clear I won't be paying when he's around. Not that I wouldn't—or can't—considering I'm worth millions, but whatever. It's not worth the argument.

Except picking a fight with Marcus might be fun.

At least the making up part...

I slip out of the cabin and lock the door. Buddy is right there, spinning circles around my feet.

"Ready?" Marcus asks, his eyes landing between my legs. Even though you can't see anything through my dress, I can tell he's trying to figure out if I followed his directions or not.

"Very ready. Let's go tow a truck," I say excitedly, stepping down the stairs and making my way to the passenger side of the vehicle.

"Actually, we're off to tow a van, as well as a car. MVA near the main entrance to the Bluff Preserves National Park. That's a motor vehicle accident," he informs me, opening the door for me to climb up. It's not huge, like a semi, but there's still a good amount of elevation between the ground and the seat I'm supposed to sit on.

Before I can ask how I'm supposed to get up there, big, warm hands wrap around my waist, and I'm practically hoisted up. A squeak slips from my mouth as I reach out for something to stabilize my weight and movement. Buddy barks, as if finding it humorous I'm being manhandled into a truck, and I suppose, in some weird sexually fueled way, it is. That big dick energy he possesses.

He's pretty good at manhandling me.

I sit in the seat, glancing around the cab of the truck. It's dirty, if I'm being honest, but not filthy gross. There's dust and maybe a bit of dirt on the dash and floorboards, probably because he drives around with the windows open all the time. And let's be real, it's not a clean job. Auto mechanics is messy. I've seen it on his clothes and under his fingernails.

Back in California, I never would have been caught dead with a man with dirt and grease embedded under his nails, but after spending just a little time with Marcus, it's not so bad. He's rugged, manly, blue-collared, as the internet would call him.

And I kind of like it.

Buddy jumps onto the driver's side floorboard before climbing up onto the seat. "Keep moving, Buddy. You can't drive."

The dog looks my way, clearly not impressed he's being relinquished to the floor for the ride instead of the passenger seat, but this truck doesn't have a bench. He moves to the floor between the seats, carefully around a bin holding papers and clipboards. He gazes up at me, big puppy dog eyes pleading for me to share.

"All right, mister," I say, sliding over and creating a little space between myself and the door.

Buddy jumps up on the seat, his head hanging out the window.

"Good to go?" Marcus asks, putting the truck in gear.

A swirl of exhilaration sweeps through me. "Yes."

We head out, Marcus driving the larger truck easily. I watch him out of the corner of my eye. Why? Because he's hot while driving. His arms are all corded muscle framed by a tight T-shirt. Not only is he radiating big dick energy, but now he's flashing the arm porn. He's like every woman's dream right now, and that's before you add in the rescued dog into the equation.

If I were wearing panties, they'd be annihilated.

Maybe that's his new nickname. Not buster.

He's the panty annihilator.

We make our way through the park, toward where the accident is. I've seen plenty of fender benders in my time. The 405 and 110 interstates are some of the worst for high traffic volume. I've even seen a car flip due to a high rate of speed. Well, I didn't actually see it flip. It passed me and then wrecked a bit ahead of me. I remember seeing the mangled wreckage left in the median and not being able to sleep that night.

Is that what I'm in for?

Because now that I think about it, I don't want to see that kind of destruction. Especially if a life was lost.

"Umm, Marcus?" I say, starting to fret a little. My hand instantly reaches out to pet Buddy, the softness of his fur having a calming effect on me.

"Yeah?" he asks without taking his eyes off the road.

"How bad is this accident? Maybe I shouldn't go," I say, hearing the hint of a quiver in my own voice.

He takes his eyes off the road for only a second, but I can see the concern. "It's not bad, I promise. Both cars are damaged enough to warrant a tow, but injuries were minor."

I exhale the breath I didn't realize I was holding. "Oh. Okay. Good."

"I wouldn't take you to the scene if it was bad, Ryan. It's not something I enjoy seeing myself, and I'd never subject you to it willingly."

A huge wave of relief washes over me, and I relax a bit in the seat. Buddy has his head out the window, his tongue dangling in delight. My hair is blowing around, and it's the first time I realize I'm not wearing my ball cap. Will people be nearby when we arrive? You know the ones. The gawkers who have nothing better to do than to stand around and watch something that doesn't pertain to them unfold?

When we finally work our way through the park to what I assume is the main entrance, I see two vehicles with a bit of damage and a police officer standing between them. Once we pull up beside them, I realize the officer is TD, Ellie's husband.

"Hey, man," Marcus greets once he stops and climbs out of the cab.

Even though I remain inside the truck, I can easily hear their conversation.

"Which one do you wanna take first?" TD asks.

"Probably the Nissan Pathfinder. It's in the way. I can get it loaded up and get the glass and debris cleaned up so you can get this intersection opened up."

"Appreciate it."

The door opens and Marcus climbs back inside. "I'm going to back up to that small SUV there. I have to position my truck in the middle of the intersection, so I'm going to have you and Buddy go over to that grassy area over there to keep you safe." He reaches behind the driver's seat and pulls out a leash.

"Okay," I answer, glancing around.

Marcus secures the leash to Buddy, who seems eager to go outside. Before I open the door to climb out, he says, "Wait. Here." I turn to find him digging a ball cap out and holding it out for me. "It may not be the cleanest, but it'll help shield your face."

My heart does this wild tippy-tap in my chest as I reach for the hat. I can tell he's worn it, probably several times. There's a smear of dirt or grease on the bill and a slight dirt ring around the inside. I'm sure it's from sweat, and as gross as I would have found this a few days ago, for some reason it doesn't bother me as much now. The fact Marcus wore this, worked hard while wearing it, makes me feel a little...happy.

I slip it on my head, and of course, it's way too big. Marcus reaches over and adjusts the plastic strap on the back before replacing it. "There."

"Thank you," I reply, feeling all warm and gooey on the inside.

In a dirty old hat.

"All right, Buddy, ready?" Marcus asks, earning a bark in return.

Smiling, I carefully get out of the truck and shut the door. Buddy and Marcus come around to the passenger side, and together, we walk to the grassy area he was referring to. Instantly, I notice it's not too close to where the vehicles are, or to where a few lookie-loos meander.

"Be right back," Marcus says as he hands over the leash and puts on thick work gloves.

Buddy barks, clearly not happy he's being left to the side, but doesn't pull on the leash to follow. Instead, he moves around on the grass, sniffing for the perfect spot to pee. While he does his thing, I watch Marcus climb back into the truck. TD goes out into the road, making sure it's clear to move the big truck into position, and watches closely.

I do the same.

I'm not sure why this seems so fascinating, but it does. From the moment he's in the street, maneuvering his truck into position, to the time he gets out and lowers the bed. When he walks over to the SUV, he gets on the ground, shifting himself to get a good look under the vehicle. Then, he attaches some sort of cord and goes back to the truck. He presses some buttons, and the next thing you know, the vehicle is being pulled onto the flatbed.

Buddy barks, as if letting his owner know he did a good job, and together, we observe Marcus securing the vehicle onto the flatbed. He finally looks our way and waves us over. "Come on, Buddy. Let's go."

We return to where Marcus waits, and instead of climbing behind the wheel, he goes to the passenger side and opens the door for us. He helps me climb in again, and I'm not sure if he's being chivalrous or just likes to have his hands on me.

Or both.

"Everything okay?" he asks when I'm in the seat. He bends down and unclips Buddy's leash before pointing into the truck.

"Yep, everything's great. He went potty."

"Good boy," he boasts, giving the dog a hearty scratch behind the ears.

He gazes up at me, and those hazel eyes turn molten in a matter of seconds. His eyes drop to my legs, which are covered by the skirt of my dress, and slowly drag up to the apex of my legs.

I smile and ask, "What are you thinking about?"

His eyes return to mine as he rips the work gloves off his hands and drops them on the floor between the seats, and there's no missing the desire embedded in them. "Just wondering if you were a good girl and listened earlier."

"You mean about the panties?" I whisper, as if it's some big conspiracy.

He nods and holds my gaze.

Leaning closer, I add, "There's really only one way to figure out the answer to that question, isn't there?"

Heat blazes in his eyes. They're burning with the intensity of an inferno, bright and urgent. Without saying a word, he places his palm on my knee and slowly moves his hand. He brushes along my thigh, angling his fingers to where I ache for his touch.

"Fuck," he curses the moment he's met with bare, wet flesh.

"Yes, that's the point, right?" I tease, wishing we weren't in the middle of a tow call and in public. Being bent over something so he can explore more sounds pretty damn good right about now.

But as quickly as his fingers brush against my pussy, they're pulled away.

"Shit," he mutters, taking a step back and putting a little distance between us. "That was a bad idea."

"Sure was," I confirm, adjusting my skirt. "Now I'm all...needy."

He groans as if in physical pain, which makes me want to grin in satisfaction. But I don't. Why? Because I'm just as worked up as he is.

He sighs and closes the truck door. The moment he does, Buddy jumps up on the seat and sticks his head out the window again. Marcus climbs in and prepares to move the truck. He throws it in gear and waves to TD. "I'll be right back for the other."

"Take your time, but not too long. I'd like to get home to my wife before too long. You shouldn't be the only one getting some, man." He taps the door of the truck.

Even though I can't see TD from my seat, I clearly watch Marcus flip his friend off and drive away. The smile I was fighting earlier spreads widely across my lips, and the temperature in the cab of this truck elevates considerably, even though the windows are open, and night is starting to fall.

It's all Marcus.

He makes things very hot with his sexy grumpiness and big dick energy.

He's the panty annihilator, and I'm not even wearing them.

CHAPTER
eighteen

MARCUS

I'm gripping the steering wheel so tightly, I swear it might break.

I should *not* have checked for panties, because now it's all I can think about—all I can picture. And if the smirk TD sent me when I was getting ready to leave is any indication, he's well aware I was about half a second away from throwing her dress over her head and burying my face between her thighs.

Now, we're on our way back to the shop so we can drop this vehicle, only to have to return to the scene of the accident and pick up the second, and all I want to do is a quick repeat of last night.

I'm sure that'll still happen, except now it's delayed. What is it they say about delayed gratification? It makes the moment that much sweeter?

Oh, hell. What do they know?

Delayed gratification sucks, and my blue balls are a testament.

"You okay over there?" she asks.

I don't miss the way her eyes drop to my lap, most likely confirming what we all know. I'm hard as hell right now, with no relief in sight. "I'm good," I respond, my words as tight as my pants.

"That was pretty neat," she says, telling me about her take on the tow. "I've never actually seen it in action."

"It's boring, I know," I reply, knowing it's not a glamorous job, but not caring much because it suits me well.

"It's not boring," she insists. "It was quite fascinating actually, and probably pretty dangerous. I've never really cared how a vehicle is transported following a breakdown or accident. I know that makes me sound spoiled and selfish, but it's true. To see it in action is eye-opening."

I nod, understanding where she's coming from. Most people don't really care how it happens, just that it does. As I move into the heart of town, heading to my shop, I say, "I'm glad you're here."

She flashes me a warm smile. "Are you just saying that because you know I'm not wearing panties?"

I bark out a laugh and shake my head, steering the flatbed into my lot. "No, Princess, that's just a bonus. A very big bonus." I glance at her and wink before returning my attention to what I'm doing.

I back up to the gated lot beside the shop and jump out to unlock the gate. Buddy follows, barking and spinning in the gravel. "You got the zoomies?" I ask, smirking as he races around the truck, yet staying close to where I am.

"What's the zoomies?"

I look over my shoulder to Ryan. "It's a term they say when a dog has a burst of energy."

"Ahh. I've never had a pet."

"None?"

She shakes her head, looking around me as I open the wide gate. "Why are you putting the vehicle in here?"

"For safety and security. So no one gets into it or messes with the vehicle before the owner can remove any personal belongings or before an insurance adjuster can do their report."

"Oh."

"I'm gonna back the truck in here and get this one unloaded," I tell her.

"Can I watch?"

I shrug my shoulders. "Sure, but stay over there," I reply, pointing just inside the gate. "I won't be able to see you, so I need to make sure you're out of the way."

She nods and moves to where I indicated. Buddy trails behind her, and since she doesn't have a leash, Ryan squats down and holds his collar.

Climbing into the truck, I slowly back through the gate. I continually check my mirrors, just to make sure Ryan and Buddy didn't move, but since I don't see them, I assume they remain where I told them to.

I stop in front of a bare spot along the fence and climb back out. Ryan approaches with Buddy but stays back and out of the way. I drop the vehicle and prep the flatbed for transporting the next one, making sure the winch is wound back up and my straps back in the toolbox.

When everything is set, I wash my hands then make my way to the passenger side of the truck. Ryan is sitting there, the door open, and her bare feet casually on the dash. She wiggles her pink-painted toes, and I can't help but get aroused all over again. And why? I don't have a foot fetish.

I think I have a Ryan fetish.

I spot Buddy lying on the mat between the seats, clearly needing a little nap after his zoomies around the lot.

"Ryan?"

"Mmm?" she replies, wiggling those damn toes.

"Are you wet?" I murmur, lifting my right foot and resting it on the step. I keep my hands to myself, which is hard. No pun intended.

"I think so," she purrs, a seductive little grin on her gorgeous face.

"You think?"

She lifts her shoulders. "I suppose if you require confirmation, you should probably check for yourself." The little vixen lifts her skirt in invitation.

What's a man to do but check?

I place my rough palm against her thigh and slide it toward her pussy. My fingers brush against smooth, wet flesh, and I waste no time. My fingers glide between the lips of her pussy as I gently spread her knees farther apart, keeping her feet planted on the dash.

"This is gonna be fast. We're out in the open. No one can see us through the wrap on the fence, but the gate's wide open. So be a good girl and come for me so we can get back to work."

With that, I press two fingers into her pussy. Ryan rocks her hips, grinding against my palm as she chases her release. I thrust my fingers in and out, sliding my thumb across her clit. She whimpers as she swirls her hips. I can feel her pussy tightening, her orgasm looming.

"You close? I can feel you starting to squeeze around my fingers. I think it makes you hot knowing we could be seen by someone at any time. Do you want someone to find us, Ryan? While I'm fingering you?"

She groans, her body moving as if entirely on its own. "I don't care who sees, as long as you don't stop."

Cracking a grin, applying a little more pressure to her clit. "I have no intention of stopping until you come on my fingers. Now, Ryan."

It's as if my words actually trigger her release. She tightens around my fingers and cries out, gripping the hell out of them and making it hard for me to move them, but I manage. I lighten my pressure on her clit but keep circling my palm over it as she rides the waves of pleasure. When the tension leaves her body, she slumps back onto the seat, a satisfied glaze in her eyes.

"Wow, that's never happened before," she practically sings, her eyes closed as she smiles. Buddy moves, having been woken up by her orgasm and rests his head on her arm.

"What? Gotten off in a tow truck in a parking lot?"

She chuckles and shakes her head. "No, silly. Well, yes, actually. That's never happened either, but I don't think I've ever felt my soul leave my body before."

A wave of pride sweeps through my body. It makes me want to pound on my chest like a caveman, but of course, I don't. The problem is all I want to do now is bury myself inside her all over again. My tongue, my cock, hell, even my fingers. I want more.

Desperately.

Unfortunately, that's not going to happen. At least not right now. I need to get back to the accident scene and clear the other car before TD comes looking for me. I won't jeopardize my business and those relationships I've built because I'm horny. Long after Ryan has returned to her life in California, I'll still be here, doing my thing.

"As much as I'd love to bend you over the seat and have my wicked way with you, I better get back and retrieve the other car."

She nods in understanding and adjusts her dress, covering herself. I'd rather she just leave herself exposed, but I'm not sure she'd go for that. Plus, I'd be too distracted and probably wreck. Wouldn't TD love to hear why I couldn't keep my eyes on the road?

I head around to the driver's side of the truck, and before I know it, we're on our way to the scene of the accident. I use the main roadway this time, since I don't need to drive through the park area, and as I drive around the curve, I spot TD standing near the car. He has a look of annoyance on his face, and his arms are crossed over his chest. I can't help but grin at the attitude I know I'm about to receive.

This vehicle doesn't require my truck to block the roadway, so I pull into the entrance and get into position. "You can hang in here this time," I tell Ryan.

"Okay." She glances at Buddy, who's hanging his head out the window, and says, "We'll stay in here."

As I step out of the truck, TD is there. He makes a big production of checking his watch.

"Sorry for the slight delay," I state, walking back to get set.

He snorts. "Yeah, that smug smirk on your face shows how sorry you are."

I can't help but laugh. "I was just being polite. I'm not sorry at all." I wink before lowering the bed and getting to work.

TD grabs one of the brooms and a bucket and starts sweeping up any debris in the roadway, while I secure the car on the trailer. By the time I have everything set to remove the car, he has the scene cleaned up.

"Thanks," I say, taking the bucket and placing it on the trailer. I hold it in place with the bungee strap and set the broom in the long toolbox.

"No problem. Thanks for helping out," he says. "Even if I was giving you shit about...you know." He glances toward the cab of the truck, letting me know he's referring to Ryan. "She seems great."

I shrug my shoulders and shove my hands in my pockets. "It's not like that. It's just...casual."

He nods in understanding. "It's always casual," he starts, stepping over and giving me a friendly slap and squeeze on the shoulders, "until it's not."

His words reach their desire target—my brain. He's reminding me that even casual flings can turn into more. He was friends with his wife for years, secretly pining away for her like a lovesick fool. Then, one day, he decided to take the leap. It wasn't always easy for them, straddling the line between friends and lovers, but they got it figured out. They were married not too long ago, and trying to have a baby.

But what happened between him and Ellie is completely different than what's before me and Ryan. First off, geography plays a huge factor. She'll be leaving in a few weeks, ending our time together. Nothing more can—or will—come of this. Plus, let's be honest. This is just fun. We're two totally different people from two totally different worlds, and unless you live in a romance novel or a cheesy rom-com movie, those two worlds don't combine. So, this arrangement will remain in the friends with benefits zone with no possibility of parole. It's just not gettin' out of there.

"Have a good night, TD," I state, making my way to the driver's door.

"You too," he hollers. TD beats me to the door and reaches in, petting Buddy. "You be a good boy." Looking up to Ryan in the passenger seat, he adds, "Good night, Ryan."

"Night. Tell Ellie I said hello," Ryan says.

"Will do." TD steps back and taps the side of the truck before heading off to his vehicle. He drives a big SUV, and when he climbs inside, he flips off the lights in the windows and the grill.

"Ready?" I ask, sitting in the driver's seat and preparing to take off.

"Yep."

As we cruise back to the shop, Ryan asks, "Is this hard to drive?"

"The flatbed? I mean, it's longer and a bit wider than a normal vehicle, so it takes some getting used to. It requires a CDL."

"What's a CDL?" she asks.

"Commercial Driver's License. It's required when a vehicle is heavier than a certain weight."

"Like a semi?" she asks.

"Yep. A semi requires a CDL," I tell her.

"Hmm." After a few seconds, she asks, "Can I drive it?"

I glance her way, finding her studying me, waiting for my reply. "You wanna drive the tow truck?"

She nods. "I've barely ever driven anything bigger than my little BMW."

"You ever driven a stick shift before?"

She giggles. "Not of the vehicle variety."

My cock jumps in my pants, eager to talk more about that.

I consider her request for a few moments, ignoring the bulge between my legs. "All right, if you want to drive it, I'll teach you. But not tonight. I don't want to do it when it's getting dark. We'll have to go out on a back road that isn't traveled often."

"Can't I just drive it around the parking lot?" she asks as we approach my shop.

"It's not big enough for that. You'd only be able to go in a little circle, and even that's not very safe. To be able to properly learn how to shift, you need space. Best to put you on a flat, open road and give it a shot."

Pulling into my lot, I swing around and back up to the fenced-in gate. I had closed it earlier, but left it unlocked since I knew I was returning quickly. After jumping out and opening the gate, I climb behind the wheel and back in. I stop directly behind the first vehicle I brought in, knowing an insurance adjuster is probably going to want to take a look at both vehicles.

While I do the next phase, Ryan climbs out of the truck and takes Buddy over to the safe area. I can feel her eyes on me, watching intently. It's a little unnerving, honestly. I've never had a passenger like this, and never one who watched my every move.

I take the bucket with broken glass and debris and set it to the side. I never pitch it right away, just in case someone is missing something from their vehicle. Once both parties have cleared out their belongings and insurance has done their thing, I'll dump the trash.

"Marcus."

"Hmm?" I ask, making sure everything is done for the night.

After a few seconds I hear her sweet voice again, this time with a little more urgency. "Marcus."

I stop and turn toward Ryan. She's standing just off to the side of the tow truck holding one of my flannels. "What's wrong?" I ask, giving her a quick onceover for injuries.

"Absolutely nothing," she says, flashing me a blinding smile. "Come here."

I do as asked, quickly since I'm trying to determine if she somehow got hurt back here. When I reach her side, she sets the flannel on the ground, places her hands against my shoulder, and moves me until my back is pressed against the fender of the truck. I'm about to open my mouth to ask what in the hell is going on when she drops to her knees.

And my brain literally goes blank.

I couldn't form a thought or a complete sentence to save my life. All I can do is watch.

Her fingers grasp for my belt buckle, for my zipper and the button on my jeans. "Ryan..." I choke out, her name sounding hoarse and strained all at the same time.

"Shhh," she insists, practically ripping open my jeans and pulling them down my thighs.

My mouth drops open, as does hers. She licks her lips, wraps her hand around the base of my cock, and draws it slowly into her mouth.

"Wh-what are you doing?" I whisper, mesmerized by the sight.

"Returning the favor," she insists before licking the head of my dick and sucking it deep into her mouth once more.

I glance around, making sure we're alone. Buddy's in the tow truck, his head hanging out the window. I don't recall when she put him in there, but it's nice to not have to worry about him getting into something in this moment. We're positioned on the passenger side of the truck, so even if someone pulls into the main lot, they won't see what's happening back here.

Reaching down, I pull off her ball cap and turn it around. This way, I can see her face while she sucks me. She doesn't even pause as I gather her hair and replace the hat on top of her head, but when I have it in place, she glances up, her mouth stretched widely around me and meets my gaze.

I almost come right then and there.

Somehow, I grapple on to any ounce of control I can find and hang on. She starts to pick up speed, twisting her hand around the base of my cock as she goes down. I know I won't last long. I've dreamed about having her mouth on me since the moment I laid eyes on her, and now that it's actually happening, I don't think I can hold off any longer.

My balls draw up and the familiar tingling sensation starts at the base of my spine. "I'm going to come, Princess," I tell her, my eyes glued to her face.

She doesn't slow her movement or pull off my cock either. In fact, she seems to bear down a little more, determined to finish me off.

I come hard, gasping for air and shooting everything I have down her throat. I don't know when I close my eyes, but I'm unable to keep them open. All I feel is the immense pleasure. All I feel is her.

"Fuck," I mutter, trying to catch my breath. I should be embarrassed by how quickly she got me off, but I'm not. It was fucking perfect.

She is fucking perfect.

Ryan finally pulls off my dick and proudly smiles up at me. She licks her lips and releases her hand. "I've been wanting to do that for a while now," she says, standing up and stretching her knees.

I snort. "Well, anytime you want a repeat, you know where to find me."

She giggles and picks up my flannel. I take the shirt, wiping off my wet cock with part of the shirt that wasn't on the ground, and toss it into the truck. I pull up my pants before taking her in my arms and pressing a firm kiss to her lips. Her mouth instantly opens for me and the kiss turns ravenous immediately. It's like we can't get enough of each other.

"Your place or mine?"

"Mine, Princess," I tell her, reaching back and slapping her ass. "Definitely mine. We're taking my truck." I open the door and let Buddy out.

She starts to walk toward the gate, heading for my old Chevy in the main lot, my dog hot on her heels. Just as she walks through the opening, she glances back and says, "Race you."

And it's on.

I couldn't get to her fast enough.

CHAPTER
nineteen

Ryan

It's been the best two weeks ever. I never expected to feel so at peace in Pine Village.

Do I miss Los Angeles and the hustle and bustle of my life there? Of course. But it feels better than I ever could have expected to slow down and recharge my battery. Not to mention I feel so much better not dealing with the press every day. No one is following me around with a camera. No one is lurking behind cars or in bushes. I don't have a microphone in my face or people screaming my name when I walk down the sidewalk.

Of course, a big part of that is no one knows where I am. I've remained hidden under the cover of my casual attire and a ball cap. My online presence is zilch, nada, and even though my phone blows up throughout the day, I don't answer many of the texts. Or when I do, I reply with a polite note I'm taking a vacation and leave it at that.

Vaughn was still reaching out—daily—and I realized after my first full week here, it was time to cut the cord. I replied to his latest message without reading it or any of the previous ones and told him—again—it was over. I stated very pointedly not to contact me again and then blocked his number. I should have done it from day one, but I think I needed a little time to clear my head. To confirm I was making the right decision in walking away from Vaughn. It didn't matter what excuse he gave. What he did—or more specifically, what he said—was all I needed to hear.

I just wish I wouldn't have heard it with the rest of the world.

Now that he's behind me, I've spent time focusing on the here and now. A big part of that is Marcus. We've spent more evenings together in the last two weeks than apart, and that doesn't upset me. Not in the least. The orgasms are plentiful, that's for sure, and then at the end of the night, we part ways. It's how we keep the lines from blurring, because this is temporary. A summer fling, as he likes to call it, and as much as I'd love to snuggle into his big, warm body at the end of the night—because something tells me that alone is something they write about in books—I'm afraid that might complicate things.

And I'm loving this completely uncomplicated thing.

Tonight, it's girls' night. I was invited to Gabe and Blair's house, where we're going to eat Mexican food, drink margaritas, and talk about guys. At least, that's what I've been told. I'm a little worried about going, only because any other night that might constitute a girls' night was always spent watching what I say so it's not used against me or what I do because I'm always being observed.

Something tells me I don't have to worry about it with these ladies, but I also don't know them well enough. They could very well share all my dirty secrets to the highest tabloid bidder.

But if they were going to do that, wouldn't they have done it after we met? After they figured out who I was, thanks to Hallie's obsession with reality television? No, my gut tells me I can trust them, but I just need to be observant and careful with what I say.

I head out of the cabin, locking the door behind me. I was told to dress casually, that I'd know everyone in attendance, but something tells me their casual and mine are two totally different things. It probably took me longer to decide what to wear when dressing down than it does when I'm going out.

As I walk to the driver's side of my rented SUV, I hear a dog bark in the distance. I stop and turn toward the path and only have to wait a few seconds before I see Buddy. The moment he spots me, he takes off running in my direction, jumping up with excitement.

"What are you doing here?" I ask, crouching down and giving him pets.

"He wanted to tell you to have a good time."

I glance up and find Marcus making his way toward us. "Hi."

"Hey," he says with a familiar smile and warm eyes. "We were going for a walk."

"Well, I was just getting ready to head out."

"Ahh, yes, girls' night," he replies with a grin. "I'm headed over to Logan's cabin. We're gonna throw a few steaks on the grill and wait for the calls for rides."

I hadn't planned on drinking more than one margarita early, since I was the only one who wasn't married or seriously dating someone and wouldn't have a ride. Hallie did tell me she and Logan would give me a ride home—or more adamantly, Marcus could give me a ride, but I didn't want to put him out. I'm not his responsibility, and since there's no car service in Pine Village, I figured the safest option was to have one drink and switch to water.

"I heard you guys will have the babies."

He runs his hand over the back of his neck. "Yeah, I won't be much help with that. I have zero baby experience. Even when Brody was a baby, I wasn't the first guy to jump in and help with the baby."

I've heard all about how everyone helped Ellie when she got pregnant in high school and her conservative parents kicked her out. She lived in the apartment above the diner where she worked to support herself and her child. The father was a douche who split the moment she told him she was pregnant, insisting it wasn't his baby. TD had loved her since high school and stood back, waiting for the right opportunity, which eventually happened when Brody was sixteen.

"Well, it's not like you'll have to babysit them while the moms are away. The dads will be there," I reassure him, sensing his uneasiness.

"Thank God," he mutters, giving me a sheepish grin. "Anyway, how are you getting home?"

"Oh, I was just going to have one drink early and then switch to water. I'll be fine to drive home later."

"I'll come get you."

"That's not necessary," I insist, but anything else I'm going to say is cut off.

"It is. Have fun with the girls. They don't do that often, so I know they're all ready to cut loose. You should too."

"Oh."

"Call me, Ryan." His gaze is intense, as if he's not going to take no for an answer.

"All right."

He nods before whistling for Buddy. "Let's go, boy. Time to head home."

Buddy looks up at me, waiting for one final pet. As soon as I reach down and scratch behind his ears, he takes off toward the path, where Marcus is heading.

Just before he disappears from sight, he hollers, "Have fun, Princess."

"Thanks. I will." I can't help but smile, and as I climb behind the wheel of my rental, it's still firmly on my face.

That smile accompanies me to Blair and Gabe's gorgeous home on the outskirts of town, not too far from where my rental cabin is located. They're not along the lake though, their backyard butting up against the acreage of timber and trails. I park in their driveway and slowly climb out, wishing I had something to contribute to tonight's festivities. But they insisted I didn't need to bring food or drinks, and I graciously accepted.

Climbing out of the driver's seat, I see the front door open and Hallie step out. "You made it!"

I nod, excited to be included in tonight's gathering. Sure, I have friends. Lots of them. But are any of them real? It sure as heck doesn't feel like it now.

"Come on," Hallie says, linking her arm through mine and leading me into the house.

"This house is amazing," I start, taking a look around as we enter.

"When my brother bought it, it was in need of a lot of TLC. He's done most of the work himself, slowly remodeling it room by room. Blair will give you a tour. She loves showing off my brother's work."

We enter the kitchen and find four more women. "She's here," Hallie declares to Blair, Ellie, Ava, and Jillian, the woman who owns the bakery and coffee shop.

"So happy you came," Blair says graciously.

"Your home is beautiful," I tell her.

"I'll give you a tour, but first, let's eat. I've been smelling this food since it was dropped off, and I'm starving," she replies.

"Me too. I skipped lunch just so I could gorge. But I wasn't expecting this. Where did you get all this Mexican food?" Ava asks, taking in the spread on the kitchen island.

"Kameron," Hallie says with a big grin.

Ava stops and glance toward Ellie. "Kameron? Kameron Markley? The man who owns the steakhouse?"

"I didn't realize he added Mexican food to the menu," Ellie says, reaching for a chip and dipping it in salsa.

Hallie grins widely. "He didn't. He did it for Jillian," she informs the group, waggling her eyebrows as she hands me a margarita.

Jillian groans. "Stop it. It's not like that. He owed me a favor."

"For sexual favors rendered?" Hallie asks, taking a sip of her drink.

"No!" Jillian declares, her face turning beet red. "It's not like that. He needed a dessert one evening at the restaurant after his order didn't arrive on time, so I whipped up a few cheesecakes. It was nothing."

"Nothing but sex," Hallie mutters behind the rim of her glass.

Everyone laughs, including Jillian. "Oh my God, stop it! That did *not* happen!"

"But you want it to. Admit it."

There's no missing the blush on Jillian's face.

"We're just...friendly. Two business owners helping each other out when needed. That's all," she insists.

"Fine, but he made this massive Mexican spread for his *friend.* Let's eat, and then we can grill Ryan about Marcus," Hallie states, grabbing a plate and starting to make a taco.

"Hey! What'd I do?" I ask, taking another drink of my strawberry margarita. I consider sipping it slowly, but Marcus said he'd pick me up, so I suppose it wouldn't hurt.

"Nothing, but we're dying to hear all the dirty details," Blair chimes in, stepping aside while everyone moves to the island to make plates of food.

My eyes widen, though I shouldn't be surprised. This group seems like one who shares—everything—even if you don't want to.

I step over to the island and get in line behind Ellie. When it's my turn, I make a soft-taco with chicken and add all my favorite toppings. This isn't a basic lettuce, tomato, and taco cheese set-up either, though those are on the counter. I spot cilantro, onions, pico de gallo, peppers, and what appears to be homemade salsa. It looks and smells amazing, and I can't wait to dive in. I also add a few tortilla chips and some queso to my plate before grabbing my margarita and joining the ladies at the table.

"I can't believe Kameron made all this, but I'm not surprised at all," Ava says between bites. "Everything I've had at the steakhouse is amazing."

"He should add this to his menu," Ellie chimes in.

"I doubt he would though. His place is too classy for Taco Tuesdays," Jillian says, dipping a chip in salsa.

Hallie nods. "True, but I'm sure it would bring in new customers."

We chat about jobs and children, but I mostly stay quiet. It's when our glasses are being refilled with more of the sweet frozen tequila mixture that all eyes finally turn my way.

"Can I ask you something personal?" Ellie asks, visibly hesitant.

"Okay," I say, taking a longer sip of my margarita.

"I watched the finale show Hallie was talking about. Did you really not know? About Vaughn?" There's nothing but sympathy reflecting in her eyes. She's not judging or accusing me of anything. She's genuinely curious, and I can respect that.

I've been waiting for this conversation to come up, ever since Hallie realized exactly who I was at their Memorial Day cookout. In fact, I've been expecting it with Marcus too, but if there's one thing I've learned in the last two weeks, he doesn't care about gossip, and he rarely watches TV.

"Had no idea," I confess. "I really did find out when the rest of the world did."

"That's...wild!" Hallie says and then bursts out laughing. "Or I guess I should say that's so wild?"

I can't help but roll my eyes as I laugh. "I said that one time, and it just...stuck."

"I love it," Jillian announces. "It's a fun catchphrase."

"It's so overused," I insist. "I was told to incorporate it into everything when we were filming. Fortunately, half of them didn't make the final cut, because otherwise, it would be all viewers would think I could say."

"That's so wild," Hallie sings, doing her best impression of me.

We all laugh as Blair gets up to make another pitcher of margaritas.

"So? What happened? After you found out what he said?"

I sigh, finishing off the liquid in my glass. "I called him, but he didn't answer. He just got the hero lead in my dad's next action movie, so he was supposedly running lines by himself and had his phone off. I didn't get to talk to him until the next day, and he completely tried to play it off as something he just said for ratings. I called his bullshit. I could see it in his eyes. Everything he said was fact and exactly how he felt. He was using me. So, I broke up with him and walked away."

"Good for you," Jillian proclaims, raising her glass to toast.

"Absolutely. What an asshole," Blair declares.

Everyone chimes in with some sort of agreement, telling me I did the right thing. Not that I needed their validation, because I already know I did. I feel it in my heart, that what Vaughn and I shared was superficial at best. Yes, I loved him, but when it was all said and done, I wasn't as torn up as I expected.

"He's in your dad's new movie? The one with what's her face? I saw some online chatter about it," Jillian says.

I shrug and drink more tequila. "He wanted to fire him, but I told him not to. He hired him because of his acting skills, not because he was my boyfriend."

"Yeah, but he doesn't deserve the role now," Hallie insists.

Even though I do agree, I don't feel it's right. "It's part of the industry," I concede, because it is. People will do *anything* for a role, including date the producer's daughter.

"So, what happens now with the show?" Ava asks, moving the conversation along.

"Well, I'm technically in a contract for two seasons, so I suppose I'll have to do one more."

"Ugh, that's tough. I'd tell them to stick it up their asses for what they did," Blair adamantly states.

I can't help but smile at their outrage, especially because it's on my behalf. Their responses feel...good. Like I have friends who truly care about me, not my name. That's rare where I come from, and a part of me wishes I could stay.

But that's silly.

Pine Village is a vacation destination. My roots are in California, as is my business. Not to mention, the show is there. Thinking I could possibly relocate to Small Town, USA is quite silly, actually.

Ridiculous.

Far-fetched.

Absurd.

I'm a city girl.

That's where I belong.

But as I look around the table at these women, I feel a sense of...belonging. They have a close relationship, one I envy. My friends and I are nothing like this.

We finish in the kitchen, and Blair gives me a tour of the rest of the house. It's such a great place, spacious and comfortable. After she shows me their home, we all move into the open living room and sit around the large sectional sofa. Even with a baby swing in the corner and glider chair where I can picture a mother rocking her baby to sleep, the room feels just as homey as the rest of the place.

Hallie hands me a fresh margarita and plops down on the couch beside me. "Okay, now let's talk about you and Marcus."

The other four heads all nod adamantly.

"Spill."

CHAPTER
Twenty

MARCUS

"So, what's going on with you and Ryan?" Logan asks.

I glance over and almost laugh. One of my oldest friends is kicked back around the fire, and instead of drinking a beer, he's got a little pink bundle cradled in his arms. It suits him though. Both him and Gabe. Fatherhood looks good on them.

My, how things have changed.

From sitting around, drinking beers, to babysitting and waiting for their women to call for a ride.

"Nothing," I reply, keeping my focus on the dancing bonfire in front of me.

TD snorts. "Definitely didn't look like nothing from my point of view."

Logan's eyebrows shoot toward the heaven. "And what point of view is that exactly?"

I snort. "You're acting more like gossiping women right now, you realize that, right?"

Logan shrugs. "You think she's not over at Blair and Gabe's talking about it with the rest of the women?"

Is she? I wonder why I never really thought about what the women are all sitting around and chatting about. I mean, I've never cared, because I've never had a woman as part of the group. Well, not that she's my woman. Ryan's just my...what? We have an arrangement, and it's fun. That's exactly what it is. It's also temporary. Something we both agreed on. So why does the thought of her hanging with my friends' wives and girlfriends make me...content?

"I'm guessing they're on the second pitcher of margaritas by now, and the conversation has turned to sex," Gabe states, holding a bottle and feeding his daughter.

"Really? They sit around and talk about that?" I ask, completely flabbergasted by this revelation.

"Of course they do. Women share everything, man," TD says.

Logan nods. "Everything."

"Everything?"

Gavin nods in agreement, smiling. "It's true."

"Huh," I reply, staring into the fire.

"Yep. Women overshare. By now, they're probably comparing the sizes of...you know."

My mouth drops open. "Seriously?"

All four of them nod.

"I don't...I, uh, I don't need to know about...that. I mean, let's not discuss the sizes of our..." I take off my hat and run my hands through my hair.

"Agreed," they all insist in unison.

"But that does bring us back to the original question. What's going on with you and Ryan?"

I shrug, wishing I were drinking a beer. Or a shot of Jack. Something. "We're hanging out. She's pretty cool."

"Cool," Logan says, as if that's the understatement of the year. "She's fucking famous, dude."

I lift my shoulders, recalling all the stuff I found online about her. I haven't searched her name since, so I'm sure I didn't even scratch the surface of information on the internet. "She's just...Ryan."

TD laughs. "Just Ryan. My friend, she's way more than *Just Ryan*. She's got her own TV show. And makeup line. And whatever else Ellie mentioned."

"Her parents are a movie producer and a former model," Logan adds.

"No shit?" Gavin asks, though it's not really a question.

"You've heard of Douglas Marcotte, right? He produced that big action movie last summer. It won the Academy Awards for Best Picture and Supporting Actress," Logan informs Gavin.

"How do you know that?" Gabe asks, his eyes dancing with humor.

Logan shrugs. "Hallie. She watches all that reality TV bullshit and entertainment shows. Plus, when she met Ryan she went all *Magnum P.I.* on the internet and read everything she could about her."

"*Magnum P.I.?*" TD asks with a chuckle.

"You know what I mean. We watched that damn finale of her show everyone's talking about the other night. I can't believe what that fucker did to her," Logan says, shaking his head as he adjusts his daughter in his arms.

"You watch her show?" Gabe asks his brother-in-law with wide eyes.

"I watch it with Hallie," Logan insists.

"Wait, go back to the first part. What happened on the show?" I ask, suddenly very interested.

"You don't know?" There's no masking the shock on his face.

"No."

"She's never talked about it?" Gabe asks, shifting his daughter to his shoulder so he can burp her. When he sees my eyes narrow, he adds, "I'm just surprised is all. It's all anyone was talking about. The nurses and office staff at the clinic were discussing it the next day."

When no one responds fast enough for my liking, I reply, "Tell me."

"Why don't you just watch the show?" Gavin asks, sensing the discomfort suddenly surrounding all of us. It's as if no one wants to be the one to tell me what happened, and I'm not sure how I feel about that.

"Come on," Logan says, standing up. "I want to change Mak's diaper and put her down. We'll watch it together."

I groan. "Or you could just tell me."

He laughs. "Come on."

Gabe stands too. "I need to change this one's diaper too." He places a kiss on Wrenlee's forehead as she dozes soundly in his arms, having filled her belly.

And judging by the stench hitting me, I'd say she filled her pants too.

We all file inside the cabin like cattle, and while Gabe changes his daughter's diaper, Logan cues up the TV with her reality show. I don't know how he does it, since the show isn't currently airing, but he manages. I'm guessing Hallie has some sort of on-demand on the TV, even the ones at the cabin.

The program starts, and I'm instantly drawn in. Her smile fills the screen, and even though I see a hint of the woman I've come to know, I can't help but notice the differences too. I enjoy the laid-back, casual Ryan, and the woman on screen now is anything but, with her designer clothes and her perfect makeup. Her hair is even styled with big curls a man could get his hands lost in, but I realize quickly I'd rather have her windblown and with a ball cap on her head.

We all watch the show, all five of us guys. When she's at work, discussing her product line and planning the marketing campaign for this fall, I can feel her passion pouring from the screen. This is what she was born to do, and you can tell she loves it. Her team appears competent, courteous, and works diligently, at least on camera.

Her friends, however, are...stuck up. When they all meet up for lunch, there's this vibe of spoiled, arrogant, and being self-absorbed. It's Ryan's show, but everyone seems to talk over her, not to her. I can't help but sense she's just there, doing what she's asked to do.

But then they start talking about parties hosted by some of the biggest names in the industry. They refer to Ryan as the Wild Child, and it blows my mind. Ryan? Wild? I mean, she gets a little wild in bed, but I have yet to see this uninhibited partier they keep referring to, laughing about whatever antic she did the weekend before. Worse, she seems even more uncomfortable than before, the brightness in her brown eyes dulling. Her posture changes. It's as if she's trying to hide under the table, all while wearing a smile on her pink lips.

Suddenly, a man walks up to the table flashing a blinding smile. He's wearing a tailored suit and screams douchebag. He's handsome in that Hollywood way, and his demeanor as he approaches instantly puts me on edge. He waves to nearby tables, stopping to shake hands with some big man in another fancy suit two tables away. When he finally reaches the table where Ryan and her friends are sitting, he leans down and presses a light kiss to her cheek. My blood boils in my veins.

It's Vaughn Cramer.

I'd recognize him anywhere.

There were photographs of him and Ryan together online, and now I'm seeing him on her show. I'm not a fan, but the world seems to be obsessed with him and his movies. He's good-looking and appears to be an all-right actor, but I can't get over his arrogance. Even in his movies, his manner just sets me on edge. When I was scrolling through photos of Ryan that first night she told me who she really was, I stumbled upon several of them together. Most of them were at premieres or other red-carpet events, since they were both dressed to the nines.

Now, seeing them together, makes me a little...ragey.

I'm jealous.

One-hundred-percent green with envy.

"You know, I'm having a hard time seeing those two together," Gavin says as we watch Vaughn as he appears to flirt with Ryan's friends.

"I mean, I get it. He's a huge actor, and she's a producer's daughter who was raised in the industry. It makes sense," TD replies. "But that kiss seemed like the kind you give your sister."

"Agreed," Gabe announces. "I suppose it could be for the cameras. You know, not wanting to slip her the tongue while grandma and the rest of the world is watching," he adds.

"The man's an actor. He's made out with women in every movie he's ever done," Logan replies.

"True," Gavin concedes. "Did you see that movie he did with Daphne Sparks? He has his tongue down her throat half the movie."

I listen to their conversation, but my eyes remain glued to the television. They're all laughing and carrying on, like friends do, but I just can't get past how fake everything feels.

"We could probably just fast forward through all this stuff," Logan suggests, but I shake my head no. I want to see it all.

The episode is only thirty minutes, so it doesn't take long to near the end. Ryan is visiting her parents' house, her mom coming into frame. I can see where Ryan gets her beauty from. Jade Holmes is every bit the sophisticated, stunning woman I recall from when I was a boy. She's a former beauty queen and model, and from what Ryan said, she's a dedicated philanthropist now.

Mother and daughter embrace before stepping inside a huge mansion. They're chatting about Ryan's makeup line and the potential of being picked up by a huge department store worldwide when Ryan's phone rings.

"Hello?" she asks, putting it on speakerphone.

"Is this Ryan Marcotte?"

"This is she," she replies, her mom's brown eyes wide with excitement.

"This is Stanley Goodman of Goodman's. I sent a proposal to your manager, but I wanted to call you personally to say congratulations. Goodman's is thrilled to carry your new winter line in our department stores worldwide."

"Oh my God," Ryan cries, her hand covering her mouth as tears fill her eyes. Jade stands beside her, clearly as excited about the phone call as Ryan. "Thank you so much."

"No, thank you. Please have Ariana get back to me once she and your legal team have reviewed the contract. We're anxious to get this deal done, Miss Marcotte."

"I am as well," Ryan replies, practically bouncing where she stands.

"We'll be in touch, Miss Marcotte. Congratulations."

The phone disconnects, leaving mother and daughter to celebrate this huge accomplishment. There's lots of hugs and tears, and when they finally pull apart, Ryan says, "Let's call Dad and tell him."

Jade nods as Ryan dials the phone.

"Hello, daughter," a booming voice greets into the phone.

"Hi, Dad. Do you have a minute?"

"I do, yes. Just finishing up a late lunch with Vaughn," the man says.

The camera cuts over to the restaurant where an older man sits with a younger one.

"Vaughn, it's Ryan. She has some exciting news to share," the man I now know as Douglas Marcotte says.

"Oh, that's wonderful," Vaughn says, but his eyes move just over Douglas's shoulder to two men sitting at a table, waving him over. "Actually, you take your call. I need to go say hello to an old friend. Excuse me one moment," he says, standing up and walking over to the other table.

Douglas remains cool, but I don't miss the way the corner of his mouth ticks with annoyance. "Well, Vaughn had to step away. Tell me, baby girl. What's the news?"

Ryan relays the information about the deal to her father, who not only congratulates her profusely, but gets a little misty-eyed himself at what she's accomplished. "I'm so proud of you, sweetheart."

"Thanks, Dad."

"Let's celebrate. Have your mom get a reservation at your favorite restaurant. I'll be home around six and we can go commemorate this day."

It cuts back to Ryan's gorgeous smile. "Sounds good."

"Congratulations, Ryan," he replies once more before hanging up the phone.

The camera doesn't cut back to Ryan and Jade the way I expect it to. Instead, it stays on Douglas for a moment, who chats animatedly with the server, telling him all about Ryan's big deal. I expect it to return to Ryan, but it still doesn't. Instead, the cameraman zooms in on Vaughn, who took a seat at the table with his two friends. With the camera being farther away, their conversation isn't as easily heard, but as the cameraman slowly moves closer, the words become audible.

"You about done with her yet?"

Vaughn, with his back to the camera, snorts and lifts his glass. "So done. It's getting exhausting." He sips whatever expensive liquor he has in the glass.

"She still thinks you're dating for love?"

"Of course she does. I'm a damn good actor," he replies with a laugh. "Now that I have the role I've been after in her father's upcoming movie, I can break it off with Ryan."

The friend smirks across the table. "Better make it fast. That redhead over there is eyeing you like you're her next meal," the friend states.

Vaughn glances to his right, clearly eyeing the redhead.

"Son of a bitch," I find myself saying out loud.

"Yeah," Logan replies.

The camera finally cuts back to Ryan and her mom, who continue to celebrate her big deal with Goodman's, all while having no clue how her boyfriend just confessed to the world he's only dating her for what he can get from her father.

"I'll never watch another Vaughn Cramer movie again," TD announces.

"Me either," Gavin says, shaking his head. "What a Grade A asshole."

Anger courses through my veins like a raging tornado. It takes all the strength I have not to jump up from the couch, climb in my truck, and drive to LA to kick his fucking ass. "She didn't know," I say as realization sets in.

"Hallie said she saw it with the rest of the viewers."

"What the hell?" Gabe asks, trying not to wake his sleeping daughter.

"That's bullshit," Gavin adds.

"I don't say this very often, but that guy deserves to get his ass kicked," TD states, shaking his head.

I nod in agreement, but my mind is spinning. She found out her boyfriend was using her by watching it on TV. That's why she's here. Why she's hiding who she is and is laying low. This isn't just a vacation or a month-long getaway.

She ran away from the mess back home.

Suddenly, phones around the room start blowing up. "Girls' night is over," TD announces, checking his phone.

Collectively, everyone starts prepping to head over to Gabe and Blair's to pick up their wives and girlfriends. I wonder if Ryan will call me. I told her to, but that doesn't mean she will. She could just as easily jump into any one of these guys' trucks. I know they'd take her back to the cabin, but dammit, I want to do it.

I'm just about to send her a message when my screen lights up.

Ryan: Party's over. I could use a ride, if the offer still stands.

Me: On my way, Princess.

Slipping my phone back into my pocket, I turn to Logan. "Thanks for having me."

He pulls his eyes away from securing his daughter into her infant carrier and nods. "Of course." I can tell he has more to say by the way he holds my gaze. "Be good to her, man. She went through a lot before she came to town."

I nod once, understanding what he's telling me. "We have an arrangement," I remind him.

I'm not sure I'm saying that more for him or myself.

Gabe is loading up his daughter in her seat as well, while TD and Gavin grab diaper bags, trash, and anything else that needs picked up before we leave. I head out to kick some dirt on the coals and make sure the fire is on its way out for the night. The guys all step outside, and Logan makes sure the cabin is locked up tight.

"Thanks for coming, guys."

Everyone replies as we make our way to our respective vehicles. I climb behind the wheel of my old Chevy and start the engine. I watch both Gabe and Logan secure their daughters into their vehicles, and the sight brings a smile to my lips.

My, how things have changed in the last few years.

TD has his stepson, Brody.

Gavin's got a daughter.

Gabe and Logan too.

And I'm sure it won't be long before more babies are added to the group.

Like a locomotive, we all file out of the driveway and head to Gabe's place. It doesn't take too long, and before I know it, we're all pulling into the lane leading up to Gabe and Blair's house. The front porch light is on and there's a slew of woman standing outside, waiting.

Blair takes off toward the garage, where Gabe pulls his truck inside, and the rest of the ladies all fan out to their rides.

"Night, Blair!" Hallie hollers, her arm thrown over Ryan's shoulder as she leads her my way. "Night, everyone!"

Ryan smiles as she approaches. "Hi."

"Marcus, you got our girl here?"

"I got her, Hallie."

"You better. Take care of her. You know, *take care* of her," Hallie says before bursting into fits of giggles.

"Come on, love. Let's get our little one home," Logan says, taking Hallie's hand and placing a kiss on her knuckles.

"Once she's to bed, then we're gonna get all sexy, Logan. Naked sexy stuff."

I can't help but smile. Yeah, they definitely enjoyed their margaritas.

"Ready?" I ask, opening the passenger door for Ryan.

Her eyes are glazed over, a sign of her intoxication. She looks very relaxed right now, and I take that as a good sign she enjoyed herself.

Ryan leans in and presses her chest to mine. I feel her fingers wrap around my hip, her nails digging into my T-shirt. Leaning in, she whispers those four little words I didn't even know I needed to hear.

"Take me home, Marcus."

CHAPTER
Twenty one

Ryan

Man, he looks gorgeous tonight. Maybe it's the tequila coursing through my blood or the fact I know exactly what he looks like naked. Probably both.

As he slips inside the truck cab and starts to back out of the driveway, there's this extra layer of tension surrounding him. He looks grumpy, and to be honest, since he started having orgasms regularly, he hasn't been all that grumpy lately. See what good O's do to a person? It turns even the grumpiest grump into a more relaxed, less grumpy grump.

It's like weed.

But better.

I giggle.

"What's so funny?"

I release my seat belt and slide to the center of the truck. My hand cups his crotch, and instantly, he starts to harden. Ignoring his question, I ask, "You ever had a blow job while driving down the road?"

His eyes widen as he takes them off the road for a brief few seconds and looks over at me. "Uhh, no."

"We should," I insist, releasing his belt buckle so I can get to the button and zipper.

"Ryan," he states, a mixture of hesitation and anticipation in that one word.

"Don't be a grumpy grump, Mr. Grumpston."

"What?" he asks with a gravelly chuckle.

"You're always so grumpy. Well, you were until you started getting O's. Orgasms and tequila are the bestest, aren't they?" I ask, digging his hard cock out of the opening of his jeans and giving him one long stroke.

He grunts, his entire body radiating tension. "We're almost back to the cabins," he says, unable to stop his hips from moving, thrusting up into my palm.

"We are," I confirm, giving his cock a squeeze as I slide my hand from root to tip. Bending down, I swipe my tongue across the head of his dick.

"Ryan." That one word comes out a plea, his tone filled with desperation.

With my tongue still dancing along the head of his dick, I look up and say, "You could pull over, you know."

To my surprise, he does. He practically slams on the brakes, swerving to the right and veering off the roadway. I have no idea where we are, and frankly, I don't care. He throws the truck into park as I shift onto my knees. My hair falls around my face like a curtain, and before I can grab it, his big hands are there, gathering the strands and holding them out of the way.

I can feel his eyes on me as I lower my mouth around him, taking his cock as deep as I can. When it hits the back of my throat, I almost gag, but I'm able to refrain. Instead, I focus on my hand movement, the twist and turn of my palm against his hardened flesh.

Marcus groans, his second hand moving to the back of my neck. It's as if he has to anchor himself to me somehow, someway. His hips move on their own, thrusting into my mouth, chasing the pleasure. There's something incredibly heady about this act, of having complete control over a man. Of having his trust.

"Fuck," he groans as I double down my efforts.

My hands are moving, my mouth wrapped tightly around his cock, as I drive him straight toward release. His body is a live wire, ready to explode, and there's only one way I want that to happen. Maybe it's the fact I'm more than a little buzzed right now, but I've never had this much fun giving a blow job. Never really wanted to feel him come as much as I do right now.

"Ryan, if you don't want me exploding down your throat, you need to stop right now," he states through gritted teeth.

I don't stop.

So when he comes hard, I'm ready. My firm hand twists and jerks, drawing every drop of cum I can get from his body, all while swallowing it with an eagerness I've never experienced.

When he slumps back in the seat, I finally release my hold on him. I sit up on my knees and wipe my mouth with the back of my hand. I expect to find his eyes closed, but instead, they're locked on me. "You're fucking incredible," he whispers, still trying to catch his breath.

All I can do is smile.

Marcus moves, leaning forward and pressing his mouth to mine. The kiss is...intense. It's fierce and protective and domineering, all at the same time. It makes all these feelings rise to the surface, threatening to completely take over my head...and my heart.

His tongue dances with mine, his hand firmly positioned at my neck. My head swims, and all I want is more. More kisses. More Marcus.

"We need to go," he whispers.

He releases his hold on me and adjusts his jeans. I notice he buttons and zips the fly, but he leaves his belt buckle open, a sign more's to come the moment we get home.

As another grin spreads across my lips, a wave of exhaustion hits me. All I want to do is lie down and not puke, so that's what I do. I curl up on my side on the bench seat, my head resting on his thigh, and close my eyes. Marcus rests his hand on my shoulder, his fingers lightly brushing against my bare skin. It's hypnotizing.

I feel the truck move but can't seem to open my eyes. Or sit up. Or speak.

The gentle movement of the truck partnered with his gentle hand are just what I need to combat the tequila.

Easily, I fall into a deep sleep.

I slowly stir awake, warmth surrounds me. I open my eyes, but don't see much. Due to the lack of light filtering through the windows, it's still night. I also can't help but notice the windows are different, as is the bed. An arm is wrapped around my side, and I don't have to look over to know it belongs to Marcus.

What I don't recall is how exactly I got here.

In his bed.

I lie still, trying to remember. I recall hanging with the girls, drinking margaritas, and laughing. There was so much laughter. It felt...amazing. And right. I could be *me* for what felt like the first time ever. No one cared what my last name was, how much money I have, or what they could get from me. They wanted my friendship, and in return, offered their own.

When we left Blair and Gabe's home, I got into Marcus's truck. I was bold, having slid over in the seat and went down on him. I'd never done that in a moving vehicle, though I suppose it wasn't moving the entire time. Thankfully, he pulled over so I didn't cause an accident by my actions. The paparazzi would have loved that one...

But after that?

I don't recall anything. Not getting to Marcus's cabin and whatever might have happened after our arrival.

Slowly, I turn my head to look at Marcus. He's fast asleep, his mouth slightly agape. He's facing me, lying on his side, and realization hits me. I spent the night. Of all the time we've spent together, I've never slept over. I always head back to my rented cabin, or he back here. This, waking up beside him, falling asleep here too—even if I don't remember that part—is new.

I take quick stock in my appearance. I'm wearing my panties and what I can assume is one of his T-shirts. It feels roomy, and it's definitely not the outfit I was wearing earlier in the evening. While I can't see what he's wearing below the sheet, his chest is bare. Even in the darkness, he looks yummy. I long to curl into his chest, to run my fingers down the hard, muscular planes, but I don't.

Instead, I watch.

I don't know how long I lie here and stare at him, but the darkness slowly transforms. It's not daybreak, but I can tell it won't be long before the sun is peeking over the horizon.

Carefully, I climb from the bed. Marcus stirs, rolling over onto his stomach and curling his arms beneath his pillow. As much as I'd love to stand here and watch the man sleep, I have something else I need to do.

Slipping silently toward the stairs, Buddy sits up, his ears on alert. "Shhh, go back to sleep, Buddy," I whisper, praying he doesn't bark.

He doesn't make a noise, but he doesn't lie back down either. Buddy gets up and follows me, as if he knows I'm doing something he wants to be part of. Together, we make our way down to the main floor of Marcus's cabin. My first stop is the coffeepot, which is ready to go to brew a pot. I press the start button and wait for the delicious scent to fill the air.

While the coffee brews, I check to see what he has in the fridge for creamer. I'm pleasantly surprised to find a bottle of the same creamer I enjoy. Pulling it from the fridge, I go in search of a mug. In the third cabinet I open, I find a few various coffee mugs, as well as a whole shelf of travel mugs, and even though the travel mug will keep the coffee hot longer, I opt for a regular mug.

When the coffee finishes, I pour the hot liquid into the mug. This one's black with bold white letters that reads "This might be whiskey." It's exactly the sort of dry sense of humor I've come to know and expect from Marcus, and it makes me smile. I add a bit of coffee creamer to the black coffee and replace the bottle in the fridge. Only when I have my cup of Joe in hand do I make my way to the back door.

Buddy is right beside me, ready to go out. "Do you need to potty?" I ask, releasing the lock and pulling the door open. He takes off toward the grass, ready to do his business. Just as I start to step out, I spot my clutch purse and phone sitting on the counter. I grab the phone, just in case I have any issues, and slip out into the early morning June air.

It's chilly, but only because I'm wearing a pair of panties and a thin T-shirt. However, I refuse to let the temperature stop me. With Buddy at my side—and let's be honest, I'm glad he's here—I walk toward the path that leads to the lake. I should one-hundred-percent turn back and get my sandals, but I don't. I want to feel the sand between my toes as I watch the sun rise over the lake.

I step on a dozen sticks, probably poking all kinds of holes in the bottoms of my feet, but I keep moving. The ground is damp, thanks to the cooler morning air and the tree coverage, but it feels good. Buddy runs ahead, finds a stick, and carries it back to show me his treasure. A squirrel runs across the path, scampering up a tree and making as much noise as an animal ten times his size. My heart rate kicks up at the thought of what might be lurking out here in the shadows, yet I still push forward.

Finally, we break through the tree line and step out onto the beach. The water moves silently as the sun starts to rise. Carefully, so I don't spill my coffee, I turn on the photo app and take a picture as the sun makes her presence known. I close my eyes and let it warm my face, but only for the briefest few seconds. I don't want to miss the rest of the sunrise. Buddy lies at my feet as I take it all in. The serene beauty that surrounds me.

Holding up my coffee mug, making sure you can read the words, I angle it just right so you catch the beautiful lake and the rising sun behind it. I snap a few pictures before lowering the device and just watching the rest of the sunrise.

When I've finally had my fill of the beautiful morning show, I pull up the photos I took. The pictures don't do it justice, that's for sure. With a deep breath, I do something I haven't done in more than two weeks. I pull up my app that posts on all my social media platforms. I load the photo into the post—the one with my coffee mug, the sunrise, and the lake—and type out my message.

"Nobody can bring you peace but yourself." -Ralph Waldo Emerson

And that's what I feel when I'm here.

Peace.

I hit post, and even though I have hundreds—probably more likely thousands—of notifications, I ignore them all and shut down the app. That alone is liberating.

Tucking my phone under my arm, I enjoy my coffee and watch the sunrise. I don't even care I'm standing out where anyone can see me in my underwear and a T-shirt. I mean, no one is around this section of the lake, and there are only a couple of cabins in this stretch—mine included.

I don't know how long I stand here, but I can't seem to take my eyes away from the view. I think back over the last few years, especially my relationship with Vaughn. Did I ever really love him? The answer is yes, but not the way I should have. It wasn't a forever kind of love, and I know it. He was comfortable, plain and simple. And while I loved him, perhaps it was the type of love you have for a friend instead of your lover.

Sighing, I wonder what will happen when I go back to Los Angeles. I have absolutely no intention of returning to my relationship, especially in light of the fact he was using me. Honestly, I think it was a blessing in disguise. No, I didn't want to find out on national television, but I'm glad I found out now. Who knows how far he would have taken it? Would he have married me? Cemented his alliance with my family name, all while being with me for all the wrong reasons. Would he have cheated?

Has he cheated?

My stomach churns as I take another sip of coffee. My mind swirls with what could have been, but I quickly shut it down. The relationship is over, so there's no reason to worry about what *might* have happened if we remained together. And if he *has* cheated, I suppose there's nothing I can do about it now. Except knee him square in the balls next time I see him, but whatever...

Buddy's ears perk up from where he lies, the stick he was nibbling on forgotten. I step closer to the timber, prepared to use the trees as camouflage. Before I can move completely out of sight, Buddy barks happily and trots over to the place where the path clears way to the beach.

"I wasn't expecting the woman who passed out in my bed last night to be gone this morning, along with my dog."

I give him a small smile and remain where I stand. "The sunrise was too beautiful to pass up, and you were sleeping."

He slowly approaches, his eyes scanning me from head to toe. I do the same, considering he's wearing a pair of jeans, open at the fly. He's without a shirt, exactly how I left him when I got out of bed, as well as nothing covering his feet. "You still should have woken me up. And put on more clothes."

I shrug. "I didn't have enough time. Coffee was more important."

He grins, running his hand through his unruly hair. He looks out at the water, where the sun is already creeping up the morning sky. "I've come out and watched plenty of sunrises in my time."

Ripping my gaze away from his hard body, I gaze out at the water. "It's beautiful."

I see him nod in my peripheral vision.

After a few seconds of silence, I glance his way and say, "I'm sorry about last night."

He turns his attention to me. "For what?"

"Well, for passing out, I suppose. I don't remember a whole lot."

"You fell asleep on the ride home. I carried you inside and set you on my bed. You stripped out of your clothes, so I grabbed one of my T-shirts to sleep in. The moment you were covered, you climbed beneath the sheets and passed out."

I don't miss the way something passes through his eyes. It's as if something else happened, something he's not telling me. "Was that all?"

He shrugs, the corner of his mouth curled up. "Well, you did tell me you wanted some of my big dick energy, but before you could say anything else, you were out and snoring."

"Oh," I reply, feeling the blush creep up my cheeks. "Sorry I passed out on you."

He lifts his shoulders before bending down and grabbing a stick. He tosses it down the beach, and Buddy takes off at a sprint to retrieve it. "I, uh, watched your show last night."

My entire body goes rigid with surprise. "You did?"

He nods, looking a bit sheepish. "Logan had watched it with Hallie and said something about what Vaughn did. He ended up playing it for us."

"Us?" I ask, dreading where this was going.

"The guys."

I swallow over the lump in my throat. Not because I was trying to hide it from any of them, but simply because I enjoyed the anonymity, the separation between that world and this one. "Okay."

After several seconds of silence, he says, "I want to ask you about him, but I don't think I should."

"You can," I reply, watching as Buddy drops the stick at Marcus's feet. He picks it up and tosses it a second time.

Marcus remains quiet, as if thinking about what exactly he wants to ask. "Wanna head back and refill your mug? This seems like a full cup of coffee conversation."

Smiling, I nod in agreement. "Sounds good."

If I'm going to talk about Vaughn with Marcus, I'm definitely going to need more caffeine.

Maybe even a shot of Jack.

CHAPTER Twenty Two

MARCUS

When we reach my cabin, I hold open the door for her to step inside. She shivers, setting her phone down on the counter and running her hand down her arm. "Here," I say, reaching for her mug and topping it off with hot coffee. Once I pour a second cup, I go to the fridge to retrieve the coffee creamer I know she likes. I happened to spot it in her fridge one night I was over at her cabin and ended up picking up a bottle when I was at the store. I don't know why exactly, but I'm glad I did.

"Thanks," she replies, pouring a good amount of creamer into her mug and taking a slow sip. "So good."

I drink a bit of my own cup of Joe, savoring the rich, heavy scent.

"Can I ask you something before we get to the other thing?"

I nod, waiting.

"Why did you have this creamer in your fridge, when I always see you drink your coffee black?"

Of course she'd find the creamer and wonder. "I bought it for you. I wanted to have some, just in case."

She gives me a slow nod, as if she's processing that piece of intel. Ryan walks over to the table and has a seat. She lifts one foot up, placing her heel on the edge of the chair. Even with the oversized shirt, I can still see flesh and a strip of the light purple satin panties she's wearing.

"Well, I appreciate it. I thought I'd just have to throw sugar and milk in my coffee this morning and was pleasantly surprised when I opened the fridge." After a few beats, she asks, "What is it you want to ask me?"

I take a sip of my bitter coffee and lean against the counter. Many questions flash through my head, but only one stands front and center in my brain. So, I just blurt out the one thing I want to know. "Did you punch that fucker in the nose?"

She's taken aback for a moment before bursting into a fit of laughter. "No, but I wanted to."

The corner of my mouth curls up. "Good. That would have been the least of what he deserved."

Her throat bobs as she lifts her head in agreement. "Yeah. I was completely pissed at Bradley too. He's the show's producer. He's the one who approved that bombshell to air."

I make sure to add this Bradley character to my list. "So...Vaughn Cramer, huh?" I pray that question came out as casual as it sounded in my head, and not like the jealous asshole I fear it mimicked.

She lowers her eyes for a second before returning that chocolate gaze back to me. "He was...charming. We ran in the same circles, so we were constantly at the same places at the same times. In a way, it felt good to be around someone and talk to them about the industry and the price of fame.

"I was always being followed and photographed, but when I started to date Vaughn, their efforts just went into overtime. The headlines always promoted the good boy and the bad girl he was going to tame."

"Bad girl?" I ask, recalling the online references to her partying and wild days.

She rolls her eyes. "That was their angle. They were always trying to photograph me doing something inappropriate. Each headline was more ostentatious than the previous one, and they played the angle to perfection."

"But he was using you."

She nods. "Yep. I've always kept people at arm's length, mostly because it's hard to know who to trust. In fact, I rarely trust anyone, with the exception of a few close friends and work confidantes, which makes his betrayal that much harder to take. Over time, I began to trust him, to see him as a man who just wanted a touch of normal in our abnormal world. He claimed to want to be Just Vaughn, not Vaughn Cramer, Hollywood Heartthrob."

"How long did you date?" I find myself asking.

"Off and on for more than three years."

My eyes widen at that response.

"We met at a party my dad was attending. I was twenty-three and his plus one, since my mom was away someplace. Vaughn came up and introduced himself to me. I knew who he was, since he had just wrapped up a movie they were promoting heavily for a summer release, and I'd seen some of his early movies. For the first time, someone seemed to be paying attention to me, not my dad. He never once asked me about him, which was different. Most guys would always dig for information, but not Vaughn. He never once talked about who my dad was or asked to meet him. I never picked up on an uneasy vibe, one that meant he was betraying me."

"He's a master manipulator," I state, wishing he were standing in the room so I could kick his fucking ass.

"He is. After I saw the show, I just shut down. I needed some time to come to terms with what I saw, as well as the fact the whole world just witnessed my humiliation."

"I'm sure that was tough."

She nods again. "Horribly. Anyway, when we finally connected, he tried to play it off as part of the show, like it was scripted, and he was supposed to say that. And when he realized he couldn't charm his way out of it, he threw every excuse at me, including that it was somehow my fault.

"My phone was going crazy; everyone was trying to find out what was going on. The media was hounding me, looking for a statement or whatever, and everywhere I turned, they were playing that clip. I wasn't in any mood to face it all head-on, so I left. I found a little cabin in the middle of Nowhere, Wisconsin, and I flew out a couple days later under the lesser-known name of Jade."

She's been through a lot in a short amount of time. Add in the fact I was a complete asshole to her in the beginning, and the only reason I have is that she got under my skin. In a way no woman ever has, and if I'm being honest, she's sort of embedded there, right under the surface. Without even knowing it, she's refusing to leave.

Except, that's not true.

Ryan is leaving.

In less than two weeks, she'll be out of here, jet-setting back to her life in California. I'll be here, continuing to do my thing. Even if I wanted her to stay, I wouldn't ask. What does Pine Village have for a woman like her? She's used to fancy, expensive, and glamor. The best she's gonna get here is the steakhouse, not that there's anything wrong with it. Kameron has done an amazing job transforming it into a great place to eat.

Of course, it's no CUT by Wolfgang Puck, which was recently featured on some dining and food show the TV was turned to.

Not that I'm trying to tally up what I have to offer. I'm not. This is a fling, nothing more or less. She's here for a short time, and I'm committed to showing her a good time. At the end of her month, we'll walk away with only memories and a smile.

"Is he bothering you? Vaughn?" I ask, redirecting my train of thought back to the conversation at hand.

She shrugs. "He's blocked. He tried to call and message a bunch, but I haven't talked to him since I broke it off and left. I don't want to either." She exhales loudly and shakes her head. "Looking back, I realize our relationship wasn't right. It wasn't what I really wanted, but it was all I knew. He was gone for lengthy periods of time for work, and I was fine with that. I shouldn't have been, you know? But I was. Looking back now, our relationship was comfortable, but it was built on lies."

Taking a sip of my coffee, I can't help but wonder, "What now?"

As she thinks, she smiles. "I want to put more into my makeup and skincare line. We have a huge reveal and celebration event coming up when I return. I want to watch it grow and am committed to putting the time and energy into doing so."

I can't help but feel her excitement, her passion. "You'll do just that. I know it."

She gives me a questioning look. "How do you know that?" Her question is hesitant, her voice laced with worry.

"Because I see it in your eyes, Princess. You've been feisty since the day I met ya, and if you want to do something, then dammit, that's what you'll do. So if you want your business to succeed, I know you'll do whatever possible to help it get there. I have faith in you."

Her eyes fill with tears. She blinks rapidly, trying to keep them at bay. Usually, I'd run away as if my ass were on fire at the first sign of crying, but with Ryan, all I want to do is take her in my arms, comfort and console her.

But that's not what I do.

I can't.

She's leaving in less than two weeks, and I can't afford to invest any more of my heart. I've already given her more than any other woman before her, sadly. I've not tried to keep myself closed off, but I realize that's probably what I've done all along. Why? Good question. It doesn't take a psychologist to realize it most likely stems from the fact everyone has left me. My dad died, my mom didn't want to be a parent and left me with my grandparents. When I was in high school, Gram passed away, and a few years back, Grandpa. Now, I have no one, and if I keep everyone at arm's length, it hurts a lot less when they go.

"What about you, Marcus? What do you see in your future?"

It would be too easy to picture her there. In such a short amount of time, I've become attached, and that's not like me. I'm a pro at keeping my distance. It's what I've done my whole life.

Needing to keep things light, I opt to pull it away from the heavy stuff.

"I see you and me naked in the shower in my future."

She giggles and lifts her feet, wiggling her toes. "My feet do probably need a good scrubbing."

Making my way toward her, I carefully grab her around the waist and lift her off the chair. Positioning her over my shoulder, I easily maneuver her like a sack of potatoes. Her squeal of laughter makes me hard, as does the anticipation of getting her naked and in the shower. Giving her a firm slap on the ass, I say, "We'll be scrubbing more than your feet, Princess."

Taking the steps two at a time, I cart her up to my bathroom to help her wash the dirt off her body, all while getting her dirtied up all over again.

"Shower. Now."

CHAPTER
Twenty Three

Ryan

I can't help but smile, looking up and letting the sun warm my face.

What a gorgeous day.

"Excuse me."

I quickly move, stepping aside on the sidewalk so I'm not blocking anyone's path. "Sorry," I reply politely to the group of young girls already moving past me.

I can't help but notice the number of people moving around. Everyone warned me about the summer tourist season, but for some reason, it seems to have doubled overnight. There are people everywhere, vehicles lining the streets and filling every parking spot imaginable.

My instincts have me lowering my head, blocking my face, thanks to the ball cap I'm wearing. I've become accustomed to wearing it, the hat part of my normal attire when I'm in public. I try not to make too much eye contact, because I'm afraid that's when I'll be recognized. If some of the locals have figured out who I am, they haven't said a word, at least to me.

I just left the small boutique, picking up a cute pair of shorts and some adorable jewelry made by a local resident, and my next stop is the bakery. Jillian is supposed to make apple turnovers, and I don't want to miss it. She said by the afternoon they'd be sold out, so I definitely want to stop before it gets too late. Though, with all the extra out-of-towners running around, I might be out of luck.

I slip inside the bakery, noting the extra-long line. I almost turn around and walk out, not wanting to wait for my sweet treat. Just as I turn to exit, Jillian looks up and spots me. Her eyes go wide, and she waves me toward her. People start turning, so I lower my head, and head in her direction. I can hear grumbles about me bypassing the line, but I ignore them as I reach the side of the counter.

Jillian reaches out and takes my hand, giving it a firm tug. "I'll be right back," she hollers to her employee, Lisa.

I'm practically dragged down the hallway to a small office. "Where in the hell have you been?" she asks before the door is even closed.

"What?" I ask, surprised by her insistent tone.

She faces me, her eyes wide with worry. "We've been trying to call you all morning."

I shrug, reaching for my crossbody bag where my phone is. "It's on silent, like always."

"Ryan!" she whisper-yells. "We have a big problem."

"What? Is it Hallie? Blair? One of the babies—"

"No, Ryan, it's you! They found out you're here," she practically cries out.

Her words hit me with the force of a sledgehammer to the chest. "What?" I ask through a gasp.

"I'm so sorry, honey. All those people? They're looking for you."

My head starts to spin. "I don't...how?" I fall into the chair she has positioned in front of her desk along the wall, my bags drop to the floor.

She leans against the desk. "You posted a picture on Sunday morning," she says, as if that's enough explanation.

"I made sure there were no identifying landmarks in the picture, Jillian," I insist, recalling how I scanned that picture several times before hitting publish.

"Umm," she says, nibbling on her bottom lip. "You had the location setting on."

Realization hits me hard. "Oh God," I whisper.

"Yeah. It posted that you were at Bluff Preserves National Park."

"No," I cry out, tears filling my eyes.

"I'm so sorry, honey," she says in a soothing voice.

A knock sounds at the door, and it's quickly followed by a familiar voice. "Jillian? It's Hallie!"

Jillian runs over to the door and rips it open, pulling Hallie inside the small room. "Did you tell her?" Hallie asks, her wild eyes frantic.

Jillian nods as Hallie walks over and drops to her knees in front of me. "Are you okay?"

"I just...I can't believe it. I really left the location setting on?"

Hallie nods. "I guess they started pouring into town late yesterday. I heard they're flooding in, without having a place to stay. Every cabin, camping spot, hotel room, Airbnb, everything...they're all rented, not that there was a lot available during the busy season."

I feel a tear slide down my cheek. "Why are they here?" Even though I ask the question, I already know the answer. They're here because I brought them. If I hadn't left my location setting on, if I wouldn't have posted on social media, this wouldn't have happened.

"Don't do that," Hallie insists.

"Do what?"

"Blame yourself for this," she replies.

I snort and shake my head. "Well, who's fault is it? If I wouldn't have posted, no one would know where I am. They wouldn't be pouring into this quiet little town, searching for me like vultures over roadkill."

Jillian giggles. "That's kinda gross. You've been hanging around Marcus too long," she teases with a wink to lighten the mood.

"You know as well as I do, anyone could have recognized you at any point. You're not exactly wearing a master disguise here, Ryan. Sure, the lack of makeup, ball cap, and regular clothes is helping, but I took one look at you and knew instantly who you were. It was only a matter of time before others started."

"Ummm, I think some of the regulars know," Jillian says with a shrug.

"They do?" I ask, still trying to wrap my head around everything.

She nods. "I've heard a few groups talking over the last handful of days. But no one was wondering who they should call or anything. They were keeping it to themselves, Ryan."

"Why?" I ask, completely dumbfounded. In Los Angeles, someone would have made a call before they even finished their coffee or pastry. There's nothing people like more than gossiping and being the keeper of the information.

"Why? Because in this town, we protect our own," Hallie insists.

My mouth falls open as I gape up at her. "But...I'm not from here."

She tsks. "What does that matter? You're with Marcus and you've made friends. That counts for something here, Ryan."

"I'm not with Marcus," I insist, shaking my head.

"Semantics. But you *do* have friends here," Jillian states with conviction. "This town is something special and they recognize that in you too. We know you came here for a reason, and they won't be the ones who out you."

"No, I did that all on my own," I grumble, wishing I had a tall caramel iced latte right about now.

"It happens. What we need to do now is get you out of here and to the cabin. From what we've all gathered, no one knows where you're staying, and the ones who do won't say a word."

I sigh and shake my head. "I hate this. I brought this on Pine Village."

"We can handle a bunch of early-twenties girls," Hallie says.

"Besides, I bet they don't hang around for long without any place close to stay. The nearest hotel is probably in St. Paul," Jillian adds, referring to the city thirty minutes away.

"Yeah," I agree, but my heart tells me that's probably not the case. Fans are resilient and determined. So are the photogs. "The paparazzi is probably already here, and they're ruthless. They won't leave until they find me."

"Well, they won't hear it from any of us. I'll make sure of it," Hallie says.

I sigh, realizing my time in Pine Village is probably up. I can't stay, letting the paparazzi wreak havoc on this lovely small town. They're used to an onslaught of people during tourist season, but they're not ready for the rudeness of California paparazzi. The pushing, shoving, trespassing, do what it takes at all costs to get your shot. I can't do that to this place.

"I'll be right back," Jillian says, slipping out the office door and closing it behind her.

"There's more," Hallie says the moment we're alone.

My shoulders sag. "What? More?"

She nods. "It's all over the news today. Your dad fired Vaughn."

"What!" I holler, unable to stop that one word from flying from my mouth.

"Yep," she says. "He released a statement that said the production company and Vaughn Cramer amicably parted ways.

They're actively searching for a replacement and don't see the start of filming to be delayed by this turn of events."

"I told him not to," I say.

"Well, being fired is the least of what he deserves," Hallie replies decisively.

I can't help but smile. "You're not the first person to tell me that." I exhale deeply. "I wonder why he didn't tell me he was going to do that," I say, yet instantly knowing the reason. He probably did try calling me, but I had my phone off.

The door opens again, and Jillian slips back inside. "Here," she says, handing me a large, iced drink. "Large caramel iced latte, with skim milk and sugar-free caramel."

I take a sip and sigh in sweet relief. "Thank you so much," I say, pulling some cash from my bag.

Jilian waves off the money. "Please," she says, shaking her head. "After the morning you've had, I think you've earned a free coffee."

"Well, thank you," I say, taking another sip.

"Oh, and I called you a ride. This way, in case someone spots you, you'll have security."

My ears perk up. "Security?"

There's another knock at the door, and when it opens, TD is standing there. "Hey, ladies." He levels his gaze at me and adds, "I hear you're causing all sorts of trouble."

A small smile stretches across my lips. "Apparently."

He nods. "Well, I'm parked in the alley. We'll slip out the back entrance, and I'll run you to your cabin. We can worry about getting your rental later, if that's all right."

What else can I do? "Sounds fine, TD. Thank you."

"Of course," he says, glancing around. "Ready?"

Standing up, I grab my shopping bags and coffee and turn to face my friends. *Friends*. That's exactly what they've become in such a short amount of time. "Thank you," I whisper, choking on tears once more.

Hallie is the first to step in and give me a hug. "I have to run and pick up Mak, but we can come out and hang with you this afternoon if you'd like. Now that I'm caught up on your show, I have nothing on my schedule but taking a nap when the baby does," she says with a small grin.

"Let's play it by ear," I say, feeling the need to be alone for a while.

"Sounds good. You can call me anytime, and I'll come over."

Jillian nods. "The bakery closes at three, so I can be there anytime after that."

Carefully, so I don't spill my drink on them, I pull the two ladies into a hug. "I appreciate you both so much. All of you."

"That's what friends are for," Hallie says sweetly, squeezing my hand. "Get back to the cabin and stay inside."

I follow TD to the door. Jillian goes out first, making sure no one is in the hallway before we slip out and head to the back of the bakery. He pushes through the exit, making sure no one is nearby, and waves for me to follow. The moment I'm outside, he has the door open and I'm ushered inside the front seat of his police SUV.

Both Hallie and Jillian wave as we pull away, driving through the alley and toward my rental cabin. I keep my head down but can't help but notice the increased amount of people in town. Guilt gnaws at me. I did this. I brought them to town.

TD's phone goes off, playing a call about a traffic accident near where we just left. The road coordinates are a block down from the bakery, closer to where Marcus's auto repair shop is located.

Marcus.

What am I going to tell him about this mess?

TD pulls into the lane, heading toward my rental. "Keep the doors locked, Ryan. I know it's nice and you'll want the doors open, but I don't think that's wise right now. If anyone shows up here, call me. If there's any sort of emergency, call 911."

I sigh, hating this. I can tell he's on edge, needing to get back to deal with the car accident, but also worrying about me out here and needing to make sure I arrive safely.

"Thanks for the ride, TD. I promise to keep the doors locked."

He stops in front of the cabin. "We'll get your SUV back to you."

I nod, not really caring about the vehicle right now. "Thank you."

I climb out of the vehicle and move quickly to the cabin. I input the security code and step inside, resetting the alarm as soon as I close the door. I watch TD pull away, returning the way he came just a minute ago.

Sighing deeply, I lean against the wall and close my eyes.

How can this be happening?

What am I going to do?

I need to call my dad, but first, I want to finish this latte. It might be the last one I have in Pine Village, so I'm going to savor it as long as possible. I head to my favorite spot in the living room and get comfy in the chair. With my coffee drink in hand, I pretend like everything is fine, that my world isn't closing in on me.

That my time in Pine Village isn't coming to an end.

He answers on the first ring. "Ryan."

"Hi, Dad." Just greeting him has my emotions lodged in my throat and on the verge of tears.

"I tried calling you," he replies gently.

"I know. I didn't see it until...after."

He sighs. "I wanted you to hear it from me, so for that, I apologize."

"I don't understand. Why now?"

He clears his throat. I can picture him sitting up tall at his home office desk, just as he would when discussing important issues while I was there. "I couldn't work with him, Ryan. I know you told me not to let personal affect business, but...I had to. The moment he walked into the pre-production meeting, I wanted to hit him. And you know me, I'm a lover, not a fighter. But I wanted to do things to that man I've only seen in a Jason Statham movie."

I can't help but giggle.

"And I've seen my fair share of action movies, Ryan."

It's true. The man's an action movie producer. He's seen and worked with the best.

"What now? You broke his contract."

"I don't give two shits about his contract. What he did was far worse. Besides, we always have a clause for stuff like this."

"You have a clause in case the actor uses the producer's daughter for career clout?" I ask curiously.

"Well, not in so many words, but I can terminate with rightful reason. This was rightful reason, Ryan. And because it was televised, his attorney won't touch it. He'll advise him to cut his losses and move on to the next movie. Unfortunately, his name is shit right now. I can't see him getting work anywhere in this town outside of daytime television or a reoccurring role as Taxi Driver number two."

I shake my head, feeling slightly freer than before.

He did this—fired his main actor—for me. Because he loves me. Because someone wanted to get in with him, and in doing so, hurt me. Dad didn't care how perfect Vaughn was for the role. What he did was inexcusable, and he refused to let him keep the coveted role he was aiming for in his duplicity.

"Tell me how you're doing. Mom saw your post. She tried to call you," Dad says, clearly done talking about Vaughn and the movie.

I sigh and close my eyes. "I posted a photo of a sunrise and accidentally left the location notification on, so it posted where I am."

He exhales. "And?"

"And the town is full of people, all looking for me."

"Ryan," he says, a hint of a warning. "I think you need security."

"It's fine, Dad. No one knows where I am, and I'll just stay hidden at my cabin until this blows over." However, even saying the words with conviction, I don't feel so sure. If one person discovers where I'm staying, I'll have people descending on my private haven in the woods faster than I'd be able to get away. I'd be stuck, and if anyone knows how relentless the media and fans can be, it's me.

"Why don't you let me send someone out there," he suggests.

"No. The local police chief is aware of what's going on. He can handle it." But again, I don't exactly believe that to be true. From what I've been told, TD is the only full-time police officer in town, and anyone else is just as needed to assist. I don't want to be the reason he has to call in help, because the crowds are out of control with reality TV show fans and the press. "It'll blow over," I add cheerfully.

He exhales. "I don't believe you, but I will respect your decision. For now. If so much as one person steps foot onto the property you're renting, I want to know. I will send a team of security personnel to ensure your vacation isn't disrupted."

The problem is, if it gets to that point, it's already disrupted. There's no way I could enjoy the quiet, the solitude, the peace that comes from Pine Village. Not with security escorts. The private bubble would be broken.

If it's not already.

"Okay," I appease.

"I'm sorry this is happening, Ryan. I admit, when you said you were going to Wisconsin for a month, I was worried. Not because you can't take care of yourself, but simply for fear of the unknown. I wouldn't be a parent if I didn't worry."

"I know."

"Good. Now, tell me about this young man."

My throat goes dry as I try to swallow. "Young man?"

"Mom and I agree. You seem...happier, and we don't think it's entirely because of you recharging your battery on a little vacation. You've met someone."

Tears burn my eyes, but I refuse to let them fall. "It's nothing, really. Just a..." I can't tell him it's a fling. Who wants to tell their dad that? "It's just a friend I've made."

"And you like him."

I think about the grumpy, borderline rude man I first met and the one I know now. They're the same man, but he's let me see his layers. The ones he hides from most people.

"Yeah, I like him."

"Well, I'd love to meet him."

I snort a laugh. "I don't think so."

"Why not? If he's a friend of yours, he's a friend of mine."

"Okay," I reply, shaking my head, because I know there's not a snowball's chance in Hell he'll ever meet Marcus. Why would he? Unless my parents show up here, there's no way. Marcus isn't accompanying me to Los Angeles when I return at the end of my time here.

"Good," he says happily, as if believing he'll be meeting Marcus someday.

A wave of sadness washes over me.

"I'll let you go, Dad."

"Keep me posted, Ryan. I want to know if you're having security issues."

"Understood," I confirm.

"Love you, sweetheart."

"Love you too, Dad."

I hang up, my head feeling heavier despite having talked to my father. Something tells me things here will get worse before they get better.

I just pray I'm wrong.

CHAPTER *Twenty four*

MARCUS

I look out the shop door, surprised by the number of people milling around out there. It seems like, overnight, the population just...boomed.

Glancing over at Dale, I ask, "Does it seem a lot busier out there today?"

He looks up from the Honda he's working on. "I guess. Probably because of the famous person," he says, going right back to work.

The hairs on the back of my neck stand up. "Famous person?"

"Yeah, I guess there's some big movie star or whatever here. Maybe they're making a movie at the park? I don't know. I just heard some people talking about it earlier at the diner when I grabbed lunch."

Fuck.

That can't be a coincidence.

"Huh," I reply, pulling out my phone and checking to see if anyone tried to contact me. Namely, Ryan. But my screen is blank of notifications, which isn't unusual.

He goes back to work, and I try to do the same. Unfortunately, I can't help but worry. Should I call Ryan and see if she's all right? I'm assuming she's the star everyone is searching for, unless there's another famous person floating around here, hiding from the paparazzi. I'd think one renting a cabin in Pine Village was pretty rare, but two? Seems impossible, really.

I spot a group of four leaving my front office, all on foot and chatting animatedly. My boot-covered feet are moving, heading in the direction where the group departed. Stepping through the door that separates the shop from the office, I find Gladys behind the counter, sorting papers. "Hey, everything okay?"

Buddy perks up from his bed behind the desk when he hears my voice. He likes to be in the shop with me and Dale, but when he naps, he prefers to be in the office with Gladys, snoozing in his dog bed in the air-conditioning.

She looks up and rolls her eyes. "Yeah, fine. I'm just over the teeny boppers searching for the TV star."

I lean against the counter, glancing around the room. Over in the waiting area, the owner of the Honda is reading a book while we complete her car repairs. No one else is in the room, so I turn my attention to Gladys. "What's going on?"

She stops what she's doing and levels me with a gaze. "Apparently, there's some reality TV star in town, and everyone is looking for her. She was dating that Vaughn Cramer guy, the one who was in that big movie last summer?"

"Why is everyone looking for her?"

"Who knows? Apparently, she has a big online presence and following. Makeup, a YouTube channel, and more. I don't know, but like I told those girls, ain't no TV star hanging around Wright's Auto Repair."

My heart drops into my shoes. "If anyone gives you a problem, let me know. We're asking everyone who isn't a customer to leave the property. We don't know anything, and even if we did, we wouldn't tell anyone."

Gladys stares at me, and I can tell the moment realization sets in. She nods. "No one will hear a peep from me, Marcus. You have my word." I turn to walk out of the office, when she adds, "Check on that girl, okay? Make sure she's all right in the midst of this chaos."

Of course Gladys would realize the woman everyone is looking for is Ryan. They only met one time, that I know of, back when Ryan stopped by to invite me to lunch. Perhaps it was the adamant and protective tone I had, but whatever the reason, it doesn't surprise me she'd figure it out.

"I will," I assure her, stepping outside and grabbing my phone. I head past the open bays and walk straight to the corner of the property, where the shop parking lot meets the tow yard.

Instead of calling Ryan, I dial someone else.

"Hey."

"You got a minute?" I ask TD.

"Super busy, man, and I'm pretty sure I know why you're calling, so that's why I answered."

"So you are aware."

He snorts. "Hallie and Jillian called me earlier. Ryan was at the coffee shop, which was crawling with people, so they asked me to come and drive her home. She said she'd stay there and keep the doors locked, but I haven't been able to check on her since I dropped her off. With the influx of people, I'm dealing with all sorts of shit, man. Traffic accidents, trespassing, and illegal parking are the top of the list right now."

"Shit, man." I swallow hard. "I'm sorry."

"Why are you sorry? You didn't do any of this," he says insistently.

"I know, but..." I pull my hat from my head and run my hand through the sweaty strands. "I hate this. For her. For you. For everyone."

"We're used to the extra tourists, but this is a whole new level, man." He sighs. "I gotta go. Call if you need me. I'll answer for you, but if I don't, I'll call back."

237

"Thanks, TD."

"Check on her." Then, he's gone.

I click over to Ryan's name and tap the screen. It rings once, twice, three times. After the fourth ring, it goes to voicemail, but it won't let me leave a message since it's full. I hang up and call a second time. When that call also goes unanswered, I tap a little too hard on the screen. "Fuck."

I look at my busy shop, and I know what I have to do. It won't take me too long to run out to the cabin and check on her, so that's what I'll do. Moving to the first bay door, I holler at Dale. "Hey, I'm gonna run home really quick. I didn't take a lunch, so we'll just call this a late lunch break."

He looks up, his eyes full of concern. "You all right?"

I nod. "I need to check on my tenant."

"That pretty lady having issues?"

"Yeah," I reply, patting my pocket to make sure I have my keys.

"All this ruckus is for her, isn't it." It's not a question. When I don't answer, he replies, "I thought she looked familiar."

My eyebrows shoot sky high. "You watch reality TV?" I find myself asking, completely surprised by this revelation.

Dale just shrugs his shoulders. "Lots of pretty girls on that show." He winks and turns his attention back to the vehicle he's working on. "Better get a movin'. Make sure Ryan is good."

"You got Buddy for me?" I ask, even though I don't need to. I know he'll be in good hands with Gladys and Dale. He waves me off, letting me know he's got my dog.

I run out to my truck and jump inside. The moment I start it up, I catch a whiff of myself. I forgot I spilled diesel fuel on my shirt earlier today and never changed. I should run back into my office and throw on a clean shirt, but that'll just add even more time to the journey. It might be easier just to swing by my own cabin and throw on a clean shirt before checking on Ryan. I'll still smell, but at least it won't have such a strong odor.

Thankfully, there doesn't seem to be extra vehicles on the road that leads to our driveways. At least they haven't caught wind of exactly where she is, because if they knew, this road would be packed with cars. I pull into my own driveway, leaving my old Chevy running as I head inside.

I don't bother heading up to my bedroom to retrieve a clean shirt. Instead, I go straight to the laundry room, where I know I left a few work shirts. I rip my dirty one off and throw it in the dirty basket and grab the first clean one I find.

As I'm pulling it over my head, I hear a knock at the front door. Thinking it's Ryan, I take off at a clipped pace, but the moment I round the corner and have a look out the open front door, I know it's not the woman I want to see.

Vaughn fucking Cramer is standing at my door.

"Can I help you?" I ask as I approach.

He pulls his sunglasses down his nose, glaring inside my house with his judgment and annoyance. "Who are you?"

"The man who's going to kick your ass if you don't answer my question." I push through the screen door and step out onto the porch, slowly approaching and forcing him to take a couple of steps back.

His eyes widen as he scans me from head to toe. "I'm looking for my fiancée," he states, lifting his nose in the air like some cocky asshole who caught a whiff of something he doesn't like. Probably the diesel soaked into my skin, but I don't give a shit.

"Well, you're at the wrong place, pal. Your fiancée isn't here," I insist, crossing my arms over my chest and leveling him with a glare.

He holds up his hands. "Sorry to intrude. I'm just looking for the woman I love. She's staying here for a little R&R and is waiting for me to join her, but she must have given me the wrong address." He scratches the back of his neck nervously.

"Must have. No one around here like that. Only a couple of places on this road, and they're all owned by locals. No out-of-towners here."

Lies. Complete lies, but I don't care.

"Oh. All right," he says, pushing his glasses back up on his nose. "Sorry to bother you," he adds with an air of dismissal, turning and walking toward a running Mercedes SUV waiting. It's a stark contrast to my old truck parked beside it.

"Prick," I say aloud to no one.

I watch as he goes, fortunately, turning left at the end of my driveway. If he would have gone right, he could have stumbled upon the lane that leads to Ryan's cabin. Making sure he's not turning around; I wait a few minutes before closing up my front door and returning to my truck. I climb inside and throw it in gear, pressing the gas pedal a little harder than necessary.

As I approach her cabin, I slow down, parking where she'd normally have her rental. I glance around, not finding anything out of the ordinary. No one lurking in the shadows, nothing to indicate something's been disturbed or messed with.

Climbing from the cab, my eyes catch movement on the porch. Ryan steps out, her entire body rigid with tension, her eyes a little swollen as if she's been crying. I move quickly, up on the porch and beside her within seconds. My hands go to her hair, which is wild and slightly matted down, probably from wearing her ball cap. I feel her slender arms wrap around my waist as she hugs me tightly.

"You okay?"

She sniffles and nods against my chest.

"Come on, let's get inside," I insist, glancing around once more.

We step inside the cabin, and I make sure the door is closed securely. "What the hell happened?" I ask, taking in her appearance. Even though she looks exhausted and emotionally wrung out, she's still pretty as fuck.

She sighs loudly and shakes her head. "Sunday, when you found me on the beach, I had posted a picture." She smiles softly, as if going back to that morning in her mind. "It was of the sunrise, with my coffee cup. I made sure there were no identifying marks on the

240

photo, but..." She closes her eyes for a moment. When she opens them, she finishes, "I accidentally left the location notification on. So, when I posted the picture, it said I was at the Bluff Preserves National Park."

"Oh. Shit."

"Yeah," she whispers, running her hands up her arms, as if she's cold. "There's so many people in town, Marcus. They're...everywhere." Her brown eyes turn frantic. "What if they find me here?"

"They won't," I insist, even though my words hold no weight. It's not like I can stop the information from getting out. I know my friends are solid and wouldn't say a peep, and while I'd like to assume the rest of the town would protect her identity and location, chances of that happening are slim. Someone will talk.

They always do.

"And my dad fired Vaughn."

My eyebrows shoot up in surprise.

"Yeah, apparently, my dad did it because of what happened on my show, even though I told him not to. He did it anyway, refusing to let him have the part he coveted and lied to get."

I can't help but smile. "Good. Fucker got what he deserved."

"Yeah," she replies, but any happiness she feels doesn't reach her eyes.

Clearing my throat, I know I need to drop the bomb. "Vaughn is here."

It takes a second for my words to register. "What?"

I reach out and pull her into my arms, needing to feel her there. "Before I came here, I stopped by my house to change my shirt because I got diesel on it."

"That's why you stink," she murmurs, wrinkling her nose in this cute way that makes me want to kiss her.

"Yep," I agree. "Anyway, there was a knock at my door, and there he was."

Her mouth is slightly agape, her eyes wide. "He's here?"

"Unfortunately."

"Oh my God!" she bellows, starting to pace.

"He, uh, well, he said he was looking for his fiancée." I hide how badly that word burns my tongue, but barely.

She stops moving and her jaw drops. "His what?"

"Fiancée."

"I am *not* his fiancée!" she proclaims. "We broke up! He's blocked on my phone, for God's sake! I want nothing to do with him and have told him that repeatedly."

"We can call TD," I inform her. "If he's in town, then he can ask him to leave."

She shakes her head. "Marcus," she practically cries. "We can't just ask him to leave. Technically, he hasn't done anything wrong."

"He's a damn douchebag. A royal fucking prick who deserves to have his ass run out of town," I insist, which earns me a small smile.

She moves, stepping toward me and practically jumping into my arms. I catch her easily, while her legs wrap around my waist. Her mouth slams into mine, her tongue slipping past my lips and delving inside my mouth. I cup her ass, gripping the globes with a bit of extra force. Ryan groans into my mouth, rubbing her chest against mine, and rocking her hips.

"Fuck," I murmur.

"Yes. That. Now, Marcus," she requests urgently. Her hands dive for my T-shirt, but since she's pressed against my chest, it's not going anywhere.

"I'm not sure—"

"I'm very sure," she interrupts. "Please."

I open my mouth, knowing there are a ton of things we need to discuss, all things considered, but now, with her rocking her hips and grinding against my dick, all those other reasons we should talk about fly out the window.

"No talking," she demands, reaching down and shifting her own shirt up and over her head.

I don't know what comes over me—actually, I take that back—I know exactly what comes over me. It has everything to do with the incredibly beautiful woman stripping naked and all but begging for me to fuck her right now. *That's* what comes over me.

So, that's what I do.

Spinning around, I carry her toward the bedroom, all while shoving my tongue down her throat. The moment we breach the threshold, she slides down my body and is practically ripping her clothes off. I'm torn between stripping my own clothes off and watching the show.

"Clothes, Marcus. Now." There's a desperation in her voice I've never heard before.

I move, unlacing my boots and pulling them off before fumbling with my belt buckle and trying to get my pants off. Ryan is naked, digging at my fly and practically ripping it open. I shimmy my jeans down my legs and go still when I feel her hand and mouth simultaneously wrap around my dick.

A gasp flies past my lips as I try to get my bearings, but with her working me over the way she is, it's hard.

No pun intended.

Ryan releases her hold on me and quickly moves to the nightstand. She pulls a single condom from within and rips it open with her teeth. I don't even have time to remove my shirt. She's covering my dick with the protection and hoisting herself back up my body moments later. Lifting herself up, I shift my cock to her entrance, and she lowers herself onto me.

I groan, feeling her tight, wet pussy grip my cock like a glove. It's perfect—*she's* perfect. Everything about her, including her bubbly personality, is exactly what I didn't even realize I was looking for. She's the positive to my negative, the sunshine to my grump. And this right here? A-fucking-mazing.

For the first time in my life, I picture my future differently. I see a woman there. And not just any woman, *this* woman. The problem is she's leaving soon. In about a week and a half she'll be heading back to California, just like she planned. And this fling will be over.

Even if I don't want it to be.

"Marcus?" she whispers, running her tongue up the side of my neck.

I grunt out a hoarse, "Yeah?"

"Move."

She doesn't have to tell me twice.

CHAPTER Twenty five

Ryan

A tear rolls down my cheek.

I've been watching him sleep for the past hour. After the first round of sex, he convinced me to go with him to his place. If people were looking for me, he felt it was safer for me to be in his cabin, where my name wasn't attached to the rental agreement. I understood his train of thought, even though I knew it wasn't necessary.

I wouldn't be staying.

I had to leave. The entire town erupted in chaos. While Marcus ran out to pick up dinner from the diner and Buddy from Dale's house, I packed up my belongings. Marcus thought I was doing it to move into his cabin for a few nights, but I knew in my heart this was it. I couldn't stay. I can't subject this beautiful, small town to the pandemonium that comes with my life. It's not fair to them.

Any of them.

Especially Marcus.

Hallie checked in with me, as did the rest of the women I consider friends. Ellie mentioned that TD was still working, trying to get order back amidst the madness. And the paparazzi? They were talking to everyone they could, trying to dig up any ounce of information they could. By now, I'm sure they found out where my rental is. It wouldn't be too hard, even if I used my middle name, and it was only a matter of time before they descended on Marcus's private little world in the timber.

When Marcus returned, we ate in the kitchen and played with Buddy. When it was time for the dog to go outside, Marcus went alone, refusing to let me join him for fear someone was lurking out there somewhere. At the end of the evening, we put Buddy to bed and went to bed ourselves. But we didn't sleep. At least not for a while. We made love. Twice more.

That's what it was, at least for me.

I'm falling in love with Marcus Wright, and *that's* why I need to go.

Not because I'm scared of the way I feel, but simply to protect him. I'm sure he'd laugh if I suggested he needs protecting, but he does. From the madness that surrounds me and my life. Marcus prefers solitude. He craves the privacy of his own cabin, surrounded by nothing but nature. His world is simple, quiet, and so unlike my own.

His world is here.

And mine isn't.

Another tear falls as I carefully slide out from under his arm. He stirs but doesn't fully wake. After a few seconds, he settles against his pillow and falls back into a deep sleep. I quickly move to retrieve my clothes. I left most of my belongings in my rental SUV after TD dropped it off, only bringing a few items inside for bed. The plan was to bring in all the luggage in the morning, but that's not what's going to happen.

I won't be here.

Silently, I dress in the bathroom. My sandals are by the front door, so as soon as I've slipped on a T-shirt and pair of shorts, I run my fingers through my hair and wipe off what little makeup might be smeared beneath my eyes. When I'm ready, I grab the Wright Auto Repair hat and place it on my head. Even if I won't be here, I'll still carry a piece of him with me.

Not only in my heart but sitting on top of my head.

That thought brings a smile to my face.

As quiet as a mouse, I flip off the light and slip from the bathroom. There's enough moonlight filtering through the big windows to illuminate Marcus in bed. He's breathtaking. Never in a million years would I have thought I'd fall for a rugged man like him, but here we are. My heart belongs to him, and probably always will. In less than three weeks' time, I fell in love with the grumpy man who rescued me on the side of the road.

But it wasn't meant to be.

And I have to protect him from the chaos that comes with being Ryan Marcotte.

As much as I'd love to walk over and kiss his lips one last time, I can't risk waking him up. So instead, I touch my fingers to my lips, close my eyes, and release the kiss into the air. In my mind, it floats softly from me to him, landing firmly on his lips in the lightest touch.

Buddy stirs, knowing something's up. Instead of begging him to stay put—and knowing he won't—I tap my leg once so he comes. We walk down the stairs together, and just before I'm too far down to see, I stop and give him one last look.

Those random tears from before?

They fall in earnest now.

I make sure my belongings are shoved inside my smaller suitcase before standing up and glancing around at the gorgeous cabin. A sad smile stretches across my lips. I don't want to leave, but I need to. Any dream I started to entertain by staying here is nothing more than that.

A dream.

Buddy presses his nose against my neck. I fling my arms around his, slipping my fingers into his soft fur. "I'm going to miss you, boy," I choke out, the emotion bubbling to the surface like a volcano. "Be good for your dad, you hear?"

He whimpers, as if feeling my heartache. He rests his jaw on my shoulder and sighs.

"I know, Buddy. I know." Forcing myself to stand up, I say, "You take care of your dad, okay? Don't let him be grumpy all the time."

His tongue hangs out, but I can still see the sadness in his eyes.

I pull the note I wrote from my pocket and place it on the coffee table. Bending down, I press a kiss on the top of Buddy's head. "I'll miss you so much."

Grabbing my suitcase, I roll it to the front door and gently release the lock. My phone and purse were left on the table beside the door for this very reason, so as soon as I have them in hand, I slip out the front door, flipping the lock on the handle as I go. The air holds a chill, one that would burn off at the first sight of the sun. But right now, in the middle of the night, it feels heavy and unsettling.

I manage to throw my suitcase into my SUV without dropping it, and just as I prepare to climb behind the wheel, I gaze back up at the cabin. Buddy is sitting in front of the door, his head still visible from where I stand. A single tear slides down my cheek, and the last thing I want to do is start crying before I even get out of the driveway.

I start the vehicle and throw it in gear. I risk a quick glance at the porch, almost expecting to see Marcus hurrying toward me, but there's no one there. Marcus is still soundly sleeping upstairs, and it's time for me to go. I changed my return flight earlier when Marcus was in the shower, and even though it doesn't leave until 6:00 a.m. I need to go now.

Because if I don't, I may never want to leave.

And once I'm gone, the people who flocked to Pine Village to find me will leave too. Everything will get back to normal. It's that simple.

Yet, it feels so complicated and hurts my heart. I don't want to leave, but I know it's the right thing to do. For everyone.

Tears accompany me the entire ride to the airport.

"I was surprised to hear you had returned a week early," my mom says in way of greeting as I step inside my childhood home. She places a motherly kiss on my cheek and shuts the door behind me.

"It wasn't fair to the small town I was staying in. The paparazzi was hounding them to no end. Plus, Vaughn showed up," I say, joining her in the kitchen on Friday morning.

"I saw the photos," she says, pouring two mugs of coffee. As she moves to the refrigerator to get the creamer, she adds, "That man has absolutely no couth."

"None," I confirm after pouring a bit of my favorite coffee creamer into the mug she places in front of me and taking a sip.

"What time did you land yesterday?" she asks, watching me over the brim of her mug.

"Eight in the morning," I confirm.

Memories of arriving at the airport yesterday morning filter through my mind. Unfortunately, my luck on remaining undetected ran out. I was spotted immediately and had to hide out in the airport security office until it was time to catch my flight. Even then, I was hounded, questions screamed at me, my photo taken a million times.

It was a confirmation that I had made the right decision to leave.

"I slept most of the morning yesterday and then went to the office to meet with Ariana."

Mom nods. "The party is coming along nicely. Everything will be set for next Saturday night."

It's my turn to nod now. "Thank you for helping."

She waves off my comment. "It was nothing. Not only do I enjoy organizing a party, but I did it for my daughter's first winter product line reveal, as well as the introduction of the face of her company. It's an honor, darling."

I give her a small smile, one that probably doesn't reach my eyes.

"Tell me about Pine Village," she says, leaning her elbows on the counter in front of me.

This time, my smile is real. "It's this quaint little town, where everyone knows everyone. It sits along a big national park, with a lake, lots of cabins, and trails for riding four-wheelers and snowmobiles."

"Four-wheelers?" she asks, her eyes dancing with delight.

I nod in confirmation. "I rode a four-wheeler."

"Wow, look at you! Our little adventurer," she quips with a beautiful smile.

Lifting my shoulders, I tell her, "It was fun."

And it was. Marcus took me all over his property and around part of the lake. He even showed me how to get to Blair and Gabe's house from the trails. It was a great time, and while I was nervous—and maybe a bit scared at first—I loved every second of it.

It was freeing and wild.

Much like my time with Marcus.

Her smile remains as she sips her coffee. "Tell me about him. Marcus."

I close my eyes, picturing him. "There's nothing much to say, really," I say lamely, making her chuckle.

"I beg to differ. It sounds like there's plenty to say, including how much you care for him."

I shrug my shoulders and keep my focus on my coffee. "I, uh, might have fallen in love with him."

When she doesn't respond, I glance up. I don't know what I was expecting to see, but her grinning from ear to ear wasn't it.

"What?" I ask.

"I'm just so happy for you," she says, taking another small sip of her hot beverage.

"Happy? Why?" I don't seem to follow her line of thought.

"Love is a beautiful thing," she insists. "I fell in love with your father almost immediately. It was a classic case of love at first sight."

"Mom, did you miss the part where he lives in Wisconsin, and I live here?" I ask incredulously.

She shrugs. "The heart wants what it wants, Ryan."

I feel my eyes well with tears as my head shakes. "It can't work, Mom. His life is...so simple there. And mine is complicated. I have the TV show and my makeup line."

"Two things you can do from Wisconsin."

I snort a very unladylike noise. "Who wants to watch a TV show set in Wisconsin?"

She shrugs. "You never know, honey. It could be a hit, just like the one here. And you and I both know your work can be done anywhere. You'd have to do some travel, sure, but it's completely doable."

Air deflates from my sails. "I understand what you're saying, but...it can't work."

"Can't? Or you won't let it?"

I open my mouth to argue, but nothing comes out.

"Listen, Ryan, I can't tell you what to do, but I can tell you this. Don't walk away from love because you're scared. Being scared is natural, normal, and frankly, it's part of life. Bravery comes from within. You already have it, sweetheart. You just need to follow your heart. Be that wild girl I remember, climbing trees in the backyard, even when she was told not to."

I crack a small smile at the memory her words evoked. "But...what if he doesn't feel the same way? I mean, it's not like we discussed any of this. Heck, we didn't discuss anything. I, uh, might have left in the middle of the night."

"Ryan," she groans, shaking her head in disappointment. "Tell me you didn't."

"I left a note," I add lamely, dropping my gaze once more to the counter.

"And I suppose this note didn't tell him how you really felt, did it?"

I shake my head. "It was just a fling." I cringe a little, wishing I weren't sharing such intimate details with my mother, of all people.

"So? Just because something started as a fling doesn't mean it has to stay that way."

I rub my forehead, to the spot where my stress headache is forming. "That's not what's happening here. I know you secretly want me to have a love at first sight moment like you had with Dad, but this is different."

She meets my eye, leveling me with a stern gaze of her own. "I want you to have everything, sweetheart. Whether that's love at first sight, a fling turned to more, or whatever hand the good Lord deals you, I want you to find love because you're so worthy of it. The man you're supposed to give your whole heart to is nothing like that Vaughn Cramer jerk. He'll make you laugh. He'll listen to you share your hopes and dreams, and he'll do his part in helping you achieve them. That's the type of love I want for you."

I don't know when I started to cry, but I swipe at the tears on my cheeks. "I want that too," I whisper, my heart aching for what I don't have.

She leans forward and reaches for my hand, giving it a gentle squeeze. "You will. I know it. The right man is out there for you, sweetie. Maybe he's the guy you left behind in Wisconsin. Maybe not. But he's out there, and he's looking for you too. When you least expect it, he'll make himself known. He'll be there for you in ways no one before ever has. That's when you'll know."

I lean down, resting my cheek on the cool quartz counter. "I wish I hadn't wasted so much time on Vaughn."

Mom sighs. "He was a life lesson. One where you'll learn a great deal about yourself and others, but he's not the end of your story."

"He showed up in Pine Village."

"Of course he did. He's a selfish, small man who needed you to try to fix his mistakes for him."

I snort. "It'll be a cold day in hell before that happens."

"According to those entertainment websites, he went looking for you in that small town to rekindle your romance. Apparently, some of your supporters were outraged by his appearance there and told him that much. Of course, with the paps being all over the place, a lot of it was caught on camera. One woman even slapped him across the face for being such a weasel of a man."

My mouth falls open. "She did?"

Mom smiles victoriously. "A feisty woman who lived there. I think they said her name was Hallie."

"Oh my God!" I whisper.

Mom grins. "Friend of yours?"

"Actually, yes. Hallie, Blair, Ava, Ellie, and Jillian are lovely women. I really enjoyed my time with them."

"Well, Vaughn screamed for the cops to arrest her for assault, but the sheriff refused. Said it was self-defense, since Vaughn poked her in the shoulder when she started yelling at him."

I bark out a laugh, knowing I'll be searching the internet later to find the clip. I can't wait to watch Hallie hand Vaughn his ass.

"Listen, Ryan, you don't have to decide anything today. Or even tomorrow. Take some time and do some soul-searching. Listen to your heart. It won't steer you wrong."

I nod, understanding what she's saying. There are a lot of different factors I need to consider before I make any final decisions, even though leaving in the middle of the night is a pretty big statement. He may not even want to talk to me after what I did, and even if he does agree to talk, that doesn't mean he'll be interested in a relationship. He could say no as easily as he could say yes.

"I will, promise."

"Good. Now, let's talk about this party we're hosting next Saturday night."

CHAPTER
Twenty six

MARCUS

Buddy alerts me to someone's arrival before my own ears pick up the sound. I don't bother turning around to see who it is, mostly because I don't care. I'm certain I know exactly who it's not.

It's been a week since I woke up alone, and I haven't heard from her, other than the note she left on my coffee table. I've wanted to reach out, just to make sure she's okay, but I haven't. What we shared was a fling, right? We set the parameters, and never once did we talk about more.

Until my heart got involved.

That's exactly why I always keep it out of the equation. Unfortunately, I wasn't expecting a prissy, high-maintenance woman to slip beneath my defenses. Between her fancy, designer shoes and her vacation wardrobe that cost more than I make in a month, I let down my guard, assuming we could have a little fun without the strings.

She perfected the sneak attack, and now I'm paying the price.

"You look like shit."

I grunt, refusing to turn to welcome the newcomer. I keep my focus on Grandpa's old truck, tinkering with the carburetor. Anything to keep my idle hands busy. It's actually the first night I haven't stayed until dark at the shop. At home, I look around and see Ryan. I expect her presence and then am sadly disappointed when I feel nothing but emptiness.

So, I work. There've been plenty of vehicles to fix and tow calls to go on, thanks to the busy tourist season. I've taken on more than my shop normally does, just to keep busy and away from home.

But tonight, I needed something different. Something that only working on my grandpa's truck could provide. I miss him like crazy, wishing he were here to offer a bit of advice. Or maybe a shot of Jack to help mend my broken heart, because there's no doubt in my mind that's what I'm suffering from. What started out as a little fling turned into something bigger.

Dammit.

"You wanna talk about it?" Gabe asks, leaning against the old truck and glancing under the hood. The man's got talent when it comes to woodworking and home remodeling projects, but if it involves an engine, he's shit.

"Nope," I tell him, giving the wrench a quarter turn.

"Great, then you can just listen."

I close my eyes and shake my head. When I said I wouldn't mind talking to my grandpa, that didn't mean I wanted my friends all up in my business.

"Have you talked to her?" he asks. I know which *her* he's referring to.

"No."

"Why not?"

"Because that wasn't our deal." I turn the wrench with a bit more aggression than necessary. "It was a fling, Gabe. Nothing more."

"You sure about that?" he asks.

Lacey Black

His words make me stop moving as anger sweeps through me. "Yes, I'm sure," I say through gritted teeth.

"Then why are you both miserable?"

That question makes me pause. For the first time, I look up at my friend. He's smiling, the fucker.

Sighing, I toss the wrench onto my cart and stand up straight. My back aches, thanks to being hunched over for extended periods of time today, but that pain has nothing on what I feel in my chest. "You've talked to her?"

"Not me, but Blair has. Hallie too. I think they all have. They became friends while she was here, and they're wanting to keep in touch."

I nod, happy for all of them. Especially Ryan. I got the impression she didn't have a lot of real friends back home, so to know she's still communicating with the ladies back here is comforting. They may not be right down the road, but they're great people and will have her back when she needs it.

"Listen, Marcus, I'm not here to tell you what to do, but I do have a little experience in this sort of situation."

My eyebrows shoot sky-high. "You had a summer fling with a reality TV star who was hiding out from the media and her ex-boyfriend who publicly told the world he was only dating her to get close to her father?"

He chuckles and shakes his head. "No."

"That's what I thought," I grumble, turning my attention back to the truck.

"I have experience in letting the woman I love go because I thought that was best for all of us."

Oh. That.

Yeah, I remember when he and Blair hooked up while she was in town, helping at her father's medical practice here. She and Gabe started this thing, and when her time was up, she went back home to Chicago, or wherever it was she was living. He was gutted.

256

"I let her go because I felt I couldn't ask her to stay. It needed to be her decision. But I also didn't give her all the information to make her choice. I'm guessing same for you. You haven't told her how you really feel, have you?"

"No."

"Why?"

"Because she left me a fucking note, Gabe. She said goodbye in a letter and snuck off while I was sleeping."

"Do you think it's possible she did that to protect herself? And maybe you?"

I groan, recalling the words she left me.

This isn't the life you signed up for, so if I go, everything will return to normal for you.

I shrug, not wanting to get into this with him.

"Listen, man, I'm not here to kick you while you're down, but I will say this. I didn't go after Blair when she left and will always regret it. Yeah, it turned out fine because she came back to me, but what if she hadn't? I'd like to think I'd have pulled my head out of my ass before too long and gone after her, but there's always a what-if in the back of my mind. Don't let the what-ifs keep you from living the life you want, Marcus. Go after her. Give her all the pieces to the puzzle, and if she wants to put it together, then that's her decision. If not, at least you'll know."

I swallow over the lump in my throat and keep my focus on the engine bay. His words have the impact I'm sure he was going for. They strike my heart and give voice to the questions I've had swirling in my brain and my heart. Was it a mistake to let her go without at least telling her how I feel? Probably. But I did it for two reasons.

One, the rules we established that first night we were together—a summer fling and nothing more—were fulfilled. I broke the rules. I fell for her hard and fast and was left to pick up the pieces when she returned home.

And two, I never gave her all the info. That's me protecting myself, if I'm being honest. Rejection fucking sucks. I experienced it as a baby, when my mom dropped me off at my grandparents' house and never looked back. Now I've handed over that same control to Ryan without realizing it, and in one moment, she could wield that exact kind of hurt. She could tell me to get lost, confirm the fear I've held on to like a shield around my heart.

But, like Gabe said, what if she doesn't...

He walks over and slaps me on the back, giving my shoulder a tight squeeze. It's the first time I noticed he's wearing scrubs, probably having just returned from a hospital visit in Hudson. "Think about it, but don't think too long, man. I'd hate to see you hold on to the regret for the rest of your life."

I nod, unable to speak words. My heart and my head are at war, as they've been for the last week, but there's one thing they can agree on. I miss the fuck out of her.

Gabe gives Buddy a little attention before walking out of the garage and heading back to his own truck. I hear it start and pull out of my driveway, but it's his words that really have my attention.

Don't let the what-ifs keep you from living the life you want, Marcus.

And dammit, I want Ryan.

In my bed, in my heart, and in my home.

Yeah, there's some serious logistics to take into consideration, but for the first time, I'm willing to consider them. All of them. Because like Ryan, I need all the pieces to the puzzle too, or it'll impact the picture. And the picture I see includes the woman I've fallen in love with.

Now it's time to do something about it.

The elevator dings, announcing my arrival. I adjust the tie around my neck for the hundredth time, wishing I could rip it off and throw it in the trash, but knowing it's part of the required attire for tonight's celebration event.

I step through the open elevator doors and am surrounded by wealth. It oozes from the attendees like sap from a tree. Their jewelry sparkles, their designer threads scream to be noticed. But my eyes are drawn instantly to the woman on stage. There stands Ryan, wearing a stunning red dress that hugs her curves in ways I dream about.

"Please help me welcome the new product ambassador of Ryan Holmes Cosmetics, Miss Desi Amora," Ryan says proudly, as the room erupts into applause.

I recognize the woman walking across the stage, moving to stand beside the woman I love. She waves to the crowd before giving Ryan air kisses and taking her position at the microphone.

"I couldn't be prouder to partner with Ryan and Ryan Holmes Cosmetics," Desi starts.

"Champagne, sir?" a man holding a tray of flutes ask.

"No, thank you," I reply, starting to make my way to the front of the room. I stick to the side, not wanting to be the guy who walks right up the middle of the room.

As I approach the stage, Ryan says, "Thank you all, again, for coming this evening. Please enjoy the champagne and hors d'oeuvres and the—" She stops talking, her eyes landing firmly on mine. Those gorgeous brown eyes register shock as she gapes down at me from her position on the stage. "Band," she finally finishes, clearing her throat. "Thank you," she adds, earning a round of applause.

The ladies stay up on stage, taking a few photographs. In between each one, she looks my way, as if trying to gauge whether or not her mind is playing tricks on her. I stand back, letting her have the spotlight and soak up all the attention she's receiving. She's earned this and deserves every bit of it.

Finally, after taking what feels like a thousand photographs, she excuses herself and heads in my direction. I can't help but notice the slight tremble in her hand as she reaches out and grabs the railing, descending the four steps on the side of the stage.

"Marcus," she whispers when she stands directly in front of me.

Reaching out, I grab her hand and bring it to my lips, placing a gentle kiss on her knuckles. I can't help but notice the way she shivers at the featherlight touch. "You look absolutely breathtaking," I tell her, noting the swell of her breasts and the way her breathing hitches in the red strapless dress.

"Thank you." She clears her throat, glancing around. No one seems to be paying us any attention. "What are you doing here?"

"I came to tell you something."

Her eyes widen. "Really? Now?"

"It couldn't wait any longer," I insist, reaching for the tie and giving it a gentle tug.

She notices my action and smiles. "You're wearing a tie."

I nod once. "It was the dress code."

She looks around, as if taking in the suits, tuxedos, and fancy dresses around the room. "Yes, I suppose it is." Her eyes hold so much confusion, yet I catch a glimmer of hope reflecting back at me. "How did you get in?"

I glance over her shoulder and smile. "They helped me."

Ryan turns and finds her parents standing across the room, watching. I have yet to meet them, but I spoke to her mom on the phone when I came up with this idea. She was positively gleeful with excitement and insisted on helping me set my plan into motion.

"My parents?"

I nod, reaching for her hand and pulling her toward the side of the stage. With the band now playing, it's a little more difficult to have a private conversation. Of course, we're standing in the middle of the ballroom, smack-dab in the center of her celebration event. "I called your mom."

Her pink lips part as her mouth falls open. "You called my mother? How?"

I chuckle and shake my head. "Believe it or not, it wasn't that difficult. I tried to reach your father first, but I quickly discovered it would probably have been easier to speak to the President of the United States on the phone than Douglas Marcotte."

She grins.

"Your mom's email address was listed on the website for the charity she runs, so I reached out to her. She called me back within an hour."

"Wow," she murmurs, as if trying to process that bit of news.

"She helped me get a ticket to tonight's event so I could tell you face-to-face what I've been needing to say."

"And that is?" she asks. I'm pretty sure she's holding her breath, and she wouldn't be the only one.

It's now or never.

"I love you."

CHAPTER
twenty seven

Ryan

"You what?" I ask, sure I've misheard him.

"I love you, Ryan," he says, reaching up and brushing his thumb over my cheekbone.

I'm still struck stupid by his unexpected presence here, so I'm having a hard time processing his words. It doesn't help he's wearing a suit that makes him look both delicious and completely uncomfortable.

I notice the change in him, and I realize my mistake. He took my silence as a rejection. Reaching out, I pull on his tie and loosen the knot. He seems confused by my actions, but doesn't say a word as I carefully lift the tie off his neck and reposition the collar on his crisp, white dress shirt.

"There," I reply with a smile. Still holding the tie in my fingers, I brush my fingers across his smooth jaw. "I don't think I've ever seen you freshly shaved like this."

His eyes burn into mine as he continues to stare at me. "Ellie told me I was looking a little scruffy. It didn't match the suit."

I grin widely at the thought of my friend telling him to shave and get a haircut. "But the scruff is you, Marcus, and I'd rather have you be *you* than trying to fit in for me."

He glances around, his nervousness palpable. "I can leave."

"Please don't," I reply quickly, realizing we're not on the same page. With my hand cupping his jaw, I state, "I love your scruff and your grumpiness and your dirty ball caps and your grease-stained nails, Marcus. Why? Because loving you means loving all of you. You don't have to wear a tie to fit into my world. You're already part of it the way you are."

His Adam's apple bobs as he swallows. "What did you say?" The corner of his mouth turns up a tick.

"I love you too."

His hands move to pull me against his body. "Even when I'm grumpy?"

"Even then," I confirm.

He moves first, pressing his lips to mine in a firm, promising kiss. "I was terrified you were going to turn me away."

I run my hand up his cheek and meet his gaze. "Never. Turns out I have a thing for the grumpy, blue-collar type."

His grin is much wider and reflects his relief. "And it seems I have a thing for the high-maintenance, spoiled type."

I can't help but smile as his arms wrap around my waist, drawing me in. I catch a whiff of his cologne and partnered with the feel of his body pressed to mine, it makes my panties a bit damp. "You're really here."

"Of course I am. Tonight's your big night. I'm sorry I missed the first part of your speech. Traffic in LA is definitely not the same as Pine Village," he says, running his hand through his freshly cut hair.

"Oh my God, no," I state with a chuckle.

"Pardon the interruption," a familiar voice says behind me.

I spin around and find both of my parents standing before us. They're both smiling, their demeanor casual and relaxed.

My dad extends his hand toward Marcus. "Douglas Marcotte."

"Marcus Wright. It's a pleasure to finally meet you, sir."

My dad waves his other hand. "Doug, please. I've been anxious to meet the man who stole my daughter's heart."

Marcus glances my way, a touch of apprehension in his hazel eyes. "Thank you, sir. I mean Doug. Your daughter has come to mean a great deal to me," he says, sending me a smile.

"And I'm Ryan's mom, Jade Holmes, and you can call me Jade," Mom says with a charming grin.

He takes her hand and gives it a polite shake. He doesn't bring it to his mouth to kiss like Vaughn used to always do or you see so much in this town. "Pleasure to meet you as well."

"Well, we'll let you two catch up. We just wanted to say hello before you two slipped away," Dad says with a jovial, knowing grin. I almost groan at the innuendo, but I also suspect it's not that far off.

I'm definitely ready to get out of here, now that Marcus has arrived.

"Let's have dinner soon," Mom says to the two of us, leaving the invitation open-ended. Considering I have no idea how long he's in town, I appreciate her not pushing to set something up now.

I nod, and as they turn to walk away, I give my attention back to Marcus. "We probably need to talk about stuff, but I can't leave yet," I tell him.

He dances his fingers up my neck, causing goosebumps to pepper my skin. "This is your night, Princess. We don't have to leave right now. I'm here for you and will proudly stand behind you as you shine like the diamond you are."

I can't help but grin and shake my head. "No, I want you beside me. I know it'll make you uncomfortable—" I start, but he cuts me off.

"Then that's where I'll stand. I'll be where you need me. Whether that's behind you, beside you, or in front of you. I won't always be able to be with you, but when I am, I'll make it count."

I know he's referring to the distance between where he lives and where I do, but I know that's something we can talk about and overcome. My mom's words from last week come back to me. I can work anywhere.

I shove his necktie into his suit jacket. "I want you comfortable. I realize you're wearing this suit for me, and I truly appreciate it. Besides, this open collar thing is kind of sexy." I run my fingers over the V at his throat, wishing I could unfasten the rest of the buttons.

"Yeah?" he asks, his eyebrow shooting upward as a smirk spreads across his kissable lips.

"Totally. Later, I'm going to strip this suit off you, but for now, I need to go back out there and mingle."

"Then that's what we'll do," he says, taking a deep breath. I know this isn't his scene, but I appreciate him trying.

"Thank you."

He leans in and whispers, "I have a confession. I'm already picturing stripping you out of that dress later and bending you over the nearest bed. I'm hoping to catch a glimpse of the *wild* later. It's what'll get me through the rest of the night." He's referring to all the media attention I used to get calling me a wild child.

A nervous, yet excited giggle spills from my mouth. "Well, I do prefer the wild. We'll add that to the list as soon as we get back to my place."

"Damn right we will." He takes my hand and gives it a squeeze.

I go up on the balls of my feet, pressing my lips to his. "I love you, Marcus. Thank you for coming, even though we decided this was just a fling."

"It was never just a fling with you, Ryan. You were always more."

I feel my cheeks heat as I give another uncontrollable grin. "Ready?"

"Lead the way, Princess."

EPILOGUE
epilogue

MARCUS

2 months later

I come home from work and find my place a disaster. I slowly take in the open boxes around the living room, the fluffy pillows on the couch and chair, and the knickknacks spread all over every surface in the cabin, and smile.

Buddy barks over the sound of music and comes running, happy to have me home. The last couple of days, he's stayed home with Ryan instead of accompanying me to the shop. I think he likes it better. You know, a comfy bed and a gorgeous woman to hang with all day? What's not to love.

After giving him a good scratching behind the ears, we take off in search of the woman who brought utter chaos into my world. I find Ryan standing at the counter, reading something on her phone screen before measuring out an ingredient and adding it to a large bowl. I lean against the doorjamb and watch, damn happy to see her making herself at home in the cabin.

This past weekend she officially moved in. It wasn't easy, considering all her stuff was in California, but we made it work. I went out to her place and helped her pack and then hired a moving company to deliver what she was keeping here. While she opted to sell a lot of her furniture, the amount of clothes this woman has is insane. Like closets and closets full. And don't get me started on the shoes...

We spent the last two months traveling back and forth, but I admit, she did most of the travel. It was much easier for her to come here, thanks to me owning my own repair shop. I did hire another mechanic to help while I was away, and it was a great decision. It gives me a bit more flexibility to be able to go see Ryan or travel with her for upcoming work trips.

Now, she lives with me.

Me.

Marcus Wright.

I fell in love and moved a woman into my place of solitude.

I never expected that to happen, but when it came to Ryan, I didn't have a choice. She owns my heart and always will.

She spins around to go to the fridge and jumps. A yelp falls from her lips as her hands go to her mouth. "Holy shit, you scared me." She runs over and turns down the pop music pumping through the speaker on the counter. "Sorry, I didn't hear you."

"I could tell," I reply, meeting her halfway and taking her in my arms. I press my lips to hers, reveling in the feel of her tongue against mine. "Hi."

"Hi."

"Whatcha making?" I ask, noticing the messy counter.

"Ummm, muffins?"

"Was that a question?" I ask with a chuckle.

"Yeah, well, I've never made them before, and Jillian swore they were easy. She sent me a recipe and everything, but I think she's a liar. This isn't easy," she proclaims, clearly frustrated with her first attempt at baking.

"I'll help you," I insist, bringing her hand to my mouth and placing a kiss on her knuckles.

"You will?"

"Of course. I just need to shower first."

She pulls back as her eyes slowly trail down my body. "I'll help you," she repeats, a big grin on her lush lips. Lips I hope will be wrapped around my cock in just a little bit.

"What about the muffins?" I ask, not caring in the least what happens to the ingredients.

"What muffins?"

Ryan

I groan and close my eyes, letting the pleasure course through me. This. Being with Marcus. Best. Feeling. Ever.

"Good?" he asks, digging his thumbs into the pads of my foot.

"Your hands are pure magic," I whisper.

"Just wait. I can do more with these hands," he says, the innuendo heavy between us.

He continues to rub my feet, the water in the huge tub lapping just below my shoulders. It's Labor Day weekend, what is dubbed as the end of the summer tourist season. The park is full of families taking advantage of the lake, trails, and cabin rentals one last time before fall approaches.

I've officially been a resident of Pine Village for a week now, and I've never felt more at home. The townspeople welcomed me with open arms, and while I'm sure fans and members of the media will eventually descend upon this small town, it shouldn't be what it was the first time.

I was able to get out of the second year of my contract. My dad's lawyers combed through the documents and found the loophole. I was able to terminate the contract without paying out the ass in penalties. I've decided to focus on my makeup line, which is showing steady gains in each report I'm presented.

I'm also returning attention to my YouTube channel. I cover a little bit of everything, from makeup and skincare tips—it's a fabulous way to promote my product—as well as throwing in random episodes, like showing pieces of what happens on the inside of the business and peeks at life inside our home. Of course, Marcus doesn't want anything to do with my on-screen presence, but he supports my desire to stay visible and relevant.

Plus, it's fun. In the last week, I've made four YouTube tutorial videos, and all received thousands of views within the first twenty-four hours. I touched on makeup techniques, skincare tips, and even discussed the muffin recipe I'm perfecting.

I'm set up to work from Pine Village. He turned the downstairs bedroom into my home office, so I can still very much be part of running and growing my business. I'll still have to travel, but at least it's not back and forth from California to Wisconsin every weekend like it was before I relocated. My first big travel is a trip to Paris. I've been a few times over the years, but this is the first time I'm doing it for my own career, not that of my mom or dad. Plus, it's Marcus's first trip out of the country, and I'm eager to show him my favorite romantic spots around Paris.

Tonight, after a long day, Marcus surprised me with a bath in his huge tub. It's not my first one, but it *is* our first one together. He even went as far as to light some candles I had around the cabin, as well as turn on some romantic country playlist he found on the internet.

"What are you thinking about?" he asks, interrupting my thoughts.

"Paris," I reply, a dreamy little smile on my lips, as I close my eyes and sink a little lower into the water.

"Yeah?" He switches feet, starting to rub the ball of my left foot.

"Are you excited?"

"To go to Paris?" he asks, then shrugs in response, water glistening off his broad shoulders. "I'm excited to go with you. And fuck you in some fancy French hotel with a view of the Eiffel Tower."

I snort a giggle and shake my head. "Typical Marcus. Always thinking about sex."

"Always," he replies, waggling his eyebrows. "Why do you think I agreed to this bath?"

After a few blissful minutes, I ask, "Are you happy?"

He looks up from his task and smiles. "Yeah, Princess. I'm happy."

I pull my foot from his hands and carefully move until I'm straddling his waist. Pressing my lips to his, I whisper, "Me too."

He deepens the kiss, his hands cupping my ass and his tongue sliding against mine. "What do you say, Princess. Wanna go get wild with me?"

"I don't know if you can handle it. I can get pretty wild," I tease.

"Well, little lady, you're in luck. I know just how to tame your kinda wild."

He stands up, completely ignoring the fact we're both soaking wet, and steps out of the tub. With his hands on my ass, he carries me into our bedroom, the one we now share. I don't know what our future holds, but as long as he's by my side, I know we can weather whatever life throws at us.

A country boy and a city girl.

Two completely different people from two opposite worlds.

Who would have guessed it would ever work so well? No one, that's who. But here we are, proving them wrong day after day.

Together.

That's so wild.

another EPILOGUE

Jillian

I almost have this recipe perfect.

As soon as I have it where I want, I'll add it to my digital cookbook. Then, I'll be one step closer to fulfilling my dream. Not that owning my own bakery and coffee shop isn't living my dream, but I've always wanted to produce my own cookbook. Maybe even have my own cooking blog or YouTube channel, like Ryan. Someday, I'll be brave enough to talk to her about it. I haven't known her that long, but she's become a great friend in a short amount of time. I'm certain she'd offer me any tips or tricks she can to get started.

I slip the pan of pastries into the oven and set the timer. I have thirteen minutes until I need to pull my latest creation from the oven, and usually I'd use the time to start cleaning up my workspace. Of course, my workspace tonight is my kitchen counter at home. Usually, I do all my creating in my bakery kitchen, having plenty of supplies and oven space to play.

However, tonight was a rash decision to bake. I had just returned home from having dinner with my parents, and that always goes about as well as you'd expect. Not that I don't love my parents—

I do—but they're ready for grandbabies, and I'm their only hope. The problem is, I'm thirty-seven and don't even have a boyfriend. I've spent every waking hour over the last decade, pouring myself into my business. Sure, having a boyfriend sounds nice—more than nice, actually—but the reality of it isn't so easy. I work a lot and the only men I meet on a daily basis want me for my cinnamon swirl bread and banana chocolate chip muffins. Oh, and the caffeine. They definitely want that too.

So those grandbabies my parents want? They're starting to get real restless and vocal in their disappointment. Tonight's dinner wasn't any different, except this time they took it a step further. Tonight, while enjoying honey-glazed pork chops, roasted Brussels sprouts, and creamy mashed potatoes, they offered up a list of available, single men in Pine Village.

A list!

Typed up and printed out on my dad's company letterhead.

I almost threw up my food right then and there. I couldn't get out of there any quicker.

That's the reason I'm baking on a Sunday night instead of relaxing and preparing for the busy week ahead of me. I glance at the timer on the oven. Five minutes left. Just as I grab the container of sugar to place in the cabinet, there's a firm knock at my door.

Hesitantly, I move toward the entryway. I'm not expecting anyone, especially at this point in the evening. All my friends would have texted or called first, so chances of the visitor being one of them are slim to none.

As I reach the door, I go up on my tiptoes and peek through the security hole. My mouth falls open when the individual on the opposite side comes into view. "Kameron?" I find myself asking, reaching down and releasing the lock.

"Hey, yeah, sorry to just drop by like this," he says, glancing over my shoulder into my house.

"Are you all right?"

He sighs and shakes his head. "No, not really. I need your help."

Worry fills my chest. I've known Kameron practically my whole life. He's a few years older than me, but we grew up down the road from each other. He may not be one of my closest friends, but if he needs something, I'd readily help. "Okay, what's up?"

He levels me with an intense look, his blue eyes full of anxiety as he drops a bomb straight in my lap. "I need you to be my girlfriend..."

Don't miss a single reveal, release, or sale! Sign up for my newsletter. **http://www.laceyblackbooks.com/newsletter**

BOOKS ALSO BY

lacey black

Rivers Edge series

Trust Me, Rivers Edge book 1 (Maddox and Avery) – FREE at all retailers

Fight Me, Rivers Edge book 2 (Jake and Erin)

Expect Me, Rivers Edge book 3 (Travis and Josselyn)

Promise Me: A Novella, Rivers Edge book 3.5 (Jase and Holly)

Protect Me, Rivers Edge book 4 (Nate and Lia)

Boss Me, Rivers Edge book 5 (Will and Carmen)

Trust Us: A Rivers Edge Christmas Novella (Maddox and Avery)

> ~ *This novella was originally part of the Christmas Miracles Anthology*

With Me, A Rivers Edge Christmas Novella (Brooklyn and Becker)

Bound Together series

Submerged, Bound Together book 1 (Blake and Carly)

Profited, Bound Together book 2 (Reid and Dani)

Entwined, Bound Together book 3 (Luke and Sidney)

Summer Sisters series

My Kinda Kisses, Summer Sisters book 1 (Jaime and Ryan)

My Kinda Night, Summer Sisters book 2 (Payton and Dean)

My Kinda Song, Summer Sisters book 3 (Abby and Levi)

My Kinda Mess, Summer Sisters book 4 (Lexi and Linkin)

My Kinda Player, Summer Sisters book 5 (AJ and Sawyer)

My Kinda Player, Summer Sisters book 6 (Meghan and Nick)

My Kinda Wedding, A Summer Sisters Novella book 7 (Meghan and Nick)

Rockland Falls series
Love and Pancakes, Rockland Falls book 1
Love and Lingerie, Rockland Falls book 2
Love and Landscape, Rockland Falls book 3
Love and Neckties, Rockland Falls book 4

Standalone
Music Notes, a sexy contemporary romance standalone
A Place To Call Home, a Memorial Day novella
Exes and Ho Ho Ho's, a sexy contemporary romance standalone novella
Pants on Fire
Double Dog Dare You
Grip
Bachelor Swap, A Bachelor Tower Series Novel
Perfect Kiss, Mason Creek Series book 9
Waiting For Love, The Love Vixen Series book 11
Quarterback Keeper, a surprise baby novella
Kissing A Stranger, book 4 in the multi-author The Kissing Games series

Burgers and Brew Crüe Series
Kickstart My Heart, book 1
Don't Go Away Mad, book 2
Same Ol' Situation, book 3
Wild Side, book 4
What's It Gonna Take, book 5
Home Sweet Home, book 6
Too Young to Fall in Love, book 7
Without You, book 8
Time For Change, book 9

You're All I Need, book 10

Pine Village Series
Pretty Remarkable, a free prequel short story
Pretty Incredible, book 1
Pretty Dependable, book 2
Pretty Drunk, book 3
Pretty Relentless, book 4
Pretty Wild, book 5

Co-Written with *NYT Bestselling* Author, Kaylee Ryan
It's Not Over, Fair Lakes book 1
Just Getting Started, Fair Lakes book 2
Can't Get Enough, Fair Lakes book 3
Fair Lakes Box Set
Boy Trouble
Home To You, a second chance novella
Beneath the Fallen Stars, Never Too Far book 1
Beneath the Desert Sun, Never Too Far book 2
Tell Me A Story
Royal – Writing as Rebel Shaw
Crying Shame – Writing as Rebel Shaw
Watch and Learn – Writing as Rebel Shaw

USA Today Bestselling Author Lacey Black is a Midwestern girl with a passion for reading, writing, and shopping. She carries her e-reader with her everywhere she goes so she never misses an opportunity to read a few pages. Always looking for a happily ever after, Lacey is passionate about contemporary romance novels and enjoys it further when you mix in a little suspense. She resides in a small town in Illinois with her husband and two children.

Website: www.laceyblackbooks.com
Email: laceyblackwrites@gmail.com

Newsletter: http://www.laceyblackbooks.com/newsletter

www.ingramcontent.com/pod-product-compliance
Lightning Source LLC
Chambersburg PA
CBHW070639260626
47161CB00007B/2764